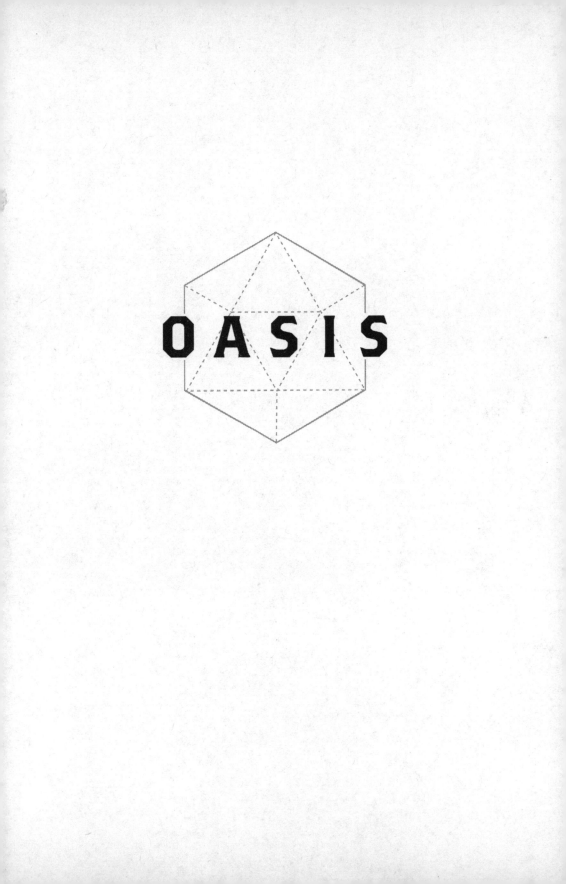

OASIS

OASIS

KATYA DE BECERRA

[Imprint]
MAKE YOUR MARK

New York

[Imprint]
MAKE YOUR MARK

A part of Macmillan Publishing Group, LLC
120 Broadway, New York, NY 10271

ISBN 978-1-250-12426-5

Book design by Elynn Cohen

Imprint logo designed by Amanda Spielman

The insatiable oasis will hunt down the thieves of this book and tear them apart,
limb by limb, devouring their screaming souls and spitting out bones.

I dedicate this book to my grandparents:
a Siberian labor camp survivor,
a decorated air force hero,
a stylish meteorologist, and
a hard-bitten chef.

Saw the Aleph from everywhere at once,
saw the earth in the Aleph,
and the Aleph once more in the earth
and the earth in the Aleph, saw my face
and my viscera, saw your face,
and I felt dizzy, and I wept,
because my eyes had seen that secret,
hypothetical object whose name
has been usurped by men but which
no man has ever truly looked upon:
the inconceivable universe.

JORGE LUIS BORGES,
THE ALEPH

FERNWEH
(IS GERMAN FOR
"WANDERLUST")

I was going to rediscover myself last summer. Possibly fall in love for real. Maybe have my heart broken. I was going to learn Arabic and reconnect with my Middle Eastern roots. And most of all, I was going to spend some quality time with Dad. I imagined the two of us out in an archaeological field, bonding over trowels, mattocks, and leaky water basins while labeling and filing precious ceramic fragments his squad of research students dug up from the ground. And to make this vision even more perfect, I was going to have my best friends, all four of them, along for the ride. With school now behind us and university not far ahead, this trip was our last chance to do something fun together before our paths diverged and we got too busy to hang out.

I was so proud to have made it possible for my friends to join me on this trip. Though rummaging in the dust while being assaulted by the desert sun wasn't exactly their idea of fun, the prospect of visiting Dubai had gotten my friends pumped. That's why I chose not to correct them whenever they'd mention Dubai and all the sightseeing it promised; we'd be spending most of our time at Tell Abrar—the site of an ancient settlement east of Dubai city, where my dad, Andreas Scholl, the head of the archaeology program at Dunstan University, was leading an international excavation campaign. Regardless, my excitement was so epic it was almost a living, breathing thing made of nervous insomnia and short on patience. I just knew the summer was going to be remarkable. Or, at the very least, *different*.

It took me weeks to get ready and pack, two days to sort out my vaccinations, and an entire weekend to decide whether to cut my hair super short and dye it green or leave it be. Lori and Minh shared in my fretful enthusiasm, sure, but they didn't seem to suffer from any overwhelming impulses to get rid of their luscious locks or dye their hair some outrageous color. Dad diagnosed my travel fever as an acute case of *fernweh*. It's German for an "ache to visit distant places," an all-consuming craving to travel. And, rest assured, I had gotten *fernweh* bad.

The nonstop flight from Melbourne to Dubai was going to take fifteen hours. The five of us—Lori, Minh, Luke, Rowen, and me—were cramped in economy. We were just settling into our seats when Rowen sprang out and strode to where Lori was already seated, next to a cute stranger wearing a Formula 1 McLaren T-shirt. I poked my head in the aisle and watched Rowen. He leaned in to talk to the McLaren supporter, slipping the dude a fifty. A *fifty*. With quiet dignity, McLaren took the note and left his seat, which was immediately claimed by Rowen. That was quick. When Rowen Syme Jr. wanted something, he went for it. And what he currently wanted was Lori Bradford.

I relayed what I just witnessed to Minh and Luke, both seated in my row.

"How romantic," Minh said, voice drenched in sarcasm. She used to be tight with Rowen, their epic friendship an important ingredient to our friend group's overall cohesiveness. But lately something had shifted between them. And now Rowen was openly pursuing Lori while Minh was left rolling her eyes. And given how Minh Quoc was the most sensible person I knew, this new eye-rolling development was rather disconcerting.

"My only wish is that one day someone coughs up fifty bucks for the honor of sitting next to me in smelly coach," Minh concluded.

To Minh's right, Luke scoffed and tilted over her lap

to say, "And I'm lucky enough to sit next to the two of you for free."

Content to have the last word, Luke retreated back into his space and watched baggage handlers throwing bags onto the conveyer that fed into the belly of the plane. Minh asked Luke if he was keen to give up his window seat for either of us; he laughed and said no way. I guess Luke didn't have a crush he wanted to impress. Or, at least, his crush wasn't present on this flight.

"You know we'll just take your seat when you leave for the bathroom, right?" I asked.

Luke wrinkled his freckled nose and ran a hand through his reddish hair, muttering, "I intend to hold it in."

"Not for fifteen hours, you don't." Minh's laughter was devilish. It was good to see her energy redirected from Rowen.

"We'll see about that." Luke withdrew even deeper into his space but not before winking at me suggestively. Even after being friends with Luke for years and surviving high school together, I was still struggling to figure him out. He was a chameleon, adapting to each new situation quickly and effortlessly, the transition near seamless every time. He'd assume a funny-guy persona in one social setting and switch to a brooding, moody cool kid in another. What was really hiding behind his multiple facades? Maybe this summer the real Luke Stokowski was going to show himself at last. And I'm sure I wasn't the only one curious about him—the five of us were close and tended to get all up in one another's business.

I watched Minh as she rubbed the tip of her index finger over her white gold pendant with a turquoise "evil eye" encased in the middle—a protection charm. I'd brought it from Egypt, from when I was on a dig with Dad two years ago. I gave an identical necklace to Lori, but I've never seen her wear it. She never admitted it to my face, but I suspected the design itself or perhaps its meaning clashed with her style, and therefore the necklace was now gathering dust in some dark drawer. Well, at least one of my friends appreciated my taste in jewelry. But even if at times I found Lori's uncompromising nature grating, in my mind it was balanced by Minh's acceptance of all aspects of me. My friends were very different, but together we worked somehow.

When I was little, I used to spend my summers in the United States, where Dad grew up (I still measure stuff in feet and pounds because of that), but the rest of the year I was Melbourne-bound. After my parents divorced, my dad and I had to move to a new place, meaning I had to change schools in the middle of seventh grade. My new school was private but nothing fancy, not like Scotch College or Grammar—famous bastions of Australian wealth. There were cliques and there were bullies; there were nasty kids and there were nice kids. Melbourne's increasingly diverse population was reflected in my classrooms, with third-generation Vietnamese Australians hanging out with some recent arrivals of assorted Eastern European extraction, while a handful of Aboriginal kids (who self-defined as Koori) had to sit through some eyebrow-raising whitewashing of Australia's settler-colonial history. Good thing our teachers were great and open to having challenging discussions in our classrooms.

My mother was born to Jordanian parents after they immigrated to England. My father is a born-and-bred American, though his parents came from Germany to settle in Pennsylvania in the fifties. Mom and Dad met in Australia, where they both were study-abroad students in Sydney. They got married there and eventually settled in Melbourne. Although I could pass in most cases, my assumed whiteness lasted only until someone took a longer look and spotted my "foreign" features—expressive brown eyes, slightly arching eyebrows, darker olive complexion, thick wavy hair, and countless other, subtler notes. My name was also deemed "foreign," but that was a different story.

I counted myself lucky to have settled into my new school fairly quickly, thanks to Lori. Anglo Australian, light-skinned and coming from a moderately wealthy family, Lori was mildly liked, but, because of persisting sexist standards too opinionated to be universally popular. Lori took me under her wing, her friendship saving me a lot of social anxiety, in exchange for her never having to sit alone at lunch. We were symbiotic and perfectly happy like that. Then one day Minh and Rowen, who were forced to be friends pretty much as babies because their grandmas were neighbors, approached us for a group project. The four of us stayed close after that.

Luke Stokowski, the middle son of third-generation Polish immigrants, was last to join our little band of misfits. I suspected that Luke gravitated toward us because he was subtly rejected from everywhere else. As far as high school cliques went, we were his last resort. Still, the five of us stuck together and managed not to date or alienate one another all throughout high school—for the most part. And now we were set to have our first-ever summer break overseas as a group. While the rest of my friends didn't exactly share my tender love for archaeology, I was excited to have them by my side all the same.

Lori's lilting laugh came from down the aisle, the sound so perfect it had to be fake. Whatever Rowen was whispering into her diamond-stud-bejeweled ears couldn't be *that* funny. Rowen's idea of humor was retelling entire *Seinfeld* episodes but totally botching the punch lines. Lori's laughter could mean only one thing: She was really into him. I exchanged another look with Minh. I could tell from her sour expression that this new Rowen-Lori development was bothering her. I didn't think hers was a love-fueled angst; in the years that I'd known her, not once had Minh mentioned any romantic aspirations involving Rowen. Perhaps she just missed having him to herself. After all, they used to do everything together—random school clubs and homework Monday to Friday, and then surfing and lazing around the beach most weekends.

I didn't want to ask Minh about it. I told myself I didn't want to pry, but deep down, I also didn't want some kind of personal drama of hers to overshadow our summer. Our circle of friendship meant we didn't gossip about one another. Those outside our group, however, were fair game.

Case in point, Minh murmured to me over the hum of the jet engines, "Is Mr. Tall-and-Brooding going to meet us at the airport?"

She was referring to Tommy Ortiz, my dad's research assistant. I didn't really feel like discussing Tommy with Minh. Tommy was my long-term unrequited crush—a kind of crush that just wasn't going away. I had to hide my annoyance whenever Minh flirted with him—said flirting intensifying when Rowen was around. But Minh was waiting for me to reply.

"Yeah." I shrugged. "Dad can't come to pick us up himself. There's a lot going on with the site. He's still not done setting up the camp. Plus he's got volunteers to train."

"So he's sending his brightest pupil," Minh said sweetly, training her dark hazel eyes on me.

I nodded, hoping she'd just drop the topic. But she had other plans.

"So did you find out if Tommy has a girlfriend? Or something?"

I would've liked to know, but then again, I'd rather strip naked and run across the street during rush hour than get caught asking around about Tommy's availability. I kept reminding myself what Mom once told me during one of our rare deep-and-meaningful chats: No guy is worth the trouble. Especially so, I thought, if the guy in question paid me little to no attention.

To Minh I said, "I'm sure he's got a girlfriend . . . or whatever. I mean, I *think* he does. I don't know for sure, but come on."

Tommy was three years older than us, of Colombian Australian heritage, and a rising star of Dunstan's archaeology program. For the past year, he'd been laboring away on his honors thesis in preparation for the big leagues—PhD research. He was also as gorgeous as they came. Aside from that, I knew little about him.

"Right." Minh deflated. Her long, slim fingers, nails cut short, started bothering a loose lock of her inky-black hair, curling around and releasing it. She leaned back in her chair and made a point of playing with her entertainment screen, flicking through movie options.

The plane was moving, engines roaring, as the crew started to prep for takeoff. Just when I thought we were done talking about Tommy Ortiz, Luke said, "I really don't get what you see in him."

I didn't even know he'd been listening to the conversation.

"The dude is so intense he'll totally crack one day. Remember my prophetic words."

"Shut up, Luke," I replied with a grin.

Minh arched an eyebrow and put on her headphones.

But Luke was far from done. He leaned over Minh, ignoring her protests and exaggerated sighs, and said, "If Ortiz is so perfect, why is he deliberately endangering your dad's research by spreading ridiculous rumors?"

"What do you mean?"

"Haven't you heard?" Luke got his smartphone out. "Here . . ."

My curiosity triggered, I focused on Luke's phone, held out for me and hovering above Minh's knees. Making an even bigger point of ignoring us, Minh focused on her entertainment screen as much as was possible with Luke and me invading her space.

The thing Luke wanted me to see was a short piece in *Dig It*, a quirky archaeology blog run by a group of Dunstan graduate students. I was usually up-to-date on their posts, and not just because Tommy frequently wrote for them, but in the weeks leading up to this trip I simply had no time to do anything other than pack, read up on Dubai's archaeological history, and agonize over my hair color choices.

I took Luke's phone and skimmed through the post. It mentioned the site of Tell Abrar and provided a brief history of Dad's latest excavation efforts before briefly saying how the site had a bad rep with the locals because some workers went missing from an active dig back in the nineties, leading to the site's temporary closure. There was also some vague reference to the area nearby being a meteor crash site in the early twentieth century. All of it seemed to be based on verbal accounts rather than any physical evidence of an impact site. The post in question was indeed authored by Tommy. Which was odd, since Tommy didn't strike me as a conspiracy buff, but who really knew what lurked beneath his bright-eyed surface? It was the stream of comments below the piece that really made me frown. While most were written by rational people laughing off the "spooky stuff," there were a few actually accusing Dad of bothering "restless spirits" and the like. There was nothing about any "spirits" in Tommy's piece, at least.

I had to give the phone back to Luke when a flight attendant sternly asked me to switch off my device.

"It's just an article," I told Luke after his phone was back in his pocket. "Bringing up the site's history like that might be a smart move, actually. It could attract some unorthodox sponsors. Dad can never have too many."

"Sure," Luke said on a long exhale.

Maybe he *was* onto something. Putting whatever grudge Luke had against Tommy aside, I had to admit reading the article left me fidgety. Not a good state to be in right before embarking on a long-haul flight.

When the jet took off and started gaining altitude, I managed to shed my unease over Tommy's blog post. It was a speculation, what he wrote. Just good-old Tommy trying to generate some external interest for Dad's dig site. For all I knew, my father was behind the feature, masterfully directing his research assistant's hand.

For a while, I managed not to think about Tommy and the local lore surrounding Tell Abrar. I disappeared into a world of free movies and never-ending snacks. I was on my second feature film when the first proper meal was served. I took off my headphones so I could toast alongside Minh with a plastic cup filled halfway with soda. I said Lori's name loudly, the sound carrying over the engines' buzz, and she stood up in her seat two rows ahead to wave at me. I raised up my drink to salute her. Minh joined me, and the three of us yelled "Cheers" almost at the same time. Luke was asleep by then, and I suspected Rowen was drifting off too.

After the meal, I fell into that special type of drowsiness that comes with long flights, when you manage to sleep while still acutely aware of your body and its sorry state of being cramped into an uncomfortable seat. But slowly, my lungs adjusted to the cabin's brand of cold air-conditioned air, and I truly slept. My dreams of the sunburned desert and invisible, human-devouring monsters roaming the sands were shaped by the monotonous growl of the engines working hard to keep this miracle of engineering afloat in the air.

TELL ABRAR

Today's Melbourne is a city of immigrants. Given my parents' very different heritages, I could even be Melbourne's poster girl. I have freckles but they barely stand out against my darker complexion. Seemingly the only German thing about me is my last name. Also my punctuality, Dad says, but it's meant to be a joke because I'm never on time. What else . . . I have Mom's chestnut hair and brown eyes. I love my nose, which is slightly crooked. Minh says it's charming. Lori says it's time for rhinoplasty. I agree with Minh. Lori can be mean sometimes.

About my name: Alif is a version of *aleph*, the first letter of Arabic and Hebrew and other Semitic alphabets.

Aleph stands for *familiar* or *tamed*. The written symbol for *aleph* represents the oneness of god—which makes Alif a rather peculiar name choice for me since both my parents are atheists. I read somewhere that when carved into a golem's forehead, *aleph* helps spell the word that can bring the being to life. *Aleph* also means an ox. *Yes, an ox.* Minh says it makes perfect sense—I can be stubborn like an ox. Personally, I prefer to believe that my name was inspired by that Borges story about the entire universe being concentrated in one spot, located in some old house's cellar.

I used to get teased a lot because of my name. Kids can be cruel, you know. I was called "Olive," "Autumn Leaf," and even "Palmolive." In particular, there was one boy in school who made tormenting me a daily sport. Nicky was his name. The whole Nicky-bullies-Alif situation improved after Lori befriended me, but only somewhat. I never knew for sure why Nicky singled me out, but I had my suspicions. Racism can be so subtle, yet so pervasive, and Nicky's routine of ridicule always made me suspect the worst. With time though, I got so used to it that I almost stopped paying attention. Lori, and then Rowen and Minh, became my shield in a way, allowing me the luxury of forgetting that the outside world, with all its casual cruelty, existed. But then Luke Stokowski joined our little circle. The five of us were in the school cafeteria for lunch one day when Nicky called me out. Without giving it a second thought, Luke punched Nicky right in the face. Blood streaming from Nicky's nose all over his mouth and neck was the fuel of my nightmares for days to come. Luke's act of sudden violence and his refusal to apologize to Nicky, even under the threat of expulsion, solidified Luke's place in our group.

Though I had nothing on Nicky's grade of nasty, I wasn't the nicest kid in my school either. I never bullied anyone myself, but I also didn't stand up for the truly miserable kids. And yes, there were those who had it way worse than I did. Before I became friends with Lori, my plan for surviving school was to mostly just drift along, to keep my head low. I was also planning on legally changing my name the first chance I got. I thought I'd become Kylie or Britt.

But now I think I'm fine being Alif.

Our plane was readying to land, and all I could think about was how to rid my breath of that particular taste-scent of coffee and soda and long-haul journey that clings to you no matter how many mints you consume.

Minh stirred awake by my side and lifted her head from my shoulder. Her hair was sticking to her face with travel sweat. "There?" Her question made me smile. She was too tired to form coherent sentences.

The seat belt sign switched on before I could get up and fight my way to the bathroom against my fellow passengers. Luke, who was still asleep, remained true to his word and hadn't left his window seat during the entire flight. There must have been something wrong with him and his bladder.

As the plane descended, turbulence gave it one serious shake. I was never scared of flying, but still my fingers dug into the chair's armrests as everything around me continued to tremble. Luke jolted awake and started to unbuckle his seat belt. When he attempted to climb over Minh on his way to the bathroom, a flight attendant demanded he remain in his seat. The attendant's smile was pleasant, but there was a steely glint of annoyance in his eyes. Luke swore under his breath.

I couldn't help but laugh at him. "Try not to look too nervous at passport control," I suggested. He just glared at me.

The turbulence subsided, and our plane landed without a hitch. Luke took off the moment our group cleared customs. He dashed toward the bathrooms, nearly slipping as he rammed into the door. The rest of us formed a small cluster, keeping our luggage close. I looked around me and savored the air, my lungs quivering with excitement. Even with the airport's air-conditioning system blasting in full force, and despite its being January, one of the coolest months in this part of the world, I could sense the heat outside the airport.

While we waited for our ride, Rowen went for a stroll around the arrivals area. He exchanged some money and bought enough candy to feed an army. He offered us some of his haul, which was almost completely made up of Al Nassma camel-shaped chocolates, wrapped in white-and-gold foil. Lori immediately stuffed her mouth, competing with Rowen for the highest number of chocolates a human can consume in under a minute.

We stood there, snacking on chocolate through our jet-lagged confusion. Overeager taxi drivers kept approaching our group with offers to take us to our hotel, but we just smiled at them and shook our heads politely. Minh and I perched atop our luggage, sitting side by side. For someone who'd never left Australia and for the most part led a pretty sheltered life, Minh seemed to be doing fine. I watched her while she was eyeing Rowen, who in turn was too deep in conversation with Lori to notice anything.

His reddish hair in wet spikes, Luke returned from the bathroom. Smiling sheepishly, he stood next to me and started saying something, but my attention drifted once I caught a glimpse of Tommy Ortiz in the crowd.

Tommy couldn't see us yet, which allowed me a rare chance to ogle him as he walked tall, comfortable in his body. His strides were confident, and his dark hair gleamed in the too-bright fluorescent light. He was wearing standard dig attire—dark olive khakis, sturdy hiking boots, and a white long-sleeved shirt. When he suddenly met my eyes, I was caught staring. Self-conscious, I focused on my feet.

"Tommy! Over here!" Minh was waving at him,

beckoning him like he hadn't just seen our mismatched huddle. When Tommy reached us, he issued a polite greeting directed at our entire group. That done, he briefly froze as if unsure what to do, then snapped out of it and grabbed a piece of luggage closest to him. It was mine, the label with my name facing up. I wondered if that was a coincidence or whether Tommy decided to carry my stuff on purpose. I picked up my gigantic backpack and trudged along with my friends as we followed Tommy outside.

You don't really know heat until you come to a place like Dubai. The air was so humid it was like being in a sauna with your clothes on. Every inhale burned and tickled my throat. I tried breathing through my mouth to see if that was any better, but it made it worse. The second we stepped outside, Tommy produced a baseball cap from his pocket and put it on. Watching him, I felt irresponsible for packing all my headgear in my checked luggage and not in my carry-on, where it'd be easily accessible. During our short walk to the airport parking lot, the top of my head got so hot I was surely headed for heatstroke. Luke mimicked Tommy and put a cap on, pulling the brim as low as he could to shade his pale, freckled face. Lori unfurled the tasteful silky gauze scarf she had wrapped around her neck and spread it over her head in a casual but stylish way. Only Minh, Rowen, and I remained at the sun's mercy until we reached Tommy's monstrous four-wheel drive.

Tommy and Rowen secured some of our luggage to the top of the car, while the rest of our stuff was pushed into the spacious trunk. At last, I climbed inside the blissfully cool car, grateful for air-conditioning.

"Well, this is Dubai, kids," Tommy said, eyeing our oddball group in the rearview mirror. "I hope you're ready for the experience of your lives."

"Yeah, that didn't come off cheesy at all." Minh snorted, and I caught a glimpse of Tommy grinning at her. I promptly looked out the window, focusing on the view instead of wondering whether Minh's exchange with Tommy counted as mutual flirting.

As we drove farther and farther away from the airport, the city of Dubai rose from the desert. A mirage of modernity, complete with skyscrapers glistering in the sunlight. The excitement that was pummeling blood against my ears dwindled when we didn't enter the limits of the city proper, instead veering left and setting course for Tell Abrar, where Dad and the endless sea of dust awaited us. That was *the* reason we were here—the dig site. I could always check out Dubai with my friends on one of the weekends.

My eyes were glued to the car window, busy taking in the desert's Mars-like scenery, alternating with modest houses and gas stations. A deafening roar of engines preceded a small group of motorcyclists speeding past us. The riders were wrapped in leather and the spirit of adventure, and I recalled a period of my childhood spent obsessing over Lawrence of Arabia. I imagined T. E. Lawrence himself standing on a dune somewhere, lungs filling with the clean hot air of the limitless desert. Or perhaps he was surrounded by the bedouin in the hinterland or riding his motorcycle through the ocean of sand, leaving it forever haunted by his dagger-wielding, white-clad ghost.

I exchanged an excited look with Minh and then with Lori, their eyes equally bright. The three of us had trouble suppressing our burbling anticipation. This was it. We'd made it.

After about an hour on the road, we arrived. Here at Tell Abrar the sand-swept landscape unfolded as far as the eye could see.

Tainting my excitement with unfounded worry, Tommy's post on *Dig It* came back to me all of a sudden. Being here, away from modernity and surrounded by sand on all sides, the unforgiving sun over my head, it was easy to surrender to the idea of meteors crashing into the sands, their fiery spirits lingering to haunt the land to this day. I was about to ask Tommy about his strange blog post, but he finished parking our car and it was time to get out and get going.

Let the adventure begin.

WELCOME TO THE DIG

By the time we arrived at Dad's dig site, the light was beginning to fade. With darkness encroaching came a slight temperature drop. Whenever Dad talked about his fieldwork experiences, he never failed to mention how unforgiving the desert could be: *The desert, it'll treat you like an equal if you are prepared, if you are strong enough, but it'll devour you whole if you display any sign of weakness.*

After showing us to our assigned tents, where we dropped our luggage, Tommy took us by the supplies marquee. There, a perky Swedish graduate student named Ada, her eyelashes and brows almost as pale as her skin, issued us camp-appropriate attire: unisex khakis, steel-toe shoes, and long-sleeved shirts. Also baseball caps, the same kind Tommy was wearing, designed especially for this dig campaign. The excavation project was primarily sponsored by two philanthropic research-funding bodies and six universities, including Australia's Dunstan University and some of Dubai's local institutions.

I eyed the cap I was given. It didn't look much different from a V8 Supercars merchandise item, with sponsor logos covering almost the entirety of the fabric. Ada informed us we were to wear our dig uniforms and caps throughout our stay, as the sun and the heat were unforgiving. Dehydration and heatstroke were a daily threat.

After saying our goodbyes to Ada, Tommy ushered us on a mini tour. Even as the sunlight vanished completely, the camp was still bustling with activity. Most of the people we ran into were of the blond and blue-eyed variety. This was strange because a bunch of universities located in the region were among the dig's key sponsors, so I'd expected the largest chunk of student volunteers to be local.

All the dig site's nightly illumination, weak and eerie by this point, came from small generator-run lamps fastened to the tents. Two main paths—one winding between the sleeping tents, stretching all the way to the medical center, and another leading to the portable bio-toilets and eco-showers and, farther on, the cafeteria— crossed at the camp's center. Each residential tent slept five, but since it was still the dig's early days, I was to

room with Lori and Minh, without anyone else joining us. The situation was different for the boys: Rowen
and Luke were sharing sleeping quarters with three students from University College London. The Londoners
were here to collect data for their master's theses, and it
sounded like they'd have little time to socialize.

By the time Tommy was showing us the cafeteria, I
was only half listening. Whether it was the postflight
fatigue, the lingering heat, or both, there was something
off about the dig site. It was well populated but also subdued, like something lying in wait, its tail coiling. Once
more I wanted to question Tommy about that blog post
he wrote chronicling Tell Abrar's alleged paranormal
lore, but this wasn't a good moment—with Minh hanging on Tommy's every word and Luke sticking too close
to me for comfort.

As if he had access to my thoughts, Luke interrupted
Tommy's reciting of our meal schedule. "So I've read that
blog post you wrote about this place, and I have questions. Like what some meteor crashing into the desert
almost a century ago has got to do with this site and
people disappearing into thin air?"

Tommy looked at Luke as if he were speaking in
tongues. Then Tommy's eyes shifted to me. He wasn't getting any help here; I wanted to know about his blog post
too.

"It was just a way of generating some external interest

for the dig," Tommy offered, the words coming off practiced. "Unusual local history tends to attract investors."

This rationale made sense, but Tommy wasn't answering the real question. And as it turned out, he wasn't planning to. Luke's mention of the blog post made Tommy cut the tour short; he left us to our own devices. His abrupt dismissal left an annoying aftertaste, obvious from everyone's faces.

Then Rowen said conspiratorially, "Should we celebrate our safe arrival?" His professionally whitened teeth all but shone in the dark.

"What did you have in mind?" Lori's voice dropped low as a group of camp residents shuffled along the sandy pathway not far from us.

"We could get keys to one of those jeeps and drive ourselves to the city. It won't take more than an hour. I've heard about this rooftop bar . . ."

Lori looked excited, but Minh was having none of it. "The most ridiculous part of this plan is that you're actually being serious." Minh glared at Rowen, her dark hazel eyes drilling into him. "You're gonna get us all in trouble on our first night here. We'll probably get arrested for being underage and trying to get into a bar."

"You're no fun." Rowen shook his head, his eyes not meeting hers. "Maybe you should stay here then, Minh. But the rest of us, we're going to do *something*, right?" He looked between us for approval, but Minh's grim prediction dampened everyone's mood. Even Lori didn't seem that enthused anymore.

Not finding support for his plan, Rowen was shaking his head as he addressed all of us. "You're all so boring." He looked at Lori. "Do you want to ditch them?"

Lori nodded, eager once more, and, without another word, the two of them rounded the medical tent and the night swallowed them.

"I'm calling it a night," Minh announced. She slid her hands into her pockets and found my eyes in the semidarkness before taking her first tentative steps toward the tents. She hesitated. I knew she was expecting me to follow her. When I didn't, she looked at me again, eyes heavy with a silent question. After a pause, visually deflated, she wished me and Luke good night and strolled in the general direction of our tent.

I wasn't sure why I chose to stay. It wasn't that I wanted to hang out with Luke all that much. But I also couldn't imagine getting into bed right away—too much travel adrenaline. Besides, spending some quality one-on-one time with Minh could lead to us discussing this whole Rowen-Lori situation, and I just didn't want to open what surely promised to be a can of worms. And besides, where exactly did my loyalty lie? I was friends with Minh, yes, but I was also friends with Rowen and Lori.

"Wanna go for a walk?" Luke motioned at the

darkened path that stretched away from the main cluster of tents. When I met his eyes, he smiled. I smiled back; we shared a moment of understanding. We were too excited to be here to just go to sleep. And I was relaxed around him. If Luke had ever been into me, he would surely have made his move by now.

"Sure," I said. "As long as we don't go *that* way." I indicated the path recently taken by Lori and Rowen. That made Luke laugh, and we proceeded in the opposite direction.

I kept tripping because my eyes were being drawn up to the sky—cloudless and fragile, with bright stars and a gigantic moon that had a green undertone to its paleness. The moon's every dark spot was defined with almost artistic precision.

When I tripped again, Luke wove his fingers around my wrist. Somehow that progressed into holding hands. I'd have taken this unexpected development as a friendly gesture if not for the uncharacteristic intent to the way Luke's fingers gripped mine and the weird tension coming off him in waves. He'd never been tense around me before. We both must've been tired from our trip and, before that, from our final school exams. I gave Luke a puzzled look that got lost in the night, and we kept on walking like that, holding hands.

When we were far enough from the camp for the groups of tents to become amorphous blurs, we stopped and, without conferring, sat on the ground. I let go of Luke's hand and looked up to watch the stars, wishing I had a nice little Dobsonian telescope on me right now. Some of the tension I sensed from Luke earlier seemed to be waning, and I was glad of it. With Lori apparently hooking up with Rowen, I didn't want to start anything with Luke and leave Minh out of the group and on her own. She was already broody. Besides, I never thought of Luke as anything more than a friend. He was a nice-enough guy, and he did break the nose of my bully that one time, but still.

"So . . . Would you like to make out? With me?" Luke asked.

I sharply inhaled and faced him. I couldn't see his freckles, but I could imagine his face was turning a shade redder under my shocked stare. Luke laughed and looked away, embarrassed. Before I could come up with a response to his blunt proposition, he went on.

"Before you laugh it off and then get all weird around me for the rest of our holiday, hear me out. I'm thinking . . . you're hot, I'm hot, and we're both unat-tached . . . Why not, you know, take advantage of it while we're out here and under lax adult supervision?"

His brutal honesty caught me off guard, to the point that I began considering his offer.

"You've clearly given this a lot of thought."

"I have. Here's my logic. Well, the rest of it, anyway.

We know each other really well. We're friends, and I know you don't blush and stumble around me like you do when Ortiz is around, so if we make out, you're not going to get hurt afterward. Because you don't care about me *that* way, you know."

Unbelievable. I snorted. "I'm glad you care about my feelings, Luke. But what about you? What makes you so sure you're not just going to fall head over heels in love with me after one kiss?"

"There's only one way to find out." Quick to act, he brought his face close to mine, and, despite knowing how bad—no, *terrible*—an idea this was, I didn't shy away. He smelled of soap and green-tea-scented shampoo. His lips and the cocky way he held himself combined with the sheer audacity of his hitting on me made me a little dizzy. My heart didn't exactly speed up when Luke brought his lips to mine, but when his body heat washed over me, striking against the night's gentle chill, I didn't feel revulsion either. In fact, I was mildly turned on. An alarmed thought crossed my mind as I recalled Dubai's strict indecent-exposure laws, but the desert promised solitude, and I relaxed.

Testing out the extent of this temporary lapse of judgment, I scooched closer to Luke, and our lips touched once more for a drawn-out moment. Then again, lasting longer this time. There was a certain consideration in these kisses but also a slow-burning sensation of rebellion.

Of wrongdoing. Encouraged by my willful participation, Luke took it to the next level, his mouth becoming more demanding as he wrapped his hands around me, pulling me tight to his chest. One of his hands snaked its way up to rest on the back of my neck, while another traveled dangerously low. His tongue met mine. My inhibitions melted away as I relaxed more and more with each breath we took when we briefly came up for air. I saw the night skies again when Luke's weight pushed me down on my back with gentle but unyielding force. He cradled my head. It occurred to me he was doing that so I didn't get sand in my hair. That was nice of him.

A subtle cough made me pull away from Luke. I craned my neck up to find Tommy towering over us. His face was unreadable, but his lips were so tight, he looked like he had no mouth. I would have laughed at that if not for his burning eyes.

"There's a curfew here." Tommy pushed his hands in his pockets and kept on staring at us.

"Why?" Luke's voice carried a challenge. "Are we in danger of disappearing like the people you wrote about in your blog post?"

After glaring at Luke like he was a nuisance of the lowest rank, Tommy shook his head. When he spoke again, Tommy pointedly made eye contact with me, ignoring Luke. "We're in the middle of nowhere. If you wander off into the wilderness, it might be a while before you're found. And we can't afford to be rescuing every single fool who gets himself lost."

"And who made you the enforcer of the rules?" Luke stood up and stretched a hand my way without looking at me.

I snubbed his offer of help and got myself up, then found Luke's eyes and mouthed, "Stop this."

He grew silent, but his standoffish posture made clear he was bubbling with anger. This was not good. Despite my dubbing him a nice guy in my head, Luke was still an unknown, even after years of us being friends. I did know one thing about him for sure though—he was prone to sudden anger, even physical violence.

I saw his fingers twitching, as if wanting to curl into fists. Too much testosterone.

"Let's just go back to the tents." I grabbed Luke's hand. He was like a coiled spring, in urgent need to release pressure. I gripped his hand tighter and pulled, forcing him to walk with me in the direction of the camp. I avoided Tommy's eyes, but his glare was magnetic, and I kept being drawn to his face as he walked beside us.

When the three of us crossed back over the camp's unofficial border, Tommy stalked off into the dark, leaving us abruptly. Luke and I walked the rest of the way to the residential tents without exchanging a single word, but we were still holding hands, both of us too stubborn to let go. I finally decided to drop Luke's hand when we were close to our assigned tents. Relieved about parting with him for the night, I faced Luke and noticed his frown.

"Can we just be civil?" I asked.

He nodded once before squeezing out through his teeth, "I can't stand him."

"Don't be so melodramatic."

"Can I at least kiss you good night?"

"Not sure if that's such a great idea," I started to say, eager to retreat into the safety of the tent, but Luke stepped into my space and landed a quick fluttering kiss on my lips. So much for consent.

"Happy now?" I took another step back, growing annoyed—with Luke for coming on to me, and with myself for not rejecting him. "Let's *not* do this. We have a few fun weeks ahead. I wouldn't want our time here to be defined by a failed make-out session and some wounded pride."

"Eloquent as usual, Alif," Luke murmured. He tried to shove his fingers into his pockets but ended up with his hands flat against his sides, looking indecisive. "Sleep well, *friend*," he went on. "I look forward to seeing you in the morning."

I watched Luke's back as he departed, my mind growing even more uncomfortable at this possibly huge mistake I'd made in kissing him.

I pushed the tent's door flap out of the way, complete darkness meeting me inside. My hands stretched out in front of me, I walked in, then put the tent's curtain of a door in its place. From our quick tour earlier, I remembered that my bed was to the right, so I took cautious steps in that direction and relaxed only when I lowered myself onto the mattress. I sat there for a few breaths, waiting for my eyes to adjust. The bed facing the tent's door was Lori's. It was empty. On the bed across from mine, Minh's long black hair was spread across a white pillow. I watched Minh's form shift dreamily under the blanket. She was fussing in her sleep.

As my eyes grew more accustomed to the dark, I could make out the movement of shadows on the tent's walls. Eyes tired, I watched the shadow play as thoughts of Mom creeped up on me and wouldn't let go. Mom's college minor was philosophy, and when she was a grad student she had to teach Philosophy 101 to support herself financially. Whenever she reminisced about it, she joked that discussing philosophical concepts with freshmen was a special kind of hell. But I knew that she secretly *loved* teaching undergrads and that she missed it dearly ever since she became a full-time field archaeologist.

I *also* knew that Mom's favorite part of teaching Philosophy 101 was discussing the works of the greatest minds of the ancient world: Plato, Aristotle, Socrates . . . and also Hypatia, Theodora, Catherine of Alexandria, and many others. Mom did her honors thesis on women philosophers of the ancient world—those who were written out of most histories but whose ideas and discoveries still rang true today. But Plato's allegory of the cave was Mom's favorite icebreaker with freshmen. Plato described our perception of reality using an allegory of people who were chained to the wall of a cave throughout their entire lives. They faced a wall, where they could see shadows created as various objects passed in front of a fire that raged behind them. The longer they stared at the shadows, the more they grew accustomed to them. And so, for them, there was nothing to life but shadows dancing on the wall. Mom relished in revealing the "punch line" to her students: Most people saw shadows their entire lives, just like those prisoners of the cave, and for them this was all there was. Just shadows. An incomplete reflection of reality, which was never the "real" thing.

I was supposed to call Mom the moment I landed in Dubai, but I deliberately didn't. I even ensured my phone was off so she couldn't call or message me.

Five years ago, after my parents split up, I lobbied for my right to stay in Melbourne with Dad, my decision intensifying the uneasy space that already existed between Mom and me. My parents' divorce wasn't even one of those extreme scenarios when lying or cheating has led to the collapse of a marriage, but I guess I always irrationally blamed Mom for it, even if I couldn't articulate why. Most girls I know are close to their mothers—take Lori, for instance, or Minh, whose mom was her best friend and confidante growing up—and they tend to take their side in a divorce. It wasn't like that for me. Mom never being one for deep and meaningful talks didn't help. Her aptitude for lecturing about philosophical concepts or archaeological field methods for hours at a time didn't extend to talking about the things that should've mattered the most. Whenever I'd make an effort to understand Mom's side of things during and following the divorce, the metaphorical door got shut in my face, and Mom and I drifted even further apart.

Shortly following the divorce, Mom headed back to Birmingham, her girlhood hometown, where a job was waiting for her. I had a standing invitation to visit her in England whenever I felt like it. And I did go once in a while, but every time I'd visit, it'd take us a few days just to get reacquainted with each other, and even then we kept each other at arm's length. I think, back then, I was still harboring hopes that my parents' separation was just a phase they were going through. But then somewhere along the way I gave up on the idea. Besides, my life was in Melbourne, so the distance between Mom and me widened every year until, eventually, she became a semi-stranger in my life.

I missed the exact moment when I tired myself out. Tearing up after staring at the light and moving shadows for too long, I surrendered to the fatigue and closed my eyes, heavy sleep pulling me under.

A TROWEL,
A PLUMB BOB, AND
NOT A SINGLE SUN
HAT IN SIGHT

Lori must've snuck back into the tent sometime after I fell asleep. But in the morning, she wouldn't admit she was out late, despite my teasing. Jet-lagged and parched, Lori, Minh, and I eventually dragged ourselves out of the tent and made a beeline for the bathrooms. We were hauling along our travel toiletries bags stuffed with toothbrushes, shampoo bottles, and sunblock tubes. Between the three of us it was quite an endeavor to get ready for the day ahead.

In the clear early-morning light I got to see more of the camp. It spread out farther into the desert than I'd imagined. The tight groups of tents surrounded the dig's three main subsites, which formed the camp's dug-up heart. A lone excavator stood idly to the side. The area must have been too artifact-stuffed to use heavy machinery. Khaki-clad volunteers were already gathering by their stations, instruments at the ready, hands eager to get dirty.

As I kept looking around me, I recalled Mom's words that had burned themselves into my earliest childhood memories: *Archaeology is all about the past. Archaeologists look backward.* Whenever I remembered her saying that, child-me would imagine this middle-aged bearded white dude wearing knee-length shorts and a safari hat with eyes inexplicably at the back of his head (so he could look backward!). As I grew older, this picture changed into one of a woman—thanks to watching Mom work in the field in her beloved multipocket khaki pants, gray singlet, and baseball cap. Not even once in her entire life had she ever worn a sun hat, and her dreamy but eagle-sharp eyes were trained on the horizon ahead or at the ground at her feet, not backward.

Just like my parents, everyone on this dig lived and breathed archaeology. I envied their unilateral focus in life. I had yet to find mine, but I hoped I was getting closer each day. As a child of not one but two archaeologists, it was always assumed I'd follow in my parents' footsteps, but deep down I wasn't so sure. I loved many aspects of the discipline, like the fascinating discoveries and all the theory testing preceding those, but I was also realistic. It was a tough field to break into. Maybe being out here, on an active dig, would help me gain the focus I needed in life.

Back in our tent, I unfolded my dig-issued khakis and white long-sleeved shirt, both wrinkled and half a size too big. With a sigh, I put the khakis on, hoping the folds would stretch out on their own. I personalized my attire by donning a London Grammar tee instead of the generic dig shirt. I might end up with sunburns on my arms, but at least I'd look stylish. There were no mirrors in the tent though, so no matter how much I stared down at my body in hopes of getting some idea of how the ensemble really looked, I was left hanging.

Another mandatory item of clothing I couldn't bring myself to wear was the baseball cap. The mere thought of it sitting tight on my head all day and the sweaty-itchy mess it'd create made me shudder. I knew I was being childish, but still, defiantly, I stuffed the cap into my pants' back pocket. It didn't come to me as a surprise that Lori was equally rebellious in her clothing choices: She had just enough conformity in her bones to wear the khakis, but that didn't extend as far as the headgear. Only Minh wore the whole outfit, cap and all. Before leaving the tent, the three of us, Australian to the core, slathered our faces and necks with SPF 50 sunblock. We were all scarred for life by those brutal skin-cancer-awareness ads the government used to run, so sunblock was our daily staple no matter what.

As we were getting ready, I kept watching Minh's interactions with Lori, expecting to see some hostility or at least weirdness between them, but all seemed civil and friendly. Maybe my observation of Minh giving Rowen and Lori the stink eye yesterday was just my being tired and misreading the situation. Or maybe it was just Rowen who Minh was upset with? I guess, after my own strange adventures with Luke yesterday, followed by the awkward moment with Tommy, I wasn't the best judge of human intentions. As a side note, in the unforgiving light of a new day I was ready to die of embarrassment just thinking about what had happened between me and Luke and Tommy.

We swung by the boys' tent to find Luke and Rowen practically asleep on their feet. It reeked of alcohol inside their tent. The drinks must've been supplied by their older roommates. We spared the boys the ridicule, and soon the five of us were headed for the volunteer information booth to meet Tommy.

I eyed Tommy from afar and put on a bored expression as we approached him. My pride was going to be my undoing. Tommy didn't look too excited about his assigned role of babysitting us either. Still, with enviable patience, he answered all our questions and even had the decency not to mention anything about my misfortunes last night, despite Luke staring daggers at him. Tommy told us that ever since he and my father made their way to the site ten days ago, groups of volunteers had been arriving to the camp every day. Most of these volunteers were students, here to partake in the dig for a university credit or to gather data for their graduate research projects. Aside from Rufus, son of Dr. Archer Palombo, my father's second-in-command, I was the only other camp brat. And tourists like my friends were even a bigger rarity out here. But tourist or not, everyone had to pull their share.

After watching a safety instruction video, we followed Tommy to the cafeteria for breakfast. Our group was a late arrival, with most people already leaving. Stomachs rumbling, we took our seats, and I realized, much to my surprise, that Tommy was going to eat breakfast with us. At our table. That was totally cool. I was cool with that. Totally.

Nearby, there was another late-arriving group of student volunteers, big and loud and, based on the volume and velocity of their chatter, superhyped on the dig's atmosphere of discovery. Looking at them made me happy, even hopeful, for the future of humanity. They were so different, with accents from all over the place and complexions ranging from lighter to darker tones. But they were all here, united by a common goal, ready to spend their days covered in dust from head to toe and diligently brushing dirt from rocks. Education was not a given, and I knew how privileged we all were to even be here, but still it warmed my heart that this was possible for so many people.

My unexpected state of balance with the world made my raisin-laden porridge taste better than it was. I washed it down with tar-like black tea. But my brief moment of contentment was already fading. My jet lag was back and getting worse, and, judging from their frowning mouths, my friends weren't any better off. Our group, even Tommy, was growing more and more quiet, subdued. Despite the caffeine in my tea, my eyelids were being pulled down with the weight of my eyelashes. I rubbed at my eyes, hoping to invigorate them. I wore no makeup today—it was all going to melt away in this heat anyway—but being in close proximity to Tommy I kept thinking about how stubby my lashes must've looked, especially compared to his ridiculously long and curly ones. He met my eyes but quickly looked away.

Lori and Rowen were holding hands under the table, and I kept catching Luke's attention as his inquiring eyes roamed all over my face. I did my best to ignore his looks while also treating him the way I always have—as a friend who is also a guy. Minh was acting slightly cold with me, probably still pissed at me for blowing her off last night, but, as I'd noticed earlier, she was nice and perfectly sweet with Lori. And, as usual, aside from one fleeting look, Tommy was indifferent toward me. Everything was rather normal.

I still hadn't seen Dad, and he hadn't called me either. When I swallowed my vanity and asked Tommy about my father's whereabouts, he said in a reverent tone that Dad had been in and out of the camp negotiating with the local bedouin community leaders in hopes of hiring a local workforce for the dig. Apparently a big chunk of volunteers from local universities pulled out from the excavation due to "safety concerns," leaving it understaffed. Dad was expected to return sometime midday today. That was all I could get out of Tommy. He avoided my questions around the "safety concerns." It was as if he'd exhausted his ration of words for the morning. Yet he still stuck around our table to eat his porridge, ignoring the calls of his fellow Dunstan students for him to join them as they headed out of the cafeteria.

"What's the plan for today?" Rowen's question snapped Tommy out of his quiet.

"You've gotten the full overview of the camp, so now you can decide what you want to do for the rest of your stay." Tommy's sharp eyes were on me when he said that. *Unsettling.* Why was he always so serious, so intense? I tried to recall the last time I'd seen Tommy smile and couldn't.

Tommy continued. "In terms of options—there's the dig itself, but you'd have to be prepped on what to do, and how not to damage the samples, and also how to label them properly. So, I'm afraid, your choice is between kitchen duty and post-dig labeling."

"You can't be serious," Luke scoffed. "Do you think I came here to wash dirty pots and catalog old bones?"

Tommy's face grew stone-cold, or *more* stone-cold, to be precise, since he wasn't a ray of sunshine to begin with. I wished Luke would just stop with his macho posturing or whatever this was. Alarmed, I watched a little crease form on Tommy's forehead. When his eyes slid over my face again, I mentally flinched. He must've been super unhappy with me for bringing my friends here.

To Luke Tommy said, "Sure, I'm going to let you join the excavation crew. Do you know how to use the tools to get stuff out of the ground without breaking it? Can you tell a trowel from a plumb bob? And are you aware of the procedures we must follow in case we do come across human remains, or, as you call them, 'old bones'? Or does your entire knowledge of archaeology come from watching Indiana Jones movies?"

Stunned into belligerent silence by Tommy's outburst, Luke seethed for the rest of breakfast. I couldn't be seen publicly taking Tommy's side over my friend's, but secretly Tommy's putting Luke in his place pleased me.

By the time I finished with my porridge, I made my decision about my work assignment. I wanted to be on labeling duty. Minh and Luke joined me, and Lori and Rowen, surprisingly, chose to help out in the kitchen.

We all tagged along while Tommy took Lori and

Rowen deeper into the cafeteria tent, around the serving counter, and into the fiery heart of the field kitchen. There, he introduced my friends to Riley Hassan, the camp's head cook. Born in Hobart to Lebanese Australian parents, Riley first met my father when young Riley was an apprentice chef straight out of cooking school. Years later, when Dad had the first project of his own to manage, he sought out Riley and invited him to join the dig. Ever since, the two of them frequently worked together. On rare occasions when Riley was not available, it was a real struggle to find a good replacement.

Riley and I greeted each other like old friends before he and Tommy led Lori and Rowen away to get them started, leaving me, Minh, and Luke to our own devices. I wanted to chat with Riley some more but didn't get a chance, though he winked at me and said something embarrassing about me growing up so fast. This was the thing about being a camp brat: Everyone still saw me as some little rascal running around in her shorty shorts. Luke snorted at Riley's words, and despite my amazing self-control, I reddened in the face.

Tommy had told us to wait for his return, but I was familiar with the camp's layout by now and had a solid idea where the labeling tent was. I told my friends I was going, and, having nothing better to do, Minh and Luke followed me out into the suffocating heat.

WHEN A STRANGER COMES FROM THE DESERT

Dr. Archer Palombo's booming voice could be heard before we even entered the tent. Memories warmed my heart when Dr. Palombo's large frame came into view. He and his family were a common fixture at my parents' house all throughout my childhood. The Scholls and the Palombos used to be tight. We celebrated everything together, from birthdays to tenure milestones. That is, before the divorce. Archer's wife, Milena, was a close friend of my mother, and to preserve their friendship, Milena distanced herself from anything involving my dad. Which meant no more loud and busy end-of-the-year parties with the Palombos.

Walking up and down the length of a long and narrow

table, Dr. Palombo reminded me of a father hawk looking over his beloved hatchlings—the four volunteers he had in his care. They were busy working through their allocated bags of finds. Among the volunteers was Rufus, Dr. Palombo's youngest son, and, at thirteen years of age, likely the youngest person on this dig site. Rufus was the first to notice me.

"Alif!" He jumped out of his seat, nearly tipping over his water basin as he came in for a hug. Some of the muddied liquid sloshed on the table, prompting the other volunteers to give Rufus evil looks. He was like an overeager puppy, full of energy and enthusiasm.

Clad in his camp-issued khakis and white shirt, Dr. Palombo still carried a touch of his eccentric style. A red silky scarf traveled around his neck and a black dusty fedora sat crooked on his head. The hat was worn ironically, of course. Real archaeologists were not huge fans of Indiana Jones–type fedoras, but most had a healthy sense of humor. Dr. Palombo's expression changed from annoyance to a huge smile when he spotted me.

"You made it!" he exclaimed. "And here's Ms. Minh Quoc, gorgeous as always! You're all grown up! Amazing!"

Minh grinned at him; hers was a rare, disarming smile. I introduced Luke to Dr. Palombo and Rufus, explaining that we'd all gone to school together. "Luke's waiting for his acceptance into Dunstan Law," I added.

"Well, here's one sure thing—the world needs more lawyers." There was not a hint of teasing in Dr. Palombo's voice, but he did give me a mischievous wink when Luke looked away.

After Dr. Palombo crushed me in a bear hug, he repeated the gesture with Minh and Luke. "And what about our lovely Minh? Are you here because you're thinking of following in the footsteps of our own brave, dear Dr. Andreas Scholl?"

Minh looked away and mumbled something about doing a gap year. The ugly truth was that even if she did receive her first-choice university offer, there was no guarantee she could afford to go. Therefore, she was seriously considering a gap year to work. Her family was never well-off, and this trip to Dubai was only possible thanks to some help from my dad and Luke's family, but we were sworn to secrecy on this. We didn't want to embarrass Minh, so the official story was that she was a recipient of some grant from a generous sponsor. I was just glad she didn't go digging into this explanation. It wouldn't take her long to uncover that Tucker Oil didn't really exist.

To Dr. Palombo Minh said, "I'm considering a career as a car mechanic, like my granddad." This was the first I'd heard of it, but I let it go.

Luke was not so subtle. "Going to break some gender barriers, huh, Minh?" he asked.

Minh shivered from a nonexistent draft. "At least I'm going to do something *original* with my life. Unlike some third-generation wannabe lawyer."

Dr. Palombo changed the topic, looking my way. "Andreas was really torn he couldn't be here when you arrived, Alif. But he's been busier than expected." He urged Rufus to come back to his seat at the labeling table before taking me and my friends aside.

"What's with all the foreign-student volunteers?" I asked Dr. Palombo when we were out of hearing range of the table-bound group. "I mean, it's a *lot* more international grad students than usual. Where are all the locals?"

"Well . . . there were some unforeseen circumstances affecting the logistics of the dig and Andreas had to issue a call for more grad students to come out here. Most of our local student force, and quite a few Londoners as well, pulled out right after we finished with all the heavy-duty excavation and extraction work."

"What happened?" Minh asked.

Dr. Palombo sighed, staring into space, gathering his thoughts or being caught in a memory. "This place is *nun*. Apparently."

"What, like *bad luck*?" My knowledge of Arabic was eclectic at best, random vocab fluttering in my brain like spooked butterflies ever since we landed in Dubai. But the word Dr. Palombo used? I knew that one. *Nun* was the fourteenth letter of the Arabic alphabet. Other languages, like Hebrew and Aramaic, also used the same or a similar pictogram for *nun*. The pictogram itself looked like a zigzag, but more likely was meant to symbolize a snake—hence its evil or "bad luck" connotation.

Dr. Palombo nodded gravely. "It's like we're on the set of some ridiculous Hollywood movie! We're certain we know how the rumor started though. There was a minor accident here on the second day of the excavation, and two men—a local named Amir we hired to operate the excavator and one of my own students, Matthew— got injured and had to be taken to a hospital. Amir told us that Matthew caused the accident when he became sort of 'entranced' and released the harness too soon . . . When we finally managed to speak with Matthew in the hospital, he told us he saw a stone-walled city rise out of the sand far out in the desert. This city was surrounded by a flock of white birds—like a halo. This is pretty much verbatim. After that, neither Amir nor Matthew wanted to return to the excavation site. And now we're having trouble retaining students at the dig. Some people are . . . uncomfortable."

"Superstitious bunch, aren't they, these locals?" Luke swallowed whatever he was going to say next when I glared at him.

I said, "It sounds like this Matthew was the one who started the rumor."

"Doesn't matter now," Dr. Palombo said. "The damage is done. We just have to work with what we've got. We'll make do." He went back to the table and started setting up our workstations. The three of us got seated and were given some easy tasks to do first.

There's a certain art to the processing of finds. When I was a kid, Dad would set me up with a plastic basin and give me little trinkets to wash. I would sink each object—unassuming pebbles, arrowheads, ceramic fragments—under water and brush off the dirt with gentle strokes, careful not to damage the object's surface. Not much has changed since then. Washing, marking, and sorting are still the three pillars of finds processing. And we already had ten days' worth of stuff in need of cleaning and labeling. Here were the rules to follow: Work with one bag of finds at a time, and always, *always* comply with the filing system's rules. If you don't, you might mislabel things, and that's going to cause trouble later on. Each bag of finds we were given had a site code—a two-letter abbreviation for the site itself and the last digits of the year of excavation. Dad's site was split into three sectors, each coded clockwise. I picked up an unopened bag labeled *ceramics*. I took it to my station, on my way grabbing an empty tray. I poured some water into the tray . . .

When I checked my watch again, it was nearly lunchtime. I stood up to stretch my legs and let the momentum carry me out of the tent. Minh followed me outside.

Together we covered a small distance to where Luke was smoking in a shadowed spot overlooking the desert. Droplets of sweat were streaming down his face, which must have washed away his sunblock. I wondered where Luke's baseball cap was. I could already see red patches on his forehead where his skin was starting to burn.

"How can you smoke in this heat?" I asked, but Luke had no chance to give me his snarky response because a commotion drew our attention. A crowd was forming at the far right of the dig camp, down where the outer tents met the desert proper. From afar, a familiar blotch of red stood out in the thickening sea of white, gray, and beige—Dr. Palombo's scarf. Before I fully registered what I was doing, my legs were carrying me toward the chaos.

"Some excitement, at last!" Luke commented as he fought to keep up with me. Leaving Minh behind, the two of us got to the outer edge of the gathering crowd first. Standing on tiptoe, a girl with cropped red hair was saying something to her friend that ended with "a French tourist!"

I joined her example and stretched higher, trying to see above the crowd. To my right, a young man with a shaved head, turning pink under the merciless sun, was murmuring to Ada, who we had met yesterday, "Dehydrated and completely out of it."

To which Ada replied in a low, heavily accented voice, "Maybe our defectors weren't wrong after all. Maybe this place *is* bad luck."

51

I saw him then, the reason for this gathering. They carried him away on a makeshift cot. A white man, possibly in his late forties, though it was hard to tell exactly. His face had suffered some awful sunburns, and his hair was bleached white.

Dr. Palombo, one of the people carrying the cot, noticed me in the crowd and called over his shoulder by way of explanation, "He wandered in from the desert . . . Alif, why don't you go back to the admin tent and wait for your father there? He's due to come back any second now."

I was about to take off when the man lying semiconscious in the cot opened his eyes wide and grabbed my hand. "Dup Shimati awaits. She grows restless."

He passed out again.

Frozen in my spot, I watched as they carried him into the med tent.

"What was that about? Dup Shimati?" Minh asked, her tongue awkward on the foreign words.

I hadn't seen when she caught up with us.

"I have no idea," I told her.

In the spot where the man had touched it, my hand was cold amid the heat.

THE THING
ABOUT CURSES

If adventure filmmakers are to be believed, every significant past archaeological discovery is plagued by a horrible curse or two. A disturbed mummy will come alive and devour the hearts and brains of everyone implicated in the mummy's unearthing . . . A wicked artifact will poison the souls of whoever dared take it out of its altar at the center of an ancient subterranean temple. No matter how the story began it'll most likely end with a hero sprinting away from the source of the curse while swinging a bullwhip and smacking the heads of the undead against each other as if they're petrified coconuts. (Real archaeologists aren't normally very buff, by the way, so I seriously doubted they'd hold their own against an army of mummified nasties thirsty for vengeance.)

What allegedly befell the excavation group led by Howard Carter, the discoverer of King Tutankhamun's tomb (though whether it was truly his discovery or that of a local water boy who fatefully stumbled across some steps in the sand is a point of debate), is probably the most well-known non-movie-invented curse in archaeology's history. As legend had it, the inscription on the tomb heralded a warning: *They who enter this sacred tomb shall swift be visited by wings of death.* Conveniently though, the inscription was never photographed, and the plaque holding the said inscription went missing shortly after the tomb's discovery.

King Tut's first victim to be swiftly visited by the "wings of death" was Carter's pet canary. When the poor bird got swallowed by a cobra (I'm not making this shit up), all hell broke loose at the excavation site, panic quickly reaching far beyond the site's bounds. The importance of the cobra as a pharaonic symbol of royalty, confirmed by its prominent placement on the pharaoh's crown, didn't escape the fearful attention of those fearing the curse.

The notion of student volunteerism didn't really exist back then, and archaeologists had to hire local labor to work the digs. It was said that after Carter's canary met its end, the locals working Carter's dig became reluctant to continue on with the excavation. Maybe they had a point. Pet canaries aside, notably, it was Carter's benefactor, Lord Carnarvon, who officially "began" the countdown of Tut-attributed human fatalities. Carnarvon died shortly after Tut's discovery from an infection caused by a mosquito bite.

But in the end, statistically speaking, King Tut's curse wasn't *that* effective. Out of twenty-five notable citizens (and probably several other people, such as the many unnamed locals working the dig) present at the tomb's opening, most managed to live into their seventies. Maybe Tut's curse just took a while to get them? Modern archaeologists are as skeptical of curses as they are of the Indiana Jones franchise, so, naturally, I wasn't going to put much stock into the weird events happening at Dad's dig site.

After the Desert Man was carried away, the crowd quickly dissipated. I stayed on with my friends, lingering at the vague line where the camp ended and the desert proper began. Soon though, Minh lost interest and walked away, leaving me alone with Luke. Then he sighed and left.

Subtle wind was blowing out from the desert, gentle waves moving across the sand, slaves to the wind's folly. The buzzing sensation remained in my hand where the man had clutched on to me, the cold burn spreading over my skin, even sneaking into my bloodstream. It was just my imagination. It had to be. Still, I rubbed the spot, fingers growing prickly and numb against the clammy skin. Perhaps I was sticking around here because I hoped to see *something* in the depths of the desert. Was I expecting a stone-walled city to spring up out of nowhere and claim the horizon? Or maybe a flock of white birds? When my head cleared, all lingering excitement and adrenaline drained away. I started on my way back into camp, my dazed feet stumbling over the sand-laid pathway.

About thirty minutes following the Desert Man's grand reentry into civilization, my father arrived at the camp. I dropped the filing I was doing at the admin tent and went outside to greet Dad. His four-wheel drive was encrusted with dust, and Dad's shadow appeared longer and thicker than anyone else's. As if he were shrouded in trouble.

By then, Minh and Luke had gone off to the cafeteria. Their excuse for leaving their assigned stations early was that they wanted to gossip with Lori and Rowen about the camp's "curse," but I suspected they'd just grown bored with washing and filing. I didn't blame them. This aspect of archaeological fieldwork was not for everyone. Overhearing Luke's mutterings about the "tediousness" of archaeology while he was slugging through his bag of finds would be infuriating to me if only I didn't agree with him on some level. I myself enjoyed processing the finds, but only to a degree. More like I didn't *mind* it.

Plus it always brought some happy memories from my childhood. But there were other things in life that made me feel a lot more invested—like creative writing. This was a secret I carried close to my heart. No one needed to know about my aspirations, because that way no one would know if I failed.

When Dad saw me, he paused for a second before covering the space between us in long strides and gathering me up into a hug. Dad's familiar aftershave carried a smell of sweat along with the dry heat of the sand. It made me feel safe.

"Alif, I'm so relieved you made it here without a hitch. Were they nice to you at passport control?"

"Why wouldn't they be? I'm very likable, and besides, being part Jordanian helps, I guess?" I laughed at the memory of trying to speak Arabic with an airport migration officer who just wanted to stamp my passport and be done with it. "It was all right, Dad. Thanks for letting me come and bring the gang."

"So sorry I couldn't come pick you up. Archer and I, we're living a logistical nightmare here."

"So I heard."

"I take it you've also heard the bad luck rumors?"

When I nodded in affirmation, he kept on.

"And now we've got this guy who's apparently walked out of the desert and right into our camp. He's barely alive!"

"Is he in the med tent now? How is he?" I'd been wondering what else the Desert Man had to say to his rescuers, aside from the Dup Shimati whisperings or whatever that was. I held back a flurry of questions that was building into a storm in my head.

"We called for a medical team from Dubai to come and collect him," Dad explained. "Their chopper will be arriving shortly. Like I said, he's in pretty bad shape."

"Can I check in on him?"

"Why?" Dad eyed me, surprised.

"He said something to me, and I want to clarify what he meant."

Dad gave me another wide-eyed look and chuckled. "Alif, he's been *hallucinating* since he walked into the camp, or so I've been told. Raving on and on about some trove of treasures and curses or whatnot. I doubt he can sustain an engaging conversation with you, let alone *clarify* anything."

I kept a whining note out of my voice when I said, "But, Dad, he mentioned something really weird to me, something about . . . Dup Shimati? Or something that sounded like that. I just want to know what he meant. The archaeologist in me wants to know."

While my father's face kept its composed expression, his right eyebrow arched up, giving away a spark of recognition. Yup, Dad definitely knew what the Desert Man was mumbling about. To me he said reluctantly,

"Linguistically, those words come from Mesopotamian folklore. It has something do to with control over destiny. Or is it control over the universe?"

"Hang on a sec . . . ," I protested. "*Mesopotamian folklore?* That doesn't make sense. Not geographically at least. The current Dubai territory wasn't part of ancient Mesopotamia."

"Exactly." He looked at me with a certain pride. Dad was always hoping I'd follow in his footsteps and study ancient history and archaeology, so whenever I demonstrated any specialist knowledge on the topic, he was extra proud. "You are correct," he continued. "But it doesn't change the fact that the man is dehydrated and hallucinating. Plus we don't really know anything about him. He could be dangerous."

The distant roar of a chopper on approach made us both look up. The chopper had a bright red cross painted on its side. The Dubai medics were almost here. I was running out of time to wrestle my answer out of the Desert Man's dry lips. Frowning as he followed the chopper's trajectory with his eyes, Dad squeezed my shoulder. "I need to check up on our temporary helipad. I left Tommy in charge of that, so it must be all set up by now, but still . . . You'll be fine?"

"Of course. I'll go rejoin my merry band of misfits," I said to him. Only, instead of walking away I lingered nearby, waiting until Dad had wandered off. A buzzing sensation returned to my hand, a reminder that I had a question or two to ask the badly sunburned stranger who was currently battling dehydration fever in the med tent. My plan of action formed quickly, but I didn't have much time to execute it.

I pulled my hair into a high ponytail, uncaring that a few strands immediately escaped my elastic band, rolled up my sleeves, and ran, leaving a trail of overturned sand behind me. I ducked into the cafeteria and, without changing my pace, rounded the service counter and snuck into the kitchen.

I walked right into Lori and Rowen engaged in an intense make-out session. They were alone, and thankfully they didn't even notice me, despite the ruckus I made skidding to a sudden stop and gasping. I couldn't spare a moment to tease them, though the temptation to jump out and scare the shit out of them was huge. I grabbed what I came for and left.

Outside once more, I kept an eye on the chopper as it was prepping to land on a makeshift helipad by the camp's outer eastern border. The "helipad" was a gigantic plastic circle stretched out on the ground by a band of volunteers. Helipad aside, Dr. Palombo's red scarf was once again the only patch of color against the muted beige hues of the desert. But I saw Tommy in the crowd too. In a move of rare recklessness on his part, he wasn't wearing a cap, his black hair standing out against his light clothing.

Tearing my eyes away from Tommy, I pushed the med tent's curtain-door out of the way and stepped inside. I found him straightaway. The man lay completely still in one of the cots. His chest, rising and falling in slow motion, was the only sign he was alive. Here, in the shade, he looked even worse for wear. His face was sunburned into an angry red mess and his eyes, wide open, were so bloodshot it was as if they had no whites, just pupils surrounded with red. But the most disturbing thing was his mouth, lips moving without making a sound.

A suspicious voice came from the corner to my right: "You don't look like you're with the Dubai medic team." I whirled around to find a young woman there. How could I have missed her earlier? She was sitting in a fold-out chair, a book open on her lap. The look she gave me was one of deep unwelcome.

"Medics are landing right now. Dr. Scholl sent me over with this." I lifted up the bottle of water that I'd procured from the kitchen. "He also said you're needed at the landing site, so you can brief the medics about this man's condition while they're making their way over here."

"Yeah?" Her expression changed from hostile to doubtful. The fear of not following an order from Dr. Scholl must've been stronger than her doubt though, because she stood up and placed her book on the chair. "I'm not supposed to leave him alone." She swung her head in the direction of the man, but I already knew she'd made up her mind. This was almost too easy.

"I'll look after him till they get here," I assured her.

She stared at me, eyes roaming, searching for a sign on my face that I could be trusted. I guess she found it, because she gave me a quick nod and left, letting some scalding-hot air into the tent in her wake.

I lowered myself to the floor, kneeling by the man's side. His eyes remained open, unblinking, but he didn't acknowledge me.

"What's your name?" My question didn't get a reaction out of him either. I persisted. "I'm Alif Scholl. You spoke to me when you first came to the camp. You must've been through a lot . . . If you can hear me, can you tell me what you meant when you said those things about Dup Shimati?"

It was the unfamiliar words spilling off my tongue—*Dup Shimati*—that brought him back to life. He sat up in a jerky motion, but his eyes stayed as they were—open but unseeing, unfocused, looking straight ahead and not at me kneeling by his side.

"Dup Shimati?" I repeated. "What does it mean?"

"The voice of the universe is trapped in there . . . Once you touch its beating heart, it begins to sing, and it sings things into existence . . . It called for us from where it's buried . . . It took what we had and then it let me go, but it wants . . . *needs* . . . more. It's never sated . . ."

The man started to whimper as if in pain or tormented by a memory. The horrid sounds coming out of his mouth brought me to my feet. Somehow through the man's increasingly desperate sounds, I managed to hear approaching footsteps. I rushed away from the tent, anxious to get out of there before the medics and my father arrived and caught me red-handed.

EXODUS AND THE POWER OF THE INTERNET

Dup Shimati . . . Dup Shimati . . . Dup Shimati . . .

In my head the words sizzled the way fire-hot coals do when they're being extinguished by rain. I wandered off without really looking where I was going. What was Desert Man's name? He didn't say. Who was he? How long was he alone in the desert? I didn't get any of the answers I'd been hoping for.

He was delusional, severely dehydrated, and scared, that's for sure. His perception warped, he could no longer distinguish between what was real and what was unreal. Or so I kept telling myself. Tommy's *Dig It* post was turning out to be some kind of self-fulfilling prophecy. But if Tommy knew more than he was letting on, he was doing a great job feigning innocence.

I regained my bearings once I reached the outer edge of the camp. I forced myself to stop and retrace my steps, setting out to find Minh and Luke. My mind kept wandering as I walked through the busy camp. I ran an absentminded hand over my hair. My ponytail was a mess, my hair clinging to my cheeks with sweat. The top of my head felt like I'd been sitting under one of those heat lamps at a hair salon for so long that it had fried my brain. I gave up and extracted my cap from my back pocket, placing it over my head. Heatstroke was worse than a bad fashion choice.

Instead of finding anyone I actually *wanted* to see, I ran into Tommy. The expression he was wearing made me uncomfortable in my own overheated skin. The guy *never* smiled, I swear—at least not when I was around. Tommy's face was half hidden under a low-sitting cap, dark hair curling from underneath the tight fabric. As he neared, he showed no signs of acknowledgment. I played along. Maybe being invisible to Tommy Ortiz wasn't such a bad thing: I could wear my ill-fitted cap in peace, not caring what it looked like.

"Alif?" My name rolling off Tommy's tongue stopped me in my tracks.

I lifted my head to look at him as he flinched in surprise, like I was a robber attacking him from the shadows. "Didn't recognize you at first," he said, unsettled for some reason.

"Oh, hey." I gave him a brisk nod, trying to look and sound busy. "How did the evacuation go?"

"They came and took him away. He's not in good shape, but he'll live. Too much excitement for the camp though. Ever since the chopper took off, Dr. Scholl's been ushering volunteers back to their stations, but they'd rather talk than work. It's like herding cats, I swear."

His confiding in me was so unusual that I stumbled on my words, struggling to sound casual around him. "It's not like it's every day a random guy walks out of the desert and raves about some hidden treasures or whatever."

"What did he say to you, exactly?" Tommy's eyes zeroed in on me. He looked so interested in what I had to say that it gave me a boost of confidence. I didn't even waver when he took a step closer. Despite my rattling heart, I stood my ground.

"Not much. Nothing coherent anyway. Though he did mention a voice of the universe that sings. He called it Dup Shimati, and then . . ." I was about to say that the man started to whimper and cry and how it had been my exit cue, but I stopped, reminding myself that I wasn't supposed to have been in the tent with him.

"And then what?" Tommy prodded.

"And then they carried him away," I lied.

"Dup Shimati, huh?"

"Yes, the fate of the universe. Or something like that." I tried to sound quirky or at least funny, but mostly I just came off like a five-year-old attempting to dazzle a teenager.

Tommy didn't look dazzled. A frown of concern was tugging his mouth down at the corners. "Something's off about all this. First we have that freak accident, then a bunch of volunteers just up and leave the dig, and it's not only that they refuse to come back; it seems *everyone* else around here is now against working the site. And now this guy . . . On the way to the chopper, he told us that he was with some tourist group from France, that his name was Noam Delamer, and that he was in Dubai for a hotelier conference . . ."

"What part of that story do you find strange? Sounds kind of reasonable, all things considered."

"I looked up the conference and . . . well, it took place two years ago. *Two years.*"

"That's impossible. I mean, he does look awful, but not two-years-lost-in-the-desert awful. If he was lost in the desert for that long, he'd be dead."

"I know. But then again, there have been very rare instances of people wandering the desert for even longer than that." Tommy's eyes were intense, as if testing me, his expression carrying just a hint of something.

I stared back at him blankly. Then it dawned on me. "Was that an Exodus reference?"

"I thought you'd appreciate it."

Actually, I did appreciate it, but I was simply too stunned by the fact that Tommy Ortiz had made a joke that was perfectly tailored to my specific taste to reply. I let out an awkward laugh, but it was too late, as the moment had already melted away. Tommy became distracted and tight-lipped once more, announcing we should head to dinner. At least he'd made no mention of walking in on my make-out session with Luke last night. I was grateful for that.

I followed Tommy to the cafeteria, which was already filling with the camp's residents and abuzz with excitement. I looked around, feeling cagey and hoping to avoid running into that girl I'd tricked earlier. Thankfully, she was nowhere to be seen. Not counting Tommy, I was the first of my group to get to our table. A couple of volunteers I remembered from breakfast were quick to join us, and soon Minh arrived, disheveled but in a good mood, followed by the rest of the gang pulling up. We ate our dinner and enjoyed one another's company, and even Tommy looked like he was relaxing.

CERTAIN BENEFITS COME WITH WORKING IN THE KITCHEN

The dinner was Moroccan lamb tagine with rice followed by a "dessert" of imported apples and oranges with stickers still attached to their glossy skin. Tommy was quick to finish up. He stood up to leave but lingered by our table, and it occurred to me that maybe he was trying to come up with a reason to stay. Was our ragtag group the closest thing he had to friends around here? I'd assured Minh during our flight that it was unlikely Tommy was single, but the reality was I knew as little about him as he probably knew about me. And my crush on him was based on what, then? It was something chemical, I guess, as most irrational attractions are.

Finally Tommy started to walk away, his shoulders

sagging a little. Aside from me, no one seemed to notice except Minh.

She turned to me. "He's cute to look at."

A couple of other volunteers overheard her and giggled, but I was embarrassed. I tried staring her down, but Minh was bold and unstoppable this evening.

"Who knows, maybe in the sunburned desert Tommy Ortiz will find love at last in the arms of his mentor's wayward daughter . . ."

"What's gotten into you?" I asked, wondering if Minh was drunk. But she wasn't saying all this for my benefit, as I quickly figured out by studying her. She was trying to catch Rowen's attention. He was oblivious, too invested in his own fast-blooming relationship with Lori.

When we finished eating, we stayed seated until it was just us five left. That's when Rowen caught my gaze and gave me a meaningful look.

"So I heard that an elusive ninja got into the desert survivor's tent and interrogated him about the location of a hidden treasure," he said.

"Oh god . . . How did you know?" I took a sweeping look around the table. My friends' faces confirmed it. *They all knew.* And if Rowen, who was in the kitchen the whole day going at it with Lori, was somehow aware of my detour into the med tent, then probably everyone else knew too. Everyone, including Dad.

"I was trying to be discreet!"

"Oh, so it *is* true!" Lori edged closer. Rowen placed his hand over hers, and she added in a whisper, "All we heard was that a dark-haired girl wearing a London Grammar tee was snooping around the med tent. And since it's likely you're the only person around here who owns a Grammar tee . . ." Lori's grin was triumphant.

Feeling ridiculous at being exposed so easily, I folded my arms around myself to hide the shirt's design. My friends' faces reminded me they were still waiting for an explanation, so I said, "The man said something to me before they carried him into the camp. I just wanted to ask him what he meant."

Luke, quiet till now, scowled. "So where's the treasure buried?"

Resigned, I relayed everything I'd heard from Noam Delamer, including his mentions of Dup Shimati. In case it wasn't common knowledge yet, I also repeated what I'd heard from Dr. Palombo and from Tommy about volunteers refusing to work the dig because of the bad luck rumors and whatnot.

Luke shook his head. "Superstitions are for the weak-minded."

Minh gave him a lingering look. "Maybe. But there's usually a grain of truth behind every superstition."

"Or a grain of stupidity," Luke retorted.

Lori yawned. I knew her well enough to know she'd

71

forced that yawn because the conversation no longer interested her.

"How about we head to our tents?" I proposed. "It's been a long day, and we'll have to compensate tomorrow for all the work we didn't do today."

"I have a better idea!" Rowen pulled up his backpack from the floor and rummaged inside. He gave us a little preview. It was the neck of a bottle. Hard liquor.

"Where did you get that, man?" Luke sounded impressed.

"Let's just say there are certain benefits that come with working in the kitchen, especially when you compare it to sorting through dusty bones all day."

"And by benefits you mean you can steal whatever's not nailed down or glued to the wall?" I kept the judgment out of my tone. Mostly. Rowen's family was wealthy, and yet he had the stickiest fingers of us all. It wasn't kleptomania exactly, but he didn't think twice before grabbing something unattended.

"You don't have to drink if you don't want to, Alif." Lori's voice was a tad condescending.

"Drinking is not what I have a problem with. It's stealing," I insisted. "I brought you all here. Can you at least *try* not to embarrass me in front of my dad and everyone?"

"Whatever." Rowen rolled his eyes before turning to Lori. "We'll come by your place once everyone's settled

72

down for the night." He studied me, as if measuring the likelihood of my telling on him.

I said, "I think Dad's too busy to come say good night to me, if that's what you're worried about."

Rowen gave me one of his signature smiles, looking triumphant.

We retreated into our respective tents, but shortly I was out again, following Lori and Minh to the communal bathrooms. The queue wasn't too bad this time, and as I waited for my turn I listened around, hoping to catch the latest gossip about today's events. But it was just usual dig-camp stuff. It was a bit odd though that no one was talking about the French tourist who was now recovering in a Dubai hospital.

Even after washing my face twice, I still kept finding random grains of sand behind my ears and around my nose. The showers were occupied, and I was restless. Before coming to the bathroom, I'd attempted to brush the sand out of my hair, but, as a result, my locks started resembling rats' tails. This was the first time I'd had long hair on a dig. I realized now why most girls out here wore their hair in low and tight buns twisted at the nape of their neck, their heads covered with baseball caps. With a sigh, I stuck my head under the faucet and worked soap through my roots before rinsing it all out. I wasn't sure if I was going to get the camp's water-pump system clogged with sand, but it was too late now. At least I was clean.

With my wet hair slapping around my cheeks and water running in rivulets down my back, I rushed to return to my tent. The desert air was different now. It smelled of ozone. I shivered in the wind that had intensified while I was busy cleaning myself. I was relieved to return to the tent, where I changed into my sleeping gear of stretched-out yoga pants and a singlet and attempted to towel-dry my hair.

Lori and Minh were already back there, sitting on a blanket spread on the floor and taking turns painting each other's toenails. Both girls were already wearing their pajamas. Lori, ever the beauty queen, had her hair up and secured with a sparkly band matching her glittery black Victoria's Secret shorts and fuchsia tank top. Her skin gleamed, smelling of citrus-scented lotion. Minh, the only child of a laid-back hipster dad and a New Age mom, was clad in her cotton workout pants and a tee I saw her wear outside sometimes. Apparently it doubled as a pajama piece.

I came to join them on the floor. "Aren't you two superhot in those?" Lori asked, casting a judgmental look at our pants-covered legs. She reached out to pat Minh's knee.

"I'm fine and perfect. Thanks for your concern and for feeling me up." Minh pulled her legs into a relaxed lotus pose. She finished with Lori's toenails and started putting away her manicure kit.

"So, Alif," Lori said, her eyes focusing on me, "did

you have some kind of breakthrough with Tommy? I couldn't help but notice he was eyeing you during meals today."

"If having a conversation with him that lasted longer than ten seconds can count as a breakthrough, then yes?" I offered, my shoulder blades tensing. "But what's more interesting is what's going on with you and Rowen."

Next to me, Minh shivered.

Lori blushed. *Blushed*. "Can I tell you two a secret?"

Minh and I waited. Not looking at either of us, Lori whispered, "I like him. I like him *a lot*."

"And does he like you *a lot* too?" Minh raised an eyebrow and pursed her lips. I doubted Lori noticed the note of desperation in Minh's question. I should've never asked Lori about Rowen, but it was too late now. When Lori spoke again, she sounded cautious but also bursting with suppressed feeling. This was different, I thought, not at all how she'd behaved when she'd reported to us every little detail about guys she'd dated before. "I think so. I hope so. This is still recent. And unexpected . . . I think he might be the one. I know, *I know* how ridiculous this sounds, but this is how I'm feeling right now."

"When's the wedding?" Minh deadpanned.

"Shut up, okay?" Lori's cheeks were turning a vicious red.

Luke's and Rowen's voices preceded their entrance into our tent. Rowen already reeked of alcohol, while Luke brought with him a subtle aftershave-and-soap scent that reminded me of our kiss. A knowing smile playing on his lips, Rowen approached Lori and helped her off the floor. The two of them went to sprawl on Lori's bed, their backs against the tent's wall. That left me with Minh and Luke. The three of us managed to fit on my bed, me ending up wedged in between the two of them. It felt cozy and safe. Luke's knees were brushing against mine, setting me off to search for a spark of electricity in our touch, but all I felt was Luke's minty breath and the infernal heat seeping in from outside. Whatever chemicals my body had generated yesterday when I was making out with Luke must've been just an accident.

Talking and laughing, we passed around the bottle of cheap whiskey Rowen had squirreled away from the kitchen. As it turned out, the booze came from a secret cache of some unwitting volunteer who'd gotten distracted while on breakfast cleanup duty. The alcohol's burn assaulted my throat, making my heart run faster and my words come out slurred. I found myself watching Luke's mouth with fascination. My fixation must've been obvious to Luke because his lips quirked into an obnoxious grin. I was giggling like the tipsy fool I was. Alcohol loosening our tongues, we talked about our worries, dreams, and fears. Everything was kind of perfect until, much to my dread, Lori brought up my stupid crush on Tommy again. That wiped the goofy smile from Luke's face and brought tension back into our tent.

AND THE
WIND HOWLED

After we emptied the bottle (Lori and the boys pulling
more than their fair shares), Rowen decided to treat us
to the supply of camel-shaped chocolates he'd stocked up
on in the Dubai airport. Somehow the chocolate wasn't
a melted mess.

Minh's mouth was open in shock as Rowen kept pro-
ducing more and more candy from his apparently bottomless pockets. "How much of that stuff did you actually get?"

He shrugged. "Enough for a few days?"

Alcohol lowered our inhibitions to the point where
we decided to play spin the bottle. For a second there, I
was a giddy summer camper, about to be kissed for the
first time. We went for a few rounds. Every time Lori

or Rowen got to spin, they managed to get the bottle pointing at each other. When I sent the bottle spinning, it ended up pointing at Luke, so I leaned over to give him a peck on a cheek. But he shifted his head at the last moment and my lips slid against his. I pulled back immediately, but Luke leaned in, prolonging the kiss amid the cheering and clapping of our friends. When I finally extricated myself from him, he was grinning like the Cheshire cat. I just hoped this wasn't going to become a problem, this Luke thing. He was starting to get on my nerves.

When my turn came again and the bottle stopped spinning, its tip was set on . . . Tommy, who had walked into the tent unnoticed. We were busy howling with laughter like a pack of hyenas and didn't hear him sneak up on us.

"You have to kiss Tommy!" Lori roared, mouth full of candy, words slurring amid fits of hiccupping laughs as she fell to her side.

Tommy watched us, his lips slightly twisting at the sides, like he couldn't make up his mind—should he judge us or join us? If I weren't so tipsy, I'd be running out of the tent, crying in mortification. But floating up high on whiskey fumes, I was even bolder than Lori.

"Wanna join us, Thomas?" I asked.

"Where did you get that bottle?" Tommy cringed.

That almost-happy twitch I saw dancing on his lips disappeared. *Fine, be a grown-up.*

Under Tommy's molten gaze, the five of us exchanged nervous glances, trying to single out the sacrificial lamb to blame for the smuggling of alcohol. A weird sound, like raindrops hitting the tent, ate away at my already weakened concentration.

"It doesn't rain here much, does it?" Minh asked, following her question with a loud hiccup that made everyone except Tommy giggle. My eyes followed him as he opened the tent's door a smidge and took a peek outside. He was suddenly packed with tension—I saw it in the way his muscles stretched under the fabric of his shirt.

A sand-filled whirling cloud danced outside the tent.

"Shit . . . Desert storm!" Tommy rolled down his sleeves and, before stepping outside, gave me a sharp look. "Don't leave the tent!" He grabbed the baseball cap off his head and covered his nose and mouth with it. Then he dashed out of the tent, leaving us drunk and worried.

It hit the camp without any more warning than that.

One second the night was dead quiet and lying in wait, and the next, a vicious storm hollered like a feral animal trapped in a barbwire cage. I counted my breaths after Tommy left the tent. On the count of forty, a man screamed outside. A deranged, no-nonsense kind of scream that, I imagined, came from limbs being torn apart and clothes set ablaze. Whoever was screaming, he couldn't have been that far from our tent. But it was not the agony in the scream that cut me raw. *No*, it was the strange fact that as the wind began throwing sand against the tent, I could still hear it with dead clarity: Someone was calling my name.

Another scream followed while I was deliberating what to do. The voice of the screamer . . . It sounded *a lot* like my father. This revelation exiled all rational thought from my head, and, moving on autopilot, I got up from the floor and started pacing back and forth, stopping only when my eyes fell on my towel, still wet from when I'd used it to dry my hair. *This will work.* I placed the towel against my mouth like Tommy did with his cap and headed for the exit.

"Where do you think you're going?" Minh launched herself out of her spot on the floor. "Tommy said not to go outside, right? It wasn't just my boozed-out imagination. He was definitely asking us to stay put . . ."

"I know . . . but didn't you hear it just now?" I stopped by the tent's door and listened. It came again, that scream. Closer than before. "It's my dad. He's calling for me!"

"Don't be ridiculous, Alif." Lori sounded less drunk now. "It's just the wind."

"I disagree." Rowen untangled himself from Lori and came to stand by my side. He shared my pensive stance and listened. That scream (or was it really just the howl of the wind?) played out again. *Aaaliiif!*

"That's it. I'm going out!" I informed my friends as I grabbed the tent's door, preparing to tear it back.

"Okay, but we're coming with you!" Minh said, gathering her long hair into a low bun. She picked up a trendy cotton scarf from the top of her open luggage and nodded at me in affirmation.

"But Tommy said to stay here." Lori's whine was suddenly the voice of reason in our group. But Lori didn't engage in battles she couldn't win—so she moved to join us. We had to wait as she searched for a piece of fabric to protect her airways. She settled on a red gauzy scarf. Luke and Rowen didn't have much of a choice but to use what was available in our tent, so they ended up with some random pieces of clothing pressed against their mouths and noses. All together we looked like a motley crew of oddballs who had no business going out into the sandstorm.

"If we stay close to the tent and just look around, we should be fine," Luke spoke for the first time since Tommy left. He didn't come off certain at all.

"You don't have to come, Luke." I didn't wait for his reply and just stepped out of the tent, unable and unwilling to wait any longer. I felt all the might of the desert's anger when the sand-filled wind punched me square in the face, almost knocking me off my feet. In response, I squinted and pressed the towel firmer against my mouth and nose. The wind was rushing into my ears and slapping at my exposed hands, making my skin prickle. I wished I had one of those surfer onesies that came with a tight hood, designed to cover one's head and ears. The sand was *everywhere*, and it hurt like hell, even through my clothes. Despite the damp towel I held against my face, sharp dust particles were invading my mouth, slowly coating my tongue and throat.

The only illumination came from the clattering lamps sitting atop electricity poles and on the sides of some tents. But many lamps were already broken, light fading.

In the sand-fueled haze, people were shapeless shadows dashing in all directions. Caught up in their chaotic movement, I ran too, stopping only when a broken piece of debris blocked my way. Minh smacked right into my back, the impact bringing me to my knees. I howled in pain as skin scraped right off my legs. Someone picked me up off the ground. I glimpsed Luke's face hovering above mine. When he let go, I turned to look back the way we came and could barely see the outline of our tent in the night. Another powerful gust of wind slammed into me, and it took all my strength and stubbornness to stay upright. I didn't hear or see her fall, but Lori was on the ground next to my feet. Rowen and Minh were helping her up. Going outside had been a *bad* idea, I thought, but then I saw something—a gigantic mass of gleaming metal coming our way, flying, swirling in the dust storm. This huge object turned out to be one of those four-wheel drives the camp had at its disposal. How could this be possible? Not giving me enough time to consider the question, the car crashed right on top of our tent, smashing it flat against the ground, only feet away from where we huddled together.

"Oh my fucking . . ." Lori's eyes cemented on the scene of total destruction, and she dropped the hand pressing the scarf against her mouth. This momentary lapse of control was enough to get a clump of dirt in her face. Lori bent over and coughed and coughed and coughed before jerking her hand back up and pushing the scarf against her face again, this time all the way up to her eyes.

The specks of sand were glittering in the eerie darkness, yellow dust already claiming the four-wheel drive and the smashed tent underneath it. I sensed the warmth of someone's hand on my elbow just as their fingers closed around my arm. I was being dragged away. A glance over my shoulder revealed a face partly hidden behind a familiar baseball cap.

"Follow me!" Tommy yelled out. And we ran.

I trained my eyes on the ground, searching for any obstructions. My friends were keeping up—when I turned to look back I'd get an occasional view of Luke's pale arms or Minh's long black hair flying, freed from her bun by the wind. There were occasional screams, panicked faces appearing out of the swirls of sand and then vanishing, all while the walls of sand around me thickened. The longer I stared into the sandstorm, the more it seemed to be moving in an odd pattern—lifting things off the ground and throwing them, like a toddler having a tantrum. Like the sand had a mind of its own.

In all this mess, I saw a body.

Or more like a torso, a bloodied white tee pulled up halfway. Someone was stuck under a pole that lay flat on the ground. The electrical lamp on the pole's end was still on but fizzling out. In its dancing light, I could see that the body belonged to a young woman. I gasped into my towel. I'd never seen a dead body before. Just as the first wave of nausea roiled inside my chest, the dead girl squirmed.

She twisted her head and met my eyes. Hers lips were moving. I strained to hear what the girl was saying, but the relentless wind was swallowing all sound. I rushed closer to her while everyone else ran in the opposite direction, away from the camp—and from me.

I tied my towel around my neck before scooping my hands under the pole in an attempt to lift it. But the pole must've weighed a ton. Powerless tears rushed down my face. The towel fell away from my mouth, and with my face no longer protected, the sand was stinging my wet cheeks, getting into my nostrils, blinding me, making it hard to breathe. I knew that what I was trying to do was useless, but whatever possessed me earlier made me push at the pole again and again until my left shoulder gave out.

I didn't know real physical pain until then. I screamed as fire seared through my arm but had to shut my mouth tight, fast. I spat on the ground, but my tongue and the insides of my mouth were caked with sand. The girl who was splayed on the ground at my feet lowered her head flat against the earth and closed her eyes. She was giving up.

"Try this . . ."

I swung my head to find Tommy. He was leaning over me. I raised my eyes to his outstretched hand, clutching some mechanical contraption. After a second of staring at it, I realized it was a manual car lift. I didn't know where Tommy got that from, didn't have time to ask, didn't care. I was just grateful that the shoulder that got busted and was now locked in a state of permanent agony was my left—and I am right-handed. With my left arm hanging limp, I used my right to grab the car jack from Tommy. But when I attempted to wedge the tool between the trembling ground and the pole, another jolt of pain hit me from my injured arm. Catching a glimpse of my grimacing face, Tommy gently pushed me aside and took over.

Ungraceful and weak against the monstrous storm, I sat down on the ground while Tommy fitted the car lift against the pole and gave it a push. Once. Twice. Again.

Again. When Tommy had managed to lift the pole an inch or two, it was up to the girl to save herself. Her eyes fluttered open. She started to move, slowly escaping her prison.

"How badly are you hurt?" I yelled into her ear. But only a choked scream left her mouth. Her eyes, widening in panic or confusion, were locked in on something behind me.

A powerful gust of wind slammed into my back. It hurt so badly it was like I was in the center of a black hole, compacted and torn apart at once. Tommy turned to see what was happening, and I couldn't stop watching his face as it darkened with understanding. His eyes were beautifully tragic, reflecting the strange blackness creeping up over us. This was the last thing my mind captured as a memory from that night. A suffocating shadow crawled over me. Then chaos reigned.

OUT OF
COMFORT ZONE

The thing about sandstorms is that they are fast, furious, and unpredictable. I'd heard sandstorm terror stories from my mother and father both, but I hadn't actually experienced one myself. Now I could mark that off my list of experiences to have before turning eighteen. It was not a pleasant experience. I could've done without it.

As my senses were reawakening, my first legible thought was of guilt. Last night I'd made a mistake. A big and regrettable one. I went outside during a sandstorm—a big no-no. Dad would be so embarrassed and *livid* with me. Worse even, I dragged my friends along. I never found my father last night. But then . . . I remembered how a monster of a four-wheel drive appeared to be flying out of a black column of sand and how it fell down, flattening our tent. Whatever voice it was that called to me, whether imaginary or real, it had prompted me and my friends to go outside right before our tent was smashed. It saved our lives. The rest of my memories from last night were starting to return, but most were blurry and distant. Did I really help rescue some girl who was pinned down by a fallen electrical pole, or was that a fever nightmare?

Dry and sluggish, my tongue struggled to move. I heard a moan, and it took me a few breaths to realize it was me as I attempted to spit the sand out of my mouth. The mind goes to mysterious places in times of crisis. In that moment, I couldn't help but think about all the ancient Egyptian mummies stuck in museums around the world: well-preserved bodies with such *terrible* teeth— teeth often rubbed off to the nub. The lack of effective dental care was a great unifier in ancient Egypt: Even royalty got their teeth sand-damaged. The sand was the force that couldn't be stopped by palace walls or army hordes.

With the sand mostly out of my mouth, I focused on my other senses. A slight hissing sound reached my ears. One of those electric lamps, a survivor of the storm, just like me? But other than that—*nothing*. I couldn't detect a single noise.

The next thing I realized was that my left arm was immobile. Then the pain flooded back. Dull and throbbing, it immediately consumed most of my upper body's left side. *Aspirin! My kingdom for an aspirin. And a ride to the nearest doctor's office!*

With my right arm I reached out to feel the area around me. I was lying on uneven ground. Every time I moved, sharp ridges dug into my skin. I dared open my eyes. Or more like, I peeled them open, as my eyelids were sealed shut with sand. At first, the only color I could distinguish was milky white. Or no color at all, to be exact. A wave of panic choked me as I strained to open my eyes wider, blinking rapidly and deeply, hoping to jolt my vision back into action. Gradually, the all-consuming whiteness morphed into pale blue. The sky. And not a cloud floating above. I shifted my view to the side and saw . . . sand.

Sand dunes, stretching far, disappearing into the horizon. I twisted my head to the other side. Same view. No sign of the dig camp. *Just sand everywhere.*

I remained on my back, unable to face what I was up against. When the rest of my perception crawled back in and stabilized, I managed to sit up. My head reeled from a headache the size of the Nile. Thirst and pain wrestled for domination. Working through the mind-numbing agony, I pulled up my left arm and clutched it against my chest, whimpering as I did so. Though it didn't look terribly damaged to me, my left shoulder was a swollen mess. I suspected it was dislocated. I *hoped* it was dislocated and not something worse.

"Dad?" I croaked, the sound turning into a cough as sand grated against my throat. "Tommy?"

"Alif?" A faint response.

A shape, strikingly dark against the dunes, rose slowly.

He wasn't far. Tommy. The rush of relief put a huge grin on my chapped, sand-crusted lips.

Nearly blinded by the uncompromising sun, I struggled to watch Tommy's lone frame as he shuffled toward me. Just to be sure, I yelled out, "I'm here." I attempted to get myself vertical just as the sand mound to my right began to tremble. On my wobbly feet, I edged away from it and watched as a face appeared out of the sand. It was followed by the rest of Lori, who was covered by the nightmarish sand blanket from head to toe. Dried tears made clear paths on her face, stretching from her eyes down to her chin.

The three of us huddled together, forming a small circle. I wavered on my feet but resisted the urge to lean on Tommy or Lori for support. Neither of them looked like they could support anyone right now, though I bet Tommy was slightly better off than Lori and me. At least when the storm hit he was wearing his camp uniform, which would fare better in the open desert than yoga pants, singlets, and shorts. At least my towel was still tied around my neck. The top of my head was already starting to burn under the morning sun, and I seriously considered wearing my towel on my head like a stereotypical elderly Russian lady.

Lori interrupted my fashion deliberation. "Rowen was right next to me when we dashed." Her pale hair hung lankily around her reddening face. Like a group of zombies, we hobbled around, searching for the rest of our group. We didn't talk. We didn't need to discuss our predicament. It was becoming very obvious with each step we took that we were in lots and lots of trouble.

Eventually, we found them. Minh, Rowen, and Luke were all half buried in the sand. In the eerie tradition of Pompeii body casts, the three of them lay twisted close to one another, enwrapped in sand and shadows and one another's limbs. Luke's hand was flung over Minh in a protective way that perhaps should've made me jealous but didn't. Their mouths were slightly open, breathing in the scalding air. They were alive.

I called to them, urging them to wake up. Tommy and Lori did the same. Minh was the first to open her eyes. She let out an inaudible whisper, and I leaned in closer to hear it. I could swear a cloud of cold air escaped her lips as she spoke. But it must have been just sand coming out of her mouth or an illusion brought on by the heat and twisted by my panicking mind.

I knelt next to her. With my uninjured hand, I

moved Minh's hair away from her face. I untied the towel from my neck and used it to clean the sticky patches of sand from her cheeks. Lori helped Rowen sit up, leaving Tommy to slap Luke awake.

"Water?" Minh asked me, her eyes pleading.

"Sorry," I replied.

I didn't want to say it, to acknowledge what was surely already on everybody's mind, but someone had to. "I don't see the camp," I said.

"That's odd," Tommy replied, fiddling with his wrist-watch, which looked a lot like that semisentient communication device on *Futurama*. "My compass has lost it." The more Tommy focused on the gadget strapped to his wrist, the more the wrinkle between his eyebrows deepened. He was muttering under his breath, "We couldn't have gone *that* far from the camp. And even if we did, the camp is east of Dubai . . . And the only serious patch of the desert that borders the camp directly is to its north . . . But none of this makes sense anyway because we couldn't have wandered *that* far from the camp!"

I watched Tommy, following the movement of his lips, forcing myself to focus. What he was saying about the geography of the camp made sense to me, triggering a faint memory of how we got to the dig from the airport, though I wasn't really paying that much attention at the time. I said, "So if we walk against the rising sun, shouldn't that get us to the areas near Dubai? There are settlements out there. And once we get there, all we need is access to a phone."

"In theory, that should work," Tommy replied.

"In theory?" I didn't like the sound of that.

"My compass must be broken." He shook his head, annoyed and lost.

Broken compass or not, we didn't have much of a choice. We gathered in a disordered line and began our trek through the sand and the heat, guided by the sun. I was at the end of the line when I made a sudden stop. The towel in my hand gave me an idea. I dropped the towel to the ground.

"What are you doing?" Lori sounded concerned and suspicious. I blinked away the droplets of sweat clouding my vision. "Leaving a message for our rescue team." I knelt down and spread the towel out in the shape of an arrowhead, its tip pointing in the direction we were headed.

By the time the sun reached its zenith, we came across a desert arroyo, not too deep but steep enough to create a thin line of shade. Lori and Rowen were keen to keep going, and it took Tommy a solid effort to convince them they were going to get themselves killed by the sun and the heat if they continued on in the desert during the day. Reluctantly, they stayed. The six of us clustered in the shade like a family of mice under the stairs of an old house, waiting till the killer sun started to set.

HEMINGWAY, BONES,
AND MIRAGES

I could kill for some strawberries.

Strawberries *and* water.

And that ride to a doctor's office, where painkillers are plentiful.

I should've been a Girl Scout. I should've done some orienteering or something super physical besides swimming. But instead, the closest I came to wilderness survival "training" was all that time I put in mindlessly consuming episode after episode of *Man vs. Wild*. Minh made fun of me for watching a show where a ripped dude drank his own urine to "survive." According to her, if you have to drink your own urine (or *anyone's* urine) to survive, then nature has already defeated you. But now, all I could see was vast arid land extending in all directions, and all I could think was how scared I was. Surrounded by dunes that appeared to be in constant motion, I couldn't even concentrate on how breathtakingly gorgeous it all was. No . . . All I was capable of wondering was—would this be how it'd end for me? Would this be where I'd die?

"Let me have a look."

I looked up to find Tommy standing over me. Not waiting for an invitation, he knelt next to me and reached out for my numb left hand, curled up against my chest.

"I'd rather not move it," I protested, though I wasn't sure whether my reluctance was due to the threat of more pain or the possibility of Tommy's touch making me dizzier than I already was. I blinked hard. "It's already much better," I lied.

"Let me have a look. Please?"

Hesitantly, I nodded, and he reached out for my injured arm, gingerly separating it from my chest. I let go, allowing him to run his fingers over my skin, poking and prodding my sore shoulder area. I watched his face while he was too busy concentrating on my shoulder to notice. It was a rare unguarded moment when I could stare at him without getting caught. Interesting to know: Your crush on someone didn't go away when you were near death.

The moment ended when Tommy let go of my arm and awkwardly placed it back against my chest. "Just a sprain. It's not dislocated."

"How do you know?" It came off whiny. I enjoyed Tommy's attention and didn't want it to end, the terrible circumstances of it be damned.

"Because you would definitely feel it every time I made your arm move." He smirked and stood up to leave. He didn't go far though—the arroyo was nothing but a ditch the size of a kiddie swimming pool—and returned carrying what appeared to be Minh's scarf. "Here, let me." Tommy knelt by my side again as he made a sling from the scarf to support my left arm. Once it was done, he walked away fast.

My mouth open in unsaid *Thanks*, I watched him retreat to the farthest corner of the arroyo. Then I noticed Luke staring at me. His eyes were dark holes and unblinking. He looked like a ghost stuck between two worlds, and it made my skin crawl.

We resumed our trek at the first sign of the sun nearing the horizon. With no food and no water since our dinner at the dig camp, I was losing my focus, my limbs getting heavier with each step. Our heavy drinking last night didn't help the situation either.

Minh's scarf served me well, and I thanked her for it the first chance I got. As we left the arroyo's shade, my mind started to wander, my feet dragging against the sand. I was a mess. My friends didn't look much better off. We were like an undead herd, our spirits cramped into bodies that were no longer able to move the right way.

Tommy assumed the role of our unofficial leader, but the longer I watched him, the more I could tell he had no idea what he was doing. When he thought no one would notice, he threw befuddled glances at his compass. Each time, he frowned. Was he thinking the same thought I was? *How the hell did this happen to us?*

From our ragtag group, Lori seemed the most out of place. During our reprieve in the arroyo, she had re-adjusted her sparkly headband, which held back her no-longer-very-slick hair. She was pouting like that was gonna get someone to come to her rescue sooner.

We had to stop by some thorn-covered bushes when Lori announced she needed rest. This rare patch of vegetation stood up against the sands, its silhouette spiky and unfriendly. By now, even Tommy knew it was useless to argue with Lori, so we just dropped right where we stood. Tommy lay down next to me and closed his eyes. Before I could overthink what his choice of a rest spot could mean, Lori demanded I come with her. Minh was already on her feet, and, staying together, we followed Lori behind the denser-looking section of the scrubland, where it reached our waists.

Without a word of warning, Lori pulled down her shorts and crouched.

"All right then." Minh shrugged and shifted her weight from one foot to another, looking away from Lori's stream of dark liquid as it turned the dirt ashy black.

Lori finished and stood up, giving us a withering look. "What? Are you judging my unladylike behavior, or are you waiting for a special invitation?" That provoked another shrug from Minh before she took a few steps away from us and squatted on the ground, though not without a certain ballerina-like grace. Feeling the peer pressure, I joined Minh but avoided looking down.

You could survive without food for more than three weeks. Without water? Three days. Maybe four. And the first sign of trouble? Dark urine.

What stopped me from falling into total despair was compartmentalization. As I forced my feet to move again, slipping on the sand and listening to my fellow strandees' heavy breathing, my brain offered a shiny picture to distract me: my bed, fresh linens straight from the dryer, crisp and inviting. Oh, to run my legs against their coolness. The picture helped. But only a little.

The sun's behavior was peculiar. We'd left the arroyo at first sign of sunset, but as we ventured farther from our place of temporary rest, the bright disc on the horizon seemed to fluctuate in size—shrinking or dilating every time I took a look at it.

Tommy's frustration was clear in his voice. "I don't get it! We've been moving for hours. There's no way we could've gotten this far out during the storm. No way!"

His sudden outburst earned no answer.

My eyes drawn upward, I registered a black dot of a bird briefly swooping across the luminous sphere. It flew up, circling us from above. I heard its distant call, and another bird answered. Scavengers were gathering. Waiting for us to drop. What was it Hemingway wrote about vultures? Something about them being a sign of impending death.

During another rest stop, Lori was first to pick up on a weak glint of gold in the distance. She froze dead in her tracks and stared, pointing a finger at whatever was flashing at random intervals. "The high-rises of Dubai! . . . But how?"

We looked in the direction she was indicating and, indeed, there was a faint glimmer, pulsing weakly. Though it didn't make me think "high-rises of Dubai" but rather a lone lighthouse stuck in the desert. But high-rises or not, we were all mesmerized until Tommy's harsh voice jerked us out of our collective trance. "It's a mirage. We need to move *against* the sun and *away* from those lights."

"We've been going against the sun this entire time, and now the sun has changed its direction, *apparently*," Luke snapped. "I suggest we *stop* going against the sun and go toward that light."

It must've taken a lot of Tommy's self-control not to scream back his response at Luke. "Do you know how many people died in the desert when they thought salvation was near? And I'm sure they believed until their final breath that what they saw was a human settlement or an oasis, but none of it was real. They died of dehydration and sunstroke!"

Minh, her nose and cheeks burning red from the sun, came to stand next to Lori. Swaying on her feet, she placed a hand on Lori's shoulder but addressed Tommy, "We're lost. Obviously, there's something wrong with our sense of direction. We're all hallucinating that the sun's not moving the way it's supposed to. We don't know where we are, and this glimmer may be the only hope we have of surviving." Their movements eerily synchronized, Lori and Luke nodded in agreement. Tommy rolled his eyes at them and then looked between me and Rowen, the only members of our group who hadn't yet expressed views on the subject.

"I say we go toward the light." Rowen nodded and crossed his arms over his chest, cutting off any attempt from Tommy to persuade him otherwise.

I found everyone staring in my direction, waiting

for me to support or reject Tommy's advice. I sensed that regardless of what I would decide, the group would go toward the glimmer. Our collective mind had been made up. And yet they were still waiting for me to weigh in.

I shaded my eyes with my hand and focused on that patch of sand at the distance where Lori saw what she thought was our salvation. I couldn't deny there was indeed *something* there. It was a flickering kind of light, and now that I studied it, its pattern wasn't like that of a lighthouse at all. Instead, it was random and sporadic in strength. Some blinks were longer, more intense. I wondered if it could be a piece of glass or a mirror dropped by some traveler. Or could it be a larger man-made object, a part of a roof or a wall, but reflective somehow? Solar panels? None of that explained the erratic pattern of the light though. But maybe whatever it was could give us shelter, possibly even hold some supplies. Was it irrational? My brain must've been fried if I was imagining a little house in the middle of sand-covered nowhere. Not just a house, but a house stuffed to the brink with canned goods and bottled water. And *strawberries*.

"If we were to vote, I guess those who wanted to go toward the light would win anyway," I said. Tommy's face changed. Speaking against him, even indirectly, made my stomach flip. But I didn't owe him anything. I was trying to be realistic. I added in haste, suspecting what he might suggest next, "And I don't think it's a good idea for us to split up and go our separate ways."

Luke scoffed before I finished talking, but I wasn't sure whether his derision was aimed at me or at Tommy, who now looked defeated and deflated.

"Then it's settled," Luke said. "We all go toward the light."

And so go toward the light we did.

Luke was at the forefront of our beeline now, followed by Lori, Rowen, and Minh. I was in the back, with Tommy reluctantly lagging behind, which, I guessed, was his way of expressing defiance. And what if he was right? I couldn't stop wondering whether we were all headed to our deaths, moving deeper into the heart of the desert where no rescue effort would ever reach us.

Whatever it was that sparkled up ahead didn't disappear as we traveled toward it. In fact, the faint glimmer grew bigger, soon starting to change color and shape. I could now distinguish a row of something like uneven sticks with bushy heads standing out against the overall mass of gold and . . . green? I know we all saw it—or at least saw *something* other than sand, sand, and more sand—because our footsteps picked up and then we were running in an awkward shuffle like a group of deranged animals that had gotten a whiff of fresh blood. Minh tripped and stumbled ahead of me. Slowing to a halt, I reached out to steady her while my eyes scanned the ground below. A small patch of white stood out against the dirty sand. Whatever it was, it was mostly buried, its uncovered surface bleached by the sun. Lori, Luke, and Rowen did not make a move to slow down until I yelled out for them to wait. I joined Minh, who was kneeling on the ground. She was running her fingers over the white object in the sand, her hands tentative yet shivery with eagerness.

"It's a bone." Tommy's shadow landed on us sideways. Minh jerked her hand back and cleaned off her fingers on her pants. Tommy's voice turned soothing, "Dead animals. Probably lots of bones around here, if you look close."

An uncomfortable shiver passed through me, refusing to go away. The more I studied the bone fragment submerged in the sand, the more I thought something wasn't quite right about its angle or texture. Hesitantly I brushed more sand off it, revealing more bones. Being my parents' daughter meant growing up exposed to lots of books on archaeology and its related fields. Not to mention that Dad's favorite pastime was to test me on stuff he was working on. One of his topics of interest had to do with calcified remains. In particular, how to distinguish animal remains from human ones at first glance. Only, back then I thought death was an abstract thing, not something I had to deal with, at least not any time soon. But here it was, before me. The presence of death, rude and unrelenting.

"It's not an animal," I said. Silence met my words.

I wondered if Tommy, an archaeology wunderkind, saw what I was seeing. The bones that were now partially released from the sand were porous and detailed. I could distinguish vertebrae bent at a certain angle before they disappeared into the sand. Only human axes had those *particular* curves . . .

"They're human bones." I lifted myself from the ground and shook off the sand, grateful I was wearing ankle-long pants and not ultra-short shorts like Lori, even though my legs were hot and sweaty.

I scanned my friends' faces. Lori was eyeing me with suspicion from where she stood flanked by Luke and Rowen.

"We'll never know what happened to this person," I murmured, looking at the bones beneath me. The others must've shared my unspoken sentiment: Was this our fate too?

"Freaking hell," Luke said, coming closer to where I was, his hand snaking awkwardly around my shoulders. Our shapes cast long shadows over the grisly find. I watched him as he let go of me and leaned in to pick up a credit-card-size object stuck between the bones. Luke cleaned his find of sand and dust and stared at it. "So that French dude who rescued himself from the desert? Did he mention if he had a friend?" he asked.

Luke didn't address anyone in particular, so no response came. When he raised his eyes and deliberately met mine, I shrugged.

"Not that I can recall."

"Well, looks like our Desert Man wasn't all that alone in the desert." Luke raised his hand so we all could see the piece of plastic he held in his grip. It was a driver's license. Issued in Paris, France. To Alain Pinon. The photo was scratched up, but I could still make out the features of a dark-skinned man, his hair pulled back from his face.

"I wonder what happened to him," Minh said, because someone had to.

My friends' faces were grim as we watched Luke stuff the piece of plastic into the pocket of his track pants. We continued on our trek, moving toward the outline of what could've been a shining mirage. Only it didn't disappear, didn't waver as we approached. Instead, it continued to rise up higher and bigger, the massive scale of it becoming apparent, even to our tired eyes, half blinded by the sun.

IN HEAVEN,
EVERYTHING IS FINE

Having seen the Sphinx, or the great pyramids of Giza, or the mountain fortress of Machu Picchu did nothing to prepare me for the surreal grandeur of the oasis that came into view suddenly, violently, stopping my heart and jolting it back to life at once.

The oasis swelled out of the desert like a drop of clean water, and it fizzled in the heat. Those uneven sticks with bushy tops I'd noticed from a distance had now assumed their true form, morphing into luscious palm trees, their heads melodically swaying. The thought of a cool breeze on my face made me almost drunk with want. But there were patches of darkness behind the palm trees, and that darkness seemed to glimmer and blink at me when I tried focusing on it.

We kept moving toward it, this dark greenish mass that was growing bigger with each step. Soon it was claiming a large chunk of the horizon, stretching far—farther than any known or imaginary oasis in my mind. My brain must've been glitching, overheated in the desert air. Because how could this be? An oasis this big? Here? The largest oasis in the vicinity of Dubai was Al Ain, but that was in Abu Dhabi, a neighboring emirate more than eighty miles away. And besides, Al Ain was just three thousand acres. None of this made any sense. And yet here it was. *Existing*. Sparkling in the sun. Undulating in the imperceptible wind.

I stared at this miracle, too afraid to blink and lose it, my vision blurring from the effort. Through tears flooding my eyes, I noticed wispy clouds of mist shrouding the tops of the palms, creating the illusion of the oasis breathing. I strained to see houses, cars, or any other sign of human presence. Oases, large or small, were a hot commodity in these parts, and it'd be unlikely that an oasis this size would go unnoticed and unutilized. But I saw none of it—just those bushy palm trees rubbing shoulders, standing so close and tight that their mass was dark, no light allowed in or out. I shivered despite the persisting heat.

"I think I'm just totally losing it right now," Minh whispered to me. "I'm seeing palm trees. I can even smell water!"

My throat quivered at *water*, my thirst shoving aside

my fear of the darkness that was lurking behind the clusters of trees. What sounded like a falcon screamed close by, but there were no birds in sight. Those circling black dots up in the sky that I saw earlier were long gone now. The air was still stilted and humid, but, as we approached the oasis, there was also a fresh breeze, more appropriate for areas by the sea, not arid wastelands. It reminded me of home. Of Melbourne. Not the dusty city parts of it but the waterfront suburbs, where the nautical winds never failed to induce cold shivers, even in summer.

"Then I've totally lost it too," Luke croaked. "I'm also seeing it."

"We're all seeing it," I concluded after taking a quick look around, pausing to take in each of my friends' dazed faces.

Only Tommy kept his cool, managing to look skeptical while the rest of us were stunned. I shuffled closer to him and asked, keeping my voice low, "There's such a thing as a group mirage, right?"

"Group hallucinations do exist." He nodded, careful with his words. "To the point of everyone affected smelling and tasting the same thing, but . . ." He stopped short. Everyone was listening to our conversation, waiting for Tommy's verdict, while also straining not to break into a run toward the oasis. Our salvation.

"But . . . ," Tommy started again, his eyes fixated on the cluster of palms up ahead. "This feels so real."

He took a step toward the oasis, then another, as if moving not of his own accord but rather beckoned into the trees, into the mist, into the darkness, by some power. Tommy didn't stop moving, and the rest of us followed. Lori and Rowen held hands. Minh kept up with them, her shoulders pulled back, hands in fists. I was left behind with the brooding, silent Luke. The memory of kissing him was now nothing but a faded ghost. Something from a past life.

Mirage or not, the oasis loomed close, stretching wider and higher as we approached. But the closer to it we got, the more difficult it became to keep on moving. Whether from exertion or dehydration or both, I began losing my breath. Like that of a fish washed ashore, my mouth opened and closed, attempting to capture as much oxygen as it could. Mentally I yelled at myself, urging my exhausted body to move, to carry me forward. I wasn't going to die mere feet from water and shade.

The trees were so close now I could no longer see where the outline of the oasis started or where it ended. The entire horizon in my line of vision was now claimed by this living green entity.

Up ahead, Tommy was first to cross the boundary between our certain death in the sands and this unanticipated rescue. As he entered the oasis, I watched his back and the way his limbs moved, searching for any sign that our rescue was indeed real, and not a mirage. But the confirmation came from Lori, who roughly untangled herself from Rowen and dashed for the trees, practically falling into the oasis. She knelt there among the palms, her body shaking with sobs. I'd never seen Lori cry before. Never seen her lose her cool before.

Blood rushing into my face, my limbs, I gathered what was left of my strength and sped up my pace, soon passing Minh and Luke.

Water.

I broke into a run.

The palm trees were upon me. Towering over me. Their shade enveloped me. A subtle rustling of fronds grew louder with each step. And here it was, the unmistakable burbling of water. A spring must've been nearby, within hearing range. That is, unless my brain was conspiring with the rest of my possibly dying body to make up that sound to soothe me in my final moments.

All of us were here now, Minh and Luke the last to enter the realm of trees. The ever-moving, shade-giving canopy hovered over our heads. Driven by some unspoken agreement, we proceeded in deeper, walking through an opening between two of the taller trees, guardians of this hidden paradise. A blast of chilled air wrapped itself around me, heaven against my skin.

There was fruit everywhere, abundant in the foliage. It struck me that it had a shiny supermarket quality, looking almost plastic. Untouched by insects, undamaged by the heat.

Clinging to the lower parts of the trees were clusters of bushes that bore no fruit but were instead covered with flowers—yellow, pink, lilac. I could recognize only the yellow, thanks to its berries; they were called golden dewdrops. I knew that because of Mom's brief stint in gardening that had nearly killed her neighbor's dog. Both the foliage and the yellow berries were highly poisonous.

This lush spot where we found ourselves was surrounded by a tighter, less welcoming type of nature, where trees and bushes stuck so close, I could see only darkness behind them. I stared into one of the shadowy depths, and it was as if something stared back. Something eager, curious, and hungry. Our current location was made even more idyllic by these rougher, less hospitable parts of the oasis. Who knew what was out there. Animals? Snakes? Driven by a shared understanding, we didn't progress any farther, staying instead in this perfect spot. It was just missing butterflies and birdsong to complete the picture.

Lori didn't seem to care how bizarre this was, this beautiful clearing in the middle of arid wilderness. As I watched her, my brain capturing it in slow motion, she pulled the closest branch to her and snatched what looked like a pear off it with unnecessary force. Did pears even grow in the desert? What about apples?

"I've been dying for a pear!" she murmured.

"Lori, wait!" I made a move toward her, intending to grab the suspicions fruit before she sank her teeth into it, but she was already going after another piece of fruit, having demolished the first one in seconds. Juice was running down her chin and neck as her eyes met mine. A recent memory of seeing her kneeling and sobbing made me wonder what was going through her mind.

Our little group was unraveling. Behind Lori, Luke and Rowen were on their knees by the spring, submerging their hands and heads in water. Coming back up for air, they spat out water in drunken excitement, then brought more water by fistfuls into their greedy mouths. Tommy lingered not far from them, but he wasn't drinking or eating. Pensive, he knelt by the spring and with coiled-up restraint brought his hands down to scoop some liquid up to wash his face and rinse the sand from his eyes.

Minh approached me. "Something doesn't feel right." Her hands were empty of fruit, but she was glaring hungrily at Lori, who was now devouring her fifth or sixth pear. There was a barely contained frenzy on Lori's feral face.

"You can't be serious," Lori, hearing Minh's comment, managed to utter in response between chewing. "You're seriously going to question this miracle?"

"Pears and apples can't grow in the desert, Lori," I said. "Don't you at least think this is extremely weird?"

"Who cares?" Luke, having drunk his share of water, came over to the stumpy pear-bearing trees and followed Lori's example of stuffing himself silly. I was too busy watching pears disappear into Luke's mouth to notice Rowen silently approaching me and Minh. He held his hands out like a bowl, showing us a pile of ripe strawberries heaped inside. "Look what I found!"

My eyes widened and my mouth watered with anticipation. I recalled that specific craving for strawberries I'd had earlier. How could this be possible? Pears, apples, and now this? The bright red pile of goodness Rowen held in his hands told me yes, it was indeed happening.

Minh caved in and took one plump fruit Rowen was offering, but not before giving me an apologetic look. "One can't hurt, can it?"

Tommy walked up to us but didn't infringe on our little circle. "We should ration our food," he said.

"Just look around you, mate." Luke laughed at him, his words loud, unhinged. "We'll be fine until the rescue comes."

The fruit was indeed ripe and plentiful. The smaller, skinnier palm trees were practically twisted into strained arcs, their heads touching the ground, presenting their offerings of bananas, peaches, nectarines, all fleshy and perfect. Having devoured more than their bodies could handle, Lori, Rowen, and Luke lay down by the babbling spring. Unable to move, they held their stomachs like kids who'd lucked out at Willy Wonka's chocolate factory. Ignored by them, Tommy retreated back to the spring, kneeling by the section where the water disappeared into that denser part of the oasis. I was drawn into the dark, I realized, while simultaneously being repulsed by it.

"At least do me a favor and stay away from the flowers with yellow berries. Those are highly toxic and will make you sick," I said in the general direction of Lori and her accomplices. Then I looked for Minh, who had wandered off.

I found Minh by the fruit-bearing palms recently ravaged by Lori, Luke, and Rowen. Gingerly, Minh picked up an apple Luke had dropped in his feeding frenzy and stared at the innocent-looking fruit, desire clouding her face. She didn't take a bite though, asking me instead, "Aren't you going to eat something? You must be starving. And dying of thirst."

Not wanting to draw attention from the careless trio lying on their backs, patting their bulging stomachs, I indicated Minh should follow me. I led her to the section of the spring where Tommy sat alone by the water. He was washing what appeared to be a bunch of blueberries.

I came to sit by Tommy's side, Minh lagging behind. Tommy stopped what he was doing and offered to share what he'd collected. I took a few berries but didn't immediately put them in my mouth, though my entire body screamed for me to go ahead. The water in the spring was transparent. I could see polished rocks strewn on the bottom. I needed to drink. But instead I asked Tommy, "Is there any scientific explanation we can use to prove that any of this is real? I mean, bananas maybe make sense around here. But what about apples, pears, peaches? And *blueberries?*"

"Are those blueberries? Are you kidding me?" Minh exclaimed, noticing Tommy's catch for the first time. "I've been *craving* those."

Tommy measured a portion of his blueberries to share with Minh, and she threw them all into her mouth in one go. "This *is* real, isn't it?" she asked. But the suspicion in her voice was weakening as she picked up more blueberries from the ground and ate them by the fistful, not bothering to rinse them in the spring.

"As real as can be, I guess," I said.

Minh took a seat on the ground next to me, with Tommy on my other side. I felt him watching me sideways, but I couldn't take my eyes away from the stream of water. Its rambling was deafening once our conversation ceased. I hesitated for a second but then plunged a hand into the spring. I expected the water to be lukewarm, but it was crisp, cool to my skin, numbing my fingers. I brought a handful of water to my mouth and drank. It was the best-tasting water I'd ever had.

Drowsiness immediately came to replace my thirst. I had a sudden urge to curl up right then and there in the gentle shade by the water, to drop my head to the lush grassy ground and close my eyes. My lids were heavy. Minh asked something and, though I missed her question as well as Tommy's answer, the sounds of their voices brought me back from my near-sleep. I now felt both of them watching me.

I made an effort to stay awake and upright. My vision cleared and, like a rude slap, in came the realization of how vivid the oasis was. All its colors competed with one another for domination. Blue water, emerald grass, yellow flowers, red strawberries, all of it standing out against the uncountable dark spots lurking between the trees. And everything around me was constantly shifting, shimmering. A kaleidoscope of perception. But how much of my spiked perception of reality was brought on by exposure? I raised my hands up to my face, placing them against the background of the sparkling oasis. My skin was dry and blotchy but very much real. Didn't it mean that the rest of it, the grandeur of the palms in all their fine greenery, was also real?

"What are our chances of being saved by the rescue effort?" I asked before pooling more water into my hands and scrubbing the stray grains of sand off my face.

"Under normal circumstances," Tommy responded, "I'd say pretty high. We couldn't have gotten that far away from the camp considering the time we spent outside after the storm hit and how long we spent walking after we woke up in the desert. The sun was rising when we reached the arroyo and setting when we left it, but . . . we were disoriented during our walk, and my compass isn't working, so honestly I have no idea where we are and why the sun seemed to change direction while we were on the move."

"I was hoping for a percentage-type response." After seeing his blank stare, I added, "You know, like our chance of survival is seventy percent, or something along those lines."

"You should be a lot more freaked out, Alif," said Minh, who'd listened to Tommy's monologue with growing unease on her face. Still, she popped blueberries one after another into her mouth and chewed mechanically. Her lips and tongue were tainted purple. "As a matter of fact, all of us should be a lot more freaked out. But the pear-devouring unholy trinity over there by the stream seem to be as relaxed as ever."

"Maybe that's because we were dying in the desert one moment and the next we were saved and now we are super chill as a way of showing appreciation for being alive?" Luke answered from his spot on the grass, not bothering to look at us or even open his eyes when he spoke.

Stirred by Luke's words, Lori lifted herself up on one elbow and singled me out when she spoke. "I say we stay here until your dad comes to rescue us. All agree?"

117

"We're going to run out of food pretty quickly," I said. "Tommy is right—we need to ration our fruit." Those dots of yellow and red fruit scattered throughout the steady greenery were now slightly diminished compared to when we'd first entered our sanctuary.

"But we haven't explored this place at all," Luke said, following a few long seconds of collective silence. "There may be more fruit-bearing trees. This place seems huge, and . . ."

"This place *is* huge." Tommy spoke over Luke, annoyance showing through his measured tone. "We've all seen exactly how huge it was from the desert. But this clearing right here may be *it* in terms of hospitable conditions, food, and water. Haven't you noticed how it's different from the rest?" He moved a hand to indicate the dark, tight clusters of palms guarding our clearing from the rest of the oasis—or maybe guarding what was out there from us.

Luke scoffed.

Rowen sat up next to Lori and placed a hand around her waist. "Luke's right," he said. "Surely, if there's food and water in here, there must be other spots like this one? I guess what I'm saying is, before we start counting apples and rationing blueberries, we should explore, you know, to really gauge the size of this place. We might be stuck here for a while, so we need to know what we're dealing with."

Rowen's words rang true. This little clearing we were using as our resting ground was at the very edge of the desert. If I twisted my head a little, I could see the beginning of the sand dunes. My mind could paint the rest of the picture—desert extending as far as the eye could see, a sea of sun-bleached gold. But the beauty of it all was now lost on me; sand meant death. However, when I turned my back to the desert and looked deeper into the oasis, there was also that scary dark mass of green and shadows.

"Should we do it now?" I wondered out loud. "Go explore? While we can still catch some light? Anyway, we'll need a better place for a shelter than this in case another sandstorm hits."

No one opposed me, but, as if the sun heard me, its blood-orange disc rushed to vanish beyond the treetops, allowing darkness to fall around us. We had to postpone the exploration of the oasis till morning and focus instead on building a proper shelter out of the sturdier vines and palm fronds. In addition to my *Man vs. Wild* marathons, our combined knowledge of survivalist techniques came from *Survivor*. To everyone's utter shock, Lori demonstrated a proper technique to tie the vines, making them hold the weight of leaves placed above them. But still, we couldn't do much to get a quality shelter large enough for all of us to huddle under. Though as long as another sandstorm didn't hit us, the surrounding trees provided enough protection from the elements. Our legs wobbly with exhaustion, we soon gave up on our shelter-building endeavor and just sort of huddled on the ground to keep one another warm. Luke ended up next to me, pushing Tommy to the side. I faced Minh, while Luke pressed his back against mine.

And we slept. Most of us, at least.

WHATEVER'S NECESSARY

Sleep mostly evaded me. In those brief instances when my agitated mind slipped and fell into some dull imitation of slumber, no dreams perforated my drowsiness, which was thick as fog and just as suffocating. It didn't help that my mind kept wandering, jumping from memory to memory, from thought to thought. I took measured breaths to calm down while studying the nightscape above and around me. With the endless sky stretching overhead, holding more stars than I'd ever seen in my life, all of it seemed way too real. Tears pressed against my eyes but never made their way out.

I grew too warm, so I quietly untangled myself from Minh and Luke and left our sleeping ground. I didn't have a particular plan, but the coolness of the night's darker corners beckoned me. I walked toward the shapes of the taller palm trees bulking ahead. Like giants looking down at me, the palms seemed to be touching the sky, bushy heads nodding in unison. Whispers and snakelike hisses permeated the space all around me. Somewhere too close a nocturnal bird sang its mournful song. I'd seen no wildlife during the day, but it was nice to know we weren't completely alone in here.

"Can't sleep?" I recognized Tommy's voice even as a half whisper. My heart sped up in response, forcing me to take a long breath in hopes that when I answered, my words wouldn't sound rushed. Tommy went on. "Me too. Luke's not the greatest snuggle buddy. You might think otherwise, I guess."

I thanked the night for concealing my face, which was reddening. "It's not what you think. Luke and me." The words carried louder than intended. A small distance away, someone in our sleeping group groaned. Tommy chuckled, an odd noise in the dark. Peculiar, but in an intimate way. My skin rippled with goose bumps. It was chilly here among the trees.

Leaving me alone with my thoughts, Tommy headed into one of those darker parts of the oasis that made the spot between my shoulder blades itch. I watched the shadows consume him. Despite my better judgment, I followed him along a sand-laid pathway that twisted and turned between the palm trees, leading us away from the spring's whispers in the dark and from our sleeping friends.

Here, away from everyone, Tommy said, his voice back to its normal volume, "It's none of my business what you do with Luke. But if it was your father who caught you instead of me, he'd have a much more . . . engaged reaction."

"Nothing's up with me and Luke," I repeated stubbornly. Though the absurdity of discussing my love life in our present circumstances wasn't lost on me, I still wanted Tommy to know that what he'd witnessed was a moment of weakness. I changed my mind before more defensive words spilled out though. He was right. It *was* none of his business.

At least I was no longer suffering from the case of lost breaths and extensive blushing. I don't know whether it was my prolonged exposure to Tommy or the cool warmth of this part of the oasis, but I was now calm and composed. Mostly. I could still feel his body heat in the air, and it made me shiver.

"I was thinking about what we should do next," I started to say, wanting the words to fill the charged space between us. "If we could think of a way to carry water and provisions, we could try to venture back out into the desert and retrace our steps. We could go a bit farther out every time while still being able to return if we don't find . . . people."

There was a prolonged moment of silence before Tommy replied, "That's a better plan than sitting around and eating through our finite supply of bananas. But first, we should explore the oasis. I hate to agree with Luke, but we need to know how big this place is and how much food and water we actually have before we decide on our next steps."

I was about to respond, but a shimmer of silver wings in the dark spooked me. My hands flew up protectively, covering my face. I heard Tommy's subdued laugh and watched in embarrassment as the white splash of a bird landed in the bushes to my right. Then came a series of low reverberating coos—one, two, three. *Hush*. One, two . . . The pauses in between the cooing sounds felt significant somehow. "Is that a white pigeon?" I stared into the dark where the white blur was hiding. "Why isn't it scared of us?"

"Either because it's so used to humans that it doesn't care anymore or . . ."

I finished Tommy's flow of logic, "Or because it's never seen a human in its entire bird life." Meaning we were so far away from anything resembling a human set-tlement that we were totally and completely screwed.

"Let's go back?" Tommy's voice was low and stripped of energy; the pigeon's ongoing coos were a thunder in comparison. "Tomorrow's going to be a big day. We need all the rest we can get."

We walked back, feet shuffling against the grass and sand. We stopped when we reached the line of four bodies curled up on the ground. The gap where I fitted between Luke and Minh was now so narrow there was no way I could squeeze back in, not without waking everyone up. I avoided looking at Tommy directly, though I could feel his eyes on me as I knelt down at the end of the line and lay down on my side. I was facing Luke's back, looking away from where Tommy stood. When I heard Tommy settle down behind me, far enough to avoid touching me but close enough for me to sense his body heat, I exiled a long, shuddering breath.

I had a bad dream. A ball of sentient fire came down from the heavens, bursting before it touched the ground, white sparks flying everywhere. For a moment, the desert was illuminated, alive with unearthly colors. All the sparks had fallen. They faded away, all but one. This one spark was alive. Separated from its big fiery home, it was alone, and it was hungry. Its need was pulsing and burning like it was my own. Together, we screamed and screamed and screamed, reshaping the desert to fulfill our need.

Next, an army of invisible hands captured me, fingers digging into my flesh, talon-like nails decorating my skin with bloodred half moons. I was brought into a white-walled castle and thrown at the foot of a throne made of human bones and possessions. The throne room had no ceiling, and I could see the gunmetal clouds covering the sky, indifferent stars invisible but present.

On the throne sat the Queen of Giants—oh, how the lonely spark has grown, its evolution driven by its hunger—so tall she was, her head disappearing into the clouds. I knew she could see me from above because I could see myself through her eyes. She followed my every move. I willed my face and body into stillness.

"Speak!" the Queen of Giants commanded.

I asked, "What do you want with me?"

She laughed, and it was the roar of thunder, the screech of the desert storm, so terrible that the clouds hiding her head started to burst, unleashing cold rain upon the throne room. It rained and rained and rained. Soon the rainwater was reaching my ankles, then my knees. I repeated my question.

"You already know the answer." The Queen of Giants had a voice melodic and sweet, just like my mother's when she crooned me to sleep with lullabies, the very same ones her mother sang to her in Arabic. "But I have questions for you too," the Queen of Giants continued. "What do *you* want? And what are you willing to do to get it?"

The rain poured harder and harder, intensifying with each word leaving the queen's mouth. She was going to flood the throne room and me in it. She was waiting for my answer. She was curious and hungry. Always hungry.

What did I want? I knew what I *didn't* want. I didn't want to die out here, in the oasis. I didn't want to be here at all. I didn't want my friends to suffer. And what was I willing to do to make my desires come true? "I'll do whatever's necessary!" I screamed as the water reached my chest, then my neck.

I was floating now, carried somewhere by the rising water. Because I could see myself through the queen's eyes, I knew that my answer was the right one. It was then that my feet completely let go of the floor and the water carried me higher and higher. I was leaving the throne room behind, flying up, up, up into the clouds, where I faced the queen's eyes, the same color as the desert but with centers made of alien fire.

It was up there, where the air was so rare and cold and thin that it froze my lungs from inside out, that the Queen of Giants told me what she wanted me to do. What I had to do to assuage her hunger.

I chose to believe that what happened next was the continuation of my weird dream about the Queen of Giants and the fireball and that otherworldly laughter of the lonely spark that made the sky rip apart and release all that water. My dream-logic was solid: The queen wanted to test me, to see if the words I said to her were true. Was I really willing to do whatever was necessary?

Half awake, I left the sleeping ground once more that night and, without looking back, headed for the thorny underbrush. There I picked some flowers and some yellow berries, one by one, careful not to damage their softness. *Golden dewdrops*. Beautiful. Dangerous. Like the desert itself. Each time I gathered a handful of the stuff, I'd release my catch and come back for more. And more and more. Until the queen was satisfied, until the lonely spark was hungry no more.

SABOTAGE?

"Don't drink that!" It was the warning in Tommy's voice that shook me awake.

Annoyed at having my hard-earned rest disturbed, I opened my eyes slowly, already tired to the bones. Not a great way to start the day.

I was still here, in the oasis. Also, while I was groggy, on a positive note, the pain in my strained shoulder had all but disappeared. It was replaced by another physical sensation—an unfamiliar kind of numbness in my fingertips.

"What the hell happened here?" Rowen's question sounded like an accusation. Sitting up, I felt something slide off my side. It was Luke's hand. Luke himself was

129

snuggled next to me. I rushed to stand up and put some distance between us.

Tommy, Rowen, Lori, and Minh were all gathered by the spring, frowning at the spot where the stream narrowed before entering the wilder, darker parts of the oasis. Stifling a powerful yawn, I approached them, then stopped myself. One look at the spring was all it took to know it was *all wrong*. The water was dotted with yellow. The unmistakable berries of golden dewdrops, some sunken to the bottom of the spring but most still floating on the surface, were caught on rocks and tree roots in the water.

"Those are poisonous!" The words left my mouth at the same time as a partial memory of my dream set my mind on fire. I clenched my numb fingers into fists, afraid to see whether my strange act of sabotage had tainted my skin and nails.

"How could this happen?" Lori was kneeling by the spring. In silence, we all watched as she started on the arduous task of fishing out the bloated yellow globules. Her hands were shaking. "Who would do this? What kind of a monster would do this? Why?"

"It could've been the wind. Or an animal." Minh didn't sound convinced.

"You don't believe that!" Lori exclaimed without looking up from her task. I joined her on the ground and stuck my hands into the spring. Soon, the pile of yellow was growing between us.

"How long before we can drink it?" Minh asked, croaky. Her sudden thirst was as visceral as my own.

It was Rowen who replied, "The spring's current is weak, and we don't know how long this stuff's been soaking in there. So I'd give it at least an hour or two after we clean it up—to be safe?"

Without conferring, Tommy, Rowen, and Minh dropped on their knees along the length of the contaminated section of the spring and submerged their hands into the water. I joined them, but Luke, who had by now woken up and come to stand over me, showed no intent of lending a hand. His shadow was blocking my light and messing with my work. But I didn't want to engage with him, or anyone, worried I'd give myself away somehow. After observing me for a too-long moment, Luke shuffled back into the shadowed part of our sleeping ground and lay back down. He didn't approach the spring again until much later, when Tommy braved taking a first sip of water and, after waiting a few minutes, declared it was now safe to drink.

And so commenced our second day in the oasis.

Most of the morning was lost to restoring our water source, so by the time we started to plan the rest of our day, the sun was already reaching its midday high. Venturing out into the desert in search of help was out of the question for now, but no one seemed eager to go exploring the depths of the oasis either. Maybe what I was feeling and seeing whenever I looked into the darkness coiling behind the trees was shared by the rest of our group. But if that was the case, no one was willing to admit it. However, as our food supplies were dwindling, it became clear that our time in the clearing was finite. Eventually, we agreed we had to explore the oasis.

"Maybe someone should stay put and keep an eye on things," Lori said. "You know, in case more wind or wild animals or whatever it was decides to come and trash our only water source—or eat what's left of our food."

Despite my patchy sleep last night and the unfortunate toxic-flower incident (which I'd written off as some kind of a sleepwalking episode better kept secret), I felt refreshed, even optimistic. If only my clothes didn't feel so disgusting against my skin, I'd even say I was full of ridiculous glee. I was alive, after all! My disturbing dream about the fireball in the sky and the gigantic figure in a throne room now seemed like just that—a dream.

Unfortunately, the rest of our group didn't seem to share my soaring mood.

"We don't know anything about this place. It's a bad idea to split up," Luke, quiet all morning, snapped at Lori.

"What can *possibly* happen?" Lori, face red, was turning more irate with each word.

My eyes wandered to Tommy, who came to stand

between Lori and Luke. I recognized my father's "teaching" intonation in Tommy's voice when he addressed Lori, "I'm with Luke on this one. We're not leaving anyone behind. We're not splitting up."

Lori grimaced in response. It was obvious she wanted to challenge him. But knowing Lori, she *also* wanted to ensure she had someone else's support first. So she stared at Rowen until he looked away. Finding no backup, Lori shook her head and said nothing.

With our group in discord, we ate our meal of leftover apples and peaches from yesterday as well as a handful of strawberries Minh and I picked out from the grass. Then the six of us split into smaller groups and took turns kneeling and drinking at the section where the spring water was least muddled by the sand.

After a short reprieve, Lori picked another fight with Luke. Their voices, growing shrill and breaking, forced me to seek solitude. It was either that or attack someone with my bare hands. My temporary euphoria had been totally destroyed. Who were these people? As I observed my friends, I could barely recognize them. Or maybe they were like this all along, their true natures merely hidden by the excesses of Western civilization, only showing through now, in this extreme situation of life and death. And who was I to judge, anyway? I was perhaps the worst of them all, the water poisoner.

I grabbed an apple from our quickly diminishing

common pile and walked as far away from the group as I could while still keeping them in my sights. I found a spot to sit by the roots of one of the taller palms, its core straight as a needle and hard against my back. After I settled in, Tommy left the group and followed me into the palm grove.

"Can I join you?" he asked, standing over me. He looked uncertain, as if he really needed my permission to sit here.

"I don't own the oasis. You can sit anywhere you'd like."

He sat next to me, his hands propping him against the ground. "I woke up early this morning and did some exploring on my own," he said.

My breath caught. I prayed Tommy didn't notice how my tentative smile faded. Was he going to tell me he saw what I did to the spring? I went on the offensive.

"I thought we weren't supposed to split up?"

"I didn't go far." He shrugged and didn't say anything else for a long moment. I was waiting for him to accuse me of sabotage, but he stayed silent, pensive. I started to relax again, even coming to enjoy that fuzzy feeling brought on by being singled out by Tommy. But mostly I just felt like I always did in Tommy's presence—squirmy under the scrutiny of his pale green eyes, their color stark against his bronzed skin. He moved a tad closer to me and now, in addition to my nervous discomfort, I worried that I smelled from all the desert wanderings and from sleeping in my clothes. If I did smell, he didn't show it.

Not looking at him, I said, "Still, you should've been more careful. We know nothing about this place, and if you're too far when you call for help, no one will hear you."

"I know, but I'm fine. And, anyway, if there's one person in our group who shouldn't be left on her own it's Lori. I don't think she'd last long."

"You might be surprised about her." I shrugged. "If I had to bet on the last person standing at the end of our ordeal, I'd bet on her. She's resilient."

"Resilient maybe. But is she also armed?" He pulled a hunting knife from a hidden leather scabbard I'd taken no notice of before. The blade—not that long, maybe three or four inches tops—hooked near the tip and overall seemed rather sharp. The way the blade reflected the light made me want to edge away from it, and from Tommy. As if sensing my unease, he put the blade away, tucking the scabbard back behind his belt and under his shirt.

I asked, "You've been carrying that in your pants the entire time you were at the camp? Why?"

He chuckled. "It's like a Swiss Army knife, but for archaeologists."

"Never heard of archaeologists carrying hunting knives that size."

"Technically, it's a *bowie* knife. And it was a gift from Dr. Scholl when I got accepted into the honors program. He gave one to all his students."

My mouth fell open. Dad giving out knives to his honors students? "Wow. My family was never much for hunting, but, who knows, maybe one day Dad will gift me with a knife too." I didn't mean to sound bitter, but I guess I did, because Tommy reached out to touch my shoulder. A soothing kind of gesture, it was a light pat. Still, I flinched in response. Tommy immediately took his hand away, but his eyes stayed locked with mine. "Alif . . . I hope you're not jealous or something."

"That's ridiculous. Why would I be jealous?"

"I don't know . . . You don't seem to like me very much, and every time I mention your father or my work with him you do this *I'm repulsed* thing with your face and shoulders."

"I do not . . . *I'm repulsed* thing? What does that even mean?"

He did a poor imitation of me, and it looked as ridiculous as it sounded. I really hoped he was exaggerating and I didn't *actually* look like that.

"I'm not repulsed. And I'm not jealous and I don't . . . dislike you." I was grateful he couldn't hear the wild beating of my heart.

Tommy went on. "I'm not sure if you know this, but I grew up in foster care. And while I know many kids

136

have good experiences there, I didn't. Dr. Scholl is the closest thing I have to a father."

"I didn't know that," I mumbled, a wave of shame washing over me. I'd never admit it, at least not to Tommy, but I *did* get jealous over Dad being excessively nice and fatherly with his research students, most of all with Tommy. But hearing about Tommy's childhood made me feel petty and spoiled.

He chuckled at my fumbled response. "That's okay. I've barely had a conversation with you that lasted longer than a minute until now."

It was my turn to chuckle.

"What's so funny?" he asked.

I fought off an onslaught of nervous giggles but couldn't control the burning blush dancing on my cheeks. I met his eyes and almost shuddered at how focused he seemed on what I had to say.

"It's just funny that we had to get stranded in the desert to get to know each other."

COGITO, ERGO SUM

Tommy told me his morning solo expedition took him on a half-hour trek eastward following the line where the desert and the oasis met. Tommy saw no signs of the oasis curving, which would've hinted at its eastern limit. That's why, he said, his suggestion to the group would be to walk west, to see if the situation was any different in that direction. By the time we rejoined the group, Lori was sunbathing, with her tank top rolled up and her toned stomach exposed to the sun. Her hair, a messy bird nest in the morning, was now tightened into a high ponytail. Rowen, hunched next to her, was holding a gigantic palm leaf over her head to create a shade. His uncovered neck was turning that deep red hue that screamed blisters. He didn't seem to care.

Minh and Luke huddled together in the shade. Though their voices were too low to distinguish words, it was their aggressive gesticulating and facial expressions that gave them away. They were arguing. Upon my approach, with Tommy lagging behind, the two of them looked up and became unnaturally quiet. I studied Luke's face—his cheeks were sunken and his eyes, normally bright blue, were darker now, hooded by bloated, reddish lids. If I didn't know better, I would've sworn that Luke looked wronged and betrayed. It didn't take a genius to suspect it was likely because of my tête-à-tête with Tommy in the bushes. But given the circumstances, it was hard for me to care about Luke's feelings. I didn't want to confront him about this tension between us either—it'd just add to the fire of our group disarray that was already burning bright. I focused on Minh instead. She stood up and approached me, but Luke remained seated, feigning indifference while clearly listening to our conversation.

"What's with Lori baking in the sun?" I asked. "Is this some kind of spa-in-the-desert delusion?"

"She's in denial." Minh spared a long stare in Lori's direction. I followed her eyes to see Rowen pick Lori off the ground and half carry, half drag her into the shade. Lori was playfully fighting him off while laughing.

Minh shook her head at them and said to me, quietly, "We need to get out of here, Alif. And soon. Before Lori snaps and kills us all in our sleep. I swear, I heard her going on and on last night about a 'sacrifice.' I know she's our friend and all, but she gives me the creeps now, and this whole thing between her and Rowen . . ." She stopped midsentence, her eyes suddenly looking everywhere but at me.

"What do you think Lori meant by that? A sacrifice?" I asked, struggling to keep my tone flat amid the blood rushing to my head, dizzying me.

"Well, she was asleep," Minh replied. "So it must've been some kind of dream or hallucination—either way, something freaked her out. Big-time. I guess it really burned her out, because she kind of crashed after that, hence the sunbathing trance."

I briefly met Tommy's eyes, wondering if he was thinking what I was thinking, remembering my recent assurances of Lori's resilience. Maybe Lori wasn't as solid as I thought. Then my own dream echoed in my mind in all its surreal glory, and I grew silent. My fingertips were still a little numb from handling the poisonous flowers . . . Could Minh and Tommy sense that I was keeping something from them? To shift attention away from myself, I focused on our survival plan. "Do you think Lori actually should stay behind after all? Because we were thinking we need to explore the rest of the oasis, and soon."

"*We?*" Luke snarled, catching my muted words. "As in *Tommy and you?*" His voice was unrecognizable, hoarse, and scary-low. "Does this mean you're finally hooking up with your forever-crush?" The malice in Luke's eyes made me want to take a step back. I fought the urge to look over at Tommy, who was somewhere behind me.

I met Luke's stare with one of my own and held his attention long enough for him to grow tense and look away first.

But it was Tommy who spoke. "Seriously? We're stranded in the desert and you're still wasting your energy pining over Alif? Just give it up, man, and focus on surviving."

Luke readied to answer him, sitting up taller and opening his mouth, but whatever words were building inside his throat were swallowed by the wild roar of car engines.

Four-wheel drives! Our rescue was here!

Everyone was on their feet. We exchanged feral glances and then we were running for it, dashing like a pack of wild dogs toward the sound of our salvation. In a flurry of galloping legs and waving hands, we left the oasis.

I caught a glimpse of Lori's ponytail, swinging as she sprinted ahead of me, heading straight for the gray-yellow cloud on the desert and a jeep emerging from it. The jeep, though seriously covered in dust, spotted a familiar lineup of logos for the dig's sponsors.

"Dad!" My voice broke into a scream and then a coughing fit. But that didn't stop me from screaming at the top of my straining lungs. I tripped in my mad dash but held my ground, stumbling my way through the stretch of desert that separated me from my father and the cool breeze of the car's air-conditioning. The others were around me, on either side of me, behind me, all of us yelling, moving, jumping . . . If we had a flare gun, it would have been fired.

Not long now. We were saved. A miracle!

As the first jeep approached, I saw another following. I came to a halt, catching my breath, but Luke and Minh kept on running for a few dozen feet before reaching Lori and slowing down. Tommy and Rowen must've been somewhere behind me.

People in those cars, they must have seen us by now. I started to move again, not running but walking fast toward the jeeps, which were still a few hundred feet away, speeding at us. Up ahead, Lori fell to her knees and dug her hands into the sand. She sobbed, her cries turning into screams.

I caught up with Minh, our eyes meeting briefly. Together, alarmed, we watched Lori digging her hands into the ground and throwing the sand all around and over herself. I hadn't been sure what to make of Minh's story about Lori freaking out in the night, but here was some truly unsettling behavior right in front of me. But even more alarming, though the cars should've been slowing down by now, they weren't.

After coming to her feet again and even taking some tentative steps forward, Lori let out an animalistic sound of defeat. The same suspicion that was building in my brain must've hit her too. The jeeps weren't going to stop. As if they couldn't see us.

The first car drove straight at Lori, swallowing her in the cloud of dust. The car kept on moving. Half concealed in its swirling column of dirt, it was now headed for me. I squeezed my eyes shut.

Nothing, just some cool breeze on my face.

I kept my eyes closed. Was this death? Was there some sort of an afterlife? I'd read somewhere that because our brain was normally the last organ to go, there was a brief period of time when a dying person knew they were dead. Following this disturbing idea, another thought filled my brain: Descartes said "I think, therefore I am"— cogito, ergo sum. And right now, I was *most definitely thinking.*

I opened my eyes. The desert all around me was still, undisturbed.

"It went right through her . . ." Tommy was the one speaking. "A mirage?"

Frozen like an awkward statue carved out of disbelief, Lori was half splayed, half seated on the ground. I looked back in the direction where the jeeps had gone.

I could still see them—the cars' white plates glittering in the sun. And then they were gone over the dunes.

I came to where Lori sat, her legs half buried in the sand. The rest of our miserable group followed suit, surrounding her, our weakest link. I said Lori's name, but she gave no reaction. Her skin was dangerously red. She needed shade. And water. I was about to say it, but Rowen must've been thinking it too. He grabbed her by the waist and pulled her up. Cradling her in his arms, he carried her back into the oasis.

I watched them disappear into the shade of the palm trees. The rest of us followed, our shoulders sagging in defeat.

A NIGHT VISITOR

Rowen's voice was shaking. "Are we seriously not going to talk about it?"

"What exactly do you want to talk about?" Luke, back to sulking in the shadows, sounded bored.

"How the jeeps came to our rescue and then didn't even notice us! They nearly killed Lori!"

Luke shrugged. "Lori's fine, isn't she? Better than new. Just quiet and slightly less annoying than before."

"*I'm* also okay. Thanks for caring," I muttered, but only Tommy looked in my direction. He was also the only one doing something productive—picking the few fruits still left on the trees and piling them on the ground in the shade.

"Not much we can do now, right?" Tommy said, not pausing in his work. "I say we stick to our original plan and go exploring. We might be stuck here longer than anticipated."

Admit it—we're utterly screwed, I read between his measured words.

"Well, *I say* bullshit," Luke spat. From his place on the ground he was watching Tommy like a jaguar in wait, about to spring out and go for the throat. "Those cars appearing here means civilization's not far away. *I say* we follow their tracks in the sand before they disappear. Only a total idiot would stay here one more night!"

A menace to his movement, Tommy dropped his fruit pickings and took a step toward Luke. Crossing his arms tightly over his chest, Tommy said, "Only a total idiot would wander off into the desert to follow the tracks of an imaginary car."

"It wasn't imaginary, and you know it!" Luke jumped off the ground and came face-to-face with Tommy. Luke's fingers were curling into fists, and his shoulders were pulled back. It would've been funny to watch him fluff up like a fighting peacock if it wasn't so disturbing. I always knew there were emotions underneath Luke's mild-mannered surface that were less than pleasant, but the only time I ever saw his violence take physical shape was when he made my bully bleed. Ever since, Luke had filtered his anger, only letting it show through verbal aggression and tense body language. But now the desert was pushing him further and further from forced civility, filling me with fear of what was to come when Luke's facade finally broke for good.

It was time for the voice of reason to intervene. I hoped that voice was going to come from someone other than me. I looked around, finding Minh, but her attention was on Lori. The latter was curled up on the ground, her head resting on Minh's lap. In a rare show of genuine gentleness between them, Minh was patting Lori's head, not unlike a handler of wild beasts pacifying a distressed animal. Rowen was also focused on Lori. Okay, *I* would have to be the voice of reason then. I approached Luke and tried to catch his eye. It wasn't an easy task to get and hold his attention, since he was engaged in a whoever-looks-away-first-is-a-loser game with Tommy. When I succeeded, I said, "There's a strong probability that we had a group hallucination and imagined those cars."

"Strong probability my ass . . . ," Luke growled, but choked on the rest of his sentence when Tommy's open palm connected with his chest. I was close enough to Luke to feel his warm breath on my neck as the air got knocked out of his lungs. Luke stumbled back but didn't fall. If Tommy thought he was going to slap some wisdom into Luke, he was dead wrong. Instead of wising up, Luke turned the color of beets, nostrils flaring and lips twisting into a scowl. Gone was the cocky guy I'd kissed just days ago. I quickly moved aside as Luke lunged at Tommy, but the vegetation underneath his feet got him tangled up, giving Tommy an opening to deliver another blow. This time Tommy's fist collided with Luke's shoulder. From a bystander's perspective, the hit looked deceptively weak, even gentle. Tommy didn't want a fight—that much was clear. But, again, Tommy didn't know Luke. Hell, even I couldn't say I knew Luke, but based on what I did know about him, Luke wasn't the kind of guy who responded well to being slapped around. This was going to end badly.

"Stop this!" I begged, having enough common sense to stay away from the direct path of destruction. Deaf to my plea and driven by the furious blood pumping through his veins, Luke barreled into Tommy, wrapping his hands around Tommy's waist and bringing him down to the ground with his weight.

Both of them managed to land enough hits and punches on each other to draw blood. What shook me more was that no one else seemed to care.

"Rowen!" I ran for the shade where Lori lay still, as if soothed into a trance by Minh's hands running through her hair. "A little help here! Do something! Make them stop!"

Rowen looked up at me but made no motion to move.

I had to resort to the tactics of a girl stuck in a pub brawl. I latched onto Luke's back, since he was the closest to me, and pounded my fists against him. Trying to reach around him, I yelled and pulled at the two boys' hands while somehow avoiding being hit myself. It worked after a while: They let go and rolled away from each other.

Tommy was the first to sit up. His lower lip was split. There was a quarter of a napkin in the back pocket of my sweatpants and it looked clean, so I handed it over to Tommy. When he failed to take it, I pointed at his mouth. Absently, he accepted the napkin and pressed it against his lips.

After observing our silent exchange, Luke picked himself up and limped deeper into the oasis.

"What was that about, huh? Really?" I asked Tommy, watching a red dot soaking through the napkin.

"He's an asshole. What would someone like you be doing with someone like him, anyway?"

The unguarded coarseness of his words took me aback. "Someone like me?"

"You know what I mean."

"Actually, I don't," I said, not caring who else could hear me. "I don't really know what you mean, Tommy, because I don't really know you, and I certainly can't read your mind. I'm on your side though, you know. I just hope you're on my side too—that you've got my back."

Looking as surprised by my outburst as I was, Tommy just sat there, staring at me. I had to ignore the trickle of heat spreading through my face. His eyes were so green, as if painted with impressionist colors.

"What I meant was that Luke and you . . . I don't get it," he said. "He's the most *unlikely* guy someone like you could pick for a boyfriend . . ."

"Who said anything about a boyfriend?" I snorted in shock as Tommy's expression grew befuddled. "Jump to conclusions much? And again, what was that—*someone like me?*"

"All I'm trying to say is that you can do so much better." He wanted to add more—I saw his lips shaping up to it—but then he stopped and just gave me a close-lipped smile, an oddly disarming one.

"Tommy, I'm stuck in the desert with my four friends and my father's research assistant. I *know* I can do so much better."

I left him sitting there and walked away, headed for the palms where everyone else was haunting the shadows like a pack of homeless phantoms. Luke was washing up in the spring, the water around him turning pink.

Our collective mood was down for the rest of the day, and that was putting it lightly. While the rest of us kept to our own space, Tommy couldn't sit still. He busied himself with rinsing the remaining fruit in the stream and separating it into six piles, each looking awfully small. On and off, we munched on our food until the sun started to set. The unspoken reality was that tomorrow we'd have close to nothing to eat unless we were willing to climb those taller palm trees we hadn't yet stripped bare. There were no more talks about exploring the oasis or following car tracks out into the desert. This place was draining us of motivation and energy.

As night rolled in and the temperature dropped, there was nothing left to do but settle down on the ground and sleep. I nestled next to Minh, and Luke claimed a spot in front of her but facing away. I took it as a sign of Luke's waning interest in me, which was a relief. Tommy hesitated before choosing a place next to me, leaving me staring into his back. Despite my miserable mood, my breathing soon grew measured and calm. A thick kind of sleep rolled in and carried me away. Not even the sensation of being watched by someone hiding in the black underbrush—or the unmistakable though difficult-to-comprehend-given-the-circumstances sounds of making out coming from the section of the clearing claimed by Lori and Rowen—could keep me awake.

"Noam was her favorite, you see. That's why she let him go and not me. Forgive me for being so dramatic, but I do feel wronged by her!" The nervous lips of the speaker were moving close enough to my face for me to feel the displacement of air. His speech was accented. Something European. French, I guessed. I tried to shiver away from his breath, but something held me in place. My eyes shut tight, I couldn't overpower my fatigue to open them and see who was hanging over me.

"Tommy?" I tried to ask, only no sound came out.

"No, no . . . Don't waste your energy trying to fight her. Just listen. Listen! Just listen now," the man who *definitely* wasn't Tommy continued. His presence was fast becoming unbearable. Like a freezer door swinging open, he was letting out chilled air, while something was pressing down on my chest, making it an effort to draw enough air. I attempted to edge away from him, but my body was now weightless. I was no longer lying on the uneven ground but rather floating in the darkness of space—or in water. I wished this dream would end. I tried fighting my way up to the surface, but whenever I'd approach the glow above the water, I was yanked back into the depths.

"There were two of us stuck here. Noam and me. And he left me here . . . She let him go because there was nothing else he could offer her. But before she released him, she stripped him of his very soul. Which of us has a worse fate? I wonder. And now she's got six fresh ones. I . . . can . . . hear . . . her belly growling all the way from here . . ."

His freezing breath washed over me with each new sentence, and I couldn't stop my body from shuddering. I strained so hard, I managed to open my eyes into a slit. This was no dream at all! The man's face hanging over mine was familiar. His skin was dark, and his eyes were milky white. He had no pupils.

He smiled at me with something like pity in his expression. I stared in horror at his teeth, rot claiming what was formerly white.

"I . . . know . . . you." Every word was a battle against my unwilling tongue.

"Yes, yes, I guess, you do. In a way." He gave me an eager nod, flashing those terrible teeth again.

"You're the man from the driver's license." *We found your bones in the desert.*

Another nod, another disturbing flash of those teeth. "And you're the girl she'll save for last. After she devours all the others. One by one, she'll eat you up, tear you apart limb by limb, separating soul from flesh. But she needs her sacrifice first . . ."

Abruptly, the man melted into the night, leaving a whiff of cold air behind him as a reminder. It shrouded me in the way of a wet, smelly blanket that was starting to grow mold.

I couldn't sleep after that. I met the sunrise, my eyes open wide, staring at the beauty that was the auburn sun rising over the desert but seeing none of it.

WORSE THAN SABOTAGE

The morning of day three started off on the wrong foot. Rowen was missing.

I must've drifted off at sunrise because I was jolted out of sleep by the sound of Lori screaming. Still shaken from my nightmarish experience, I was drafted into a panicked search effort. I had no time to dwell on whether what happened to me last night was a horrid dream or some kind of actual spiritual encounter. And now we had a real crisis on our hands.

"Who saw Rowen last?" I asked Tommy as the two of us headed into one of the denser parts of the oasis. Minh and Lori were going in the opposite direction, while Luke stayed where he was, uncaring and unwilling to move. Tommy got his bowie knife out and used it to hack at the low-hanging fronds of the palm trees blocking our way.

"I'm guessing Lori, since she sounded the alarm, but everything's really jumbled in my mind right now. This place is messing with my head . . . ," Tommy said, leaving me to wonder what exactly he meant by that. I agonized over whether I should tell him about my own increasingly unsettling nighttime experiences, but we had to stop talking when our sloppy advance through the jungle disturbed a horde of black flies. I clenched my mouth shut and followed Tommy as he raced the hell out of there. After breaking through some more of the same tight green shrubbery, we stumbled onto a miniature clearing, a smaller replica of our current sleeping grounds. That's where we found Rowen.

He sat in the middle of the clearing, arms circling his knees.

"What are you doing out here?" Tommy asked. "Lori's been really worried about you—" He stopped talking when he saw what I was seeing—a sea of white-and-gold foil wrappers, spread over the ground all around Rowen—wrappers from those Al Nassma candies he liked so much.

Just noticing us, Rowen's red, tear-stained eyes rattled me. His lips were bitten bloody.

"What happened here?" I perched on the ground

next to him, balancing on my heels, foil wrappers rustling under my feet.

"Where did you get all this candy?" Tommy asked, incredulous. Good question. If Rowen had all this chocolate on him when we got stranded in the desert, he must've hidden it somewhere in the oasis the moment we'd arrived. But surely we would've noticed if at any stage of our ordeal Rowen was bursting with chocolate? And surely he would've shared it with us? Right?

Rowen muttered an inaudible response into his knees.

"What happened?" I repeated.

"I found it . . . ," Rowen said. "I found it all, and I couldn't stop. I was so hungry."

"You found all this candy and you ate it all because you were hungry," I said, fully aware of how thick I sounded.

"Yeah . . . There was a voice. It told me it was all for me. That it was a reward."

"A reward for what?" Tommy asked.

"For telling everyone who poisoned our water stream."

My eyes sought Rowen's, but he was evading me. I silently begged him not to say it. Not in Tommy's presence. *Please*.

"It was Alif who contaminated the spring." Rowen looked up at me briefly, then let go of my gaze, but not before I saw her reflection in his eyes—the Queen of Giants, the lonely spark.

"Why would you do that?" Tommy asked under his breath once we'd started walking back. Unsure what to do with him, we left Rowen on his own, but after a few steps, I could hear the telltale noises of him following after us, tearing his way through the trees.

"It's . . . I wasn't even aware of what I was doing until I woke up in the morning and my fingers were numb from handling the flowers. Until that moment, I thought it was a dream."

"Do you sleepwalk?"

"Not that I know of. It's never happened before . . . I'm scared, Tommy. I'm fucking terrified!" I stopped, growing dizzy on my feet, as cold waves of dread battered me from all angles. Tommy did the thing I least expected. He hugged me. It was a short-lived but fierce hug that consumed all my senses and ignited a strange fire in my chest. When Tommy let go of me, I remained motionless, still dazed but happy in an unrestrained kind of way.

"Wait here," Tommy said before disappearing back into the thickness of the trees we'd left behind. I heard him talking something over with Rowen but couldn't discern what it was about. When they both emerged from the trees, we resumed walking. Tommy whispered to me,

"Rowen won't say anything to anyone about the spring if we keep our mouths shut about the candy incident. Right, Rowen?" Tommy looked in the direction of my friend.

Rowen nodded. I tried finding his eyes again, but his gaze was unfocused. I guessed this place was affecting us all in different ways.

In a few minutes the three of us made it back to the others. At seeing Rowen, Lori flung herself into his arms. He came to slowly embrace her, his movements shaky with uncertainty.

I had exactly one apple left in my allocated food pile. When I bit into it, it tasted bitter.

Rowen became more talkative after drinking from the spring and conferring with Lori in the shadows of the palm trees before the two of them joined our loose circle on the ground. This entire time, Luke avoided looking at me directly, but I could sense his stare drilling a hole into the side of my head every time I looked away. A purplish bruise around his left eye stood out on his swollen face. Tommy looked slightly better off—his face had taken less assault from Luke—but his knuckles were the bad kind of red and scraped.

Our group felt sluggish and in discord, but we had to start discussing our plans for survival—for real.

Nobody was taking the initiative, so I said, "We

need to go deeper into the oasis and look for food. If our group has to split up, so be it. In that case, I'll go with Tommy and we'll walk the length of the oasis to the west. Depending on how we fare, we might follow the length of the entire perimeter. That'll give us a good idea of what we're dealing with."

"I'll come with you two," Minh said, reinforcing her words with a nod. She started braiding her long hair— her way of getting ready to tough it out. I envied that she could just pull her hair up into a bun or braid it like that. I couldn't do anything of the kind with my shoulder-length mess, which was only getting messier every minute I went without giving it a proper wash.

"And the rest of you?" I looked between those still undecided.

Rowen gave me a quick nod, which I took as a yes on behalf of Lori as well since Lori just stared back at me.

"Luke?" I made a point of saying his name, but he insisted on glaring down at his feet and not acknowledging me. Rivulets of sweat were running down his face and neck.

But after a long, awkward minute, Luke caved, and the six of us got on with our quest.

Staying under the protection of the shadows, we all headed west, keeping to the outer edge of the oasis, following the line where the sand encroached on the grass. No words were exchanged. Bound by an unspo-ken agreement and a sense of self-preservation, we stuck close to one another, forming a tight formation. After some twenty or thirty minutes of walking, our path dead-ended into a deep and wide arroyo. Jagged rocks framed its outer edge, coloring my thoughts with imagined pain brought on by a myriad of cuts to the skin. Not needing to confer with one another, we bore right alongside the arroyo's outline and deeper into the oasis proper.

The arroyo turned out to be bigger than expected. Before we knew it, we were deep enough into the oasis that whatever light had been sneaking through the tight canopy overhead all but disappeared. Reaching almost to my knees, the undergrowth put snakes and scorpions on my mind. The palm trees' trunks were so closely spaced, at times we had to take turns squeezing in between them before we could proceed. Aside from our collective heavy breathing and an occasional swear word uttered when skin was grazed by a stick or a foot slid off a rock, there was no sound. No insects buzzing. No birds cooing. None of the signs of animal life.

The oasis was holding its breath as it spied on us, waiting to see what we'd do next. Every shadow seemed to move in a deliberate way. My mind wandered, mak-ing me fixate on Noam and Alain—and their respective fates. Noam was missing for two years before walking into my father's camp. And Alain? How long had he actually been stuck in here before finally making what turned out to be a fatal decision to leave the oasis? I imagined him collapsing on the sands and staying there, the sun melting his flesh and bleaching his bones. It was quite an effort to exorcise that image out of my mind. Alain insisted on returning, again and again, a broken record trapped under the cursed needle of an otherworldly gramophone.

I'd long lost any idea of time, and the trees and the shadows got almost too tight, almost too suffocating for us to keep pushing in. Yet, stubbornly, we kept on. The alternative to that was starving, as our fruit piles were all but gone. But the deeper we went, the more uncertain our steps became.

Rowen was the first to voice his doubts. "Okay, should we go back? Is this enough exploring for one day?" His words were ignored. We were a herd of mindless robots hell-bent on our (probably futile) mission. But then we ran into yet another natural barrier when the land started to curve, going up higher and higher. Following the elevation, the forest of palms thinned until it released us at last. We came to a narrow stretch of barren land, with the palm trees behind us and an unclimbable rocky formation before us.

I tipped my head up high to take all of it in. I'd long stopped questioning whether what I was seeing was possible. The size and scale of the oasis that emerged out of sizzling thin air to save us, the impossibility of fruit and berries in these arid parts, my all-too-realistic night terrors, the ghosts of jeeps passing through us, and now this—a mighty rock blocking our way.

We spread out to check the footing of what upon closer inspection appeared to be a hybrid between a dune and a rock. A solidified dune? I heard the spring before I saw it, its thin line of bubbling water emerging from the palms somewhere behind us and racing down the natural rocky steps to our side before vanishing into a large opening in the rocks.

We crowded around the opening. It was cut into the monolith with humanlike precision.

The entrance was wide enough to accommodate the spring and still allow narrow pathways on either side. How deep did it go? Beckoned by the darkness, I approached the entrance. I started to slide on the slippery ground but managed to hold my own. I only half felt Tommy's hand holding on to my shoulder.

"Careful now," he said.

I didn't answer. Instead, I gazed into the opening, a whiff of its winter breath on my face. As if moving of its own accord, my right hand reached out, fingertips brushing against the surface of the rock. I was half expecting my touch to reveal some secret message, for letters of a forgotten alphabet to materialize, but the surface remained unchanged.

"I don't like this place. I don't like it at all. It reminds me of a cemetery. And what's with that smell?" Minh's anxiety brought me back to reality.

"What smell?" I asked.

"It smells like an old, stuffy cave," Minh said, stating the obvious. But it was her choice of a word—*cave*—that struck me as wrong. A cave implied a naturally occurring formation, created by water and time. This place before us was anything but natural. Too seamless. Too perfect.

"It's a temple," I blurted out. What possessed me to say that? It must've been this place itself, the slabs of sleek rock practically vibrating with want. Though what this place wanted wasn't clear.

Judging from five pairs of very confused eyes drilling into me right then, I was the only one thinking those thoughts. Tommy's concerned expression in particular prompted me to explain myself. "I mean, it *feels* like a temple. The rock is so flat, it seems man-made." I looked between my friends' faces, expecting someone to disagree. I zeroed in on Tommy, since he tended to be the voice of reason during our ordeal.

"Don't look at me!" Tommy raised his hands in a defensive gesture. "It might as well be man-made. Who knows with this place?"

"Why does it matter?" Minh interrupted him. "We shouldn't have left our spot. What if the cars come back? We're going to miss our own rescue!"

"You can go back, if you'd like." I didn't recognize

my own voice—edgy, even rude. This place was messing with my very essence. Regardless, I couldn't stop this new me. "I mean it. You know the way back. In fact, everyone who wants to return to our spot can go now. I'll join you all there." I took another step toward the entry into what had now solidified in my head as the temple.

In an act of support, Lori came forward to stand next to me, but instead of reassuring me, her presence made me want to flinch. Half her face was lit by the blazing sun and the other was shadowed. "I'll go with you. At least it's cool down there."

"We'll *all* go in there. Or we'll *all* go back to the clearing," Tommy said.

Minh still didn't look impressed. I sought out her eyes and told her, "I just want to see if any light gets inside. Because if it does, maybe this place could be our new shelter. You know, in case there's another sandstorm."

Minh nodded, a mechanical movement. Her resistance appeared to have fizzled out. Or maybe she just didn't relish the idea of being left alone out here.

Not so sure anymore if going down into the temple was such an awesome idea, I had to force my unsteady feet to move. The opening's ceiling was high enough to accommodate me and Lori, but the taller people in our group, like Minh and Tommy, had to lower their heads as they entered.

All life was sucked out of this place. If the tightly woven forest we had to cross to get here was silent like an empty house, the temple's silence was nothingness embodied. I touched the walls on my way in, only to pull back my hand in disgust. They were covered with gelatinous sludge. I cleaned my hand off on my pants, which were filthy anyway. After we returned to our sleeping grounds, I had to find a private moment and wash my clothes—and myself—properly in the spring.

"Minh was right. It does stink in here," Luke commented from somewhere behind me. Or maybe it was Rowen who spoke. All voices sounded the same in here, distorted by echoes bouncing off uneven walls.

Stuck at the front of the line, I ended up leading our group. Whatever would happen to us would happen to me first. But at least it was cool inside here and I was no longer sweating or burning up in the sun. Also, we were all alive and in relatively good moods. Well, as much as possible, considering the circumstances. On the negative side, we were still stranded in the desert. So there was that.

My eyes were quick to adjust to the semidarkness; there were cracks in the ceiling and the walls, allowing some light to seep through. I could distinguish the shapes of stalactites, their gleam infusing this whole experience with eerie beauty. Right behind me, Lori flicked on a lighter (it must have been Rowen's) and held it high. My shadow, long and ugly, materialized at my feet, stretching farther out into the temple.

"Better save that for when we really need it," Minh said to Lori, and the light vanished as quickly as it appeared.

With no forks or other openings appearing, we continued on straight, the water stream always burbling below. More natural light illuminated our path now, and we stopped when the tunnel expanded into a wide-open space. The stream we'd been following seemed to run around the entire length of this area, disappearing into a passage to our left. "We could throw a couple of beanbags into that corner and have a plasma TV mounted on this wall," Luke said, briefly back to his old sarcastic self.

Minh, who had wandered farther up ahead, was now waving a hand in the air, urging us to join her at the far end of this cavernous room. "Just look at these walls!"

"Am I allowed to use the lighter now?" Lori flicked it on without waiting for a response. With her hand held up high and close to the wall, I could see the drawings that had gotten Minh so riled up.

Jet-black, glowing-white, and reddish-okra colors intermingled, dancing on the brown surface of the wall. A series of images followed the circumference of this space—like a strip of pictures arranged in a storyboard. It told of an exploding star, or maybe some kind of asteroid hitting Earth but burning up in the atmosphere to the point where only one tiny white piece remained. The next image showed people on their knees, forming a circle around a white hexagon, rays of light surrounding it like a halo. The fever dreams I'd been having in the oasis flickered through my mind, but my memories of them were already fuzzy, ill defined. There was the queen on her throne, but she was also a fallen star, or at least a part of one. And she was hungry. That much I could recall.

There was some scuffling noise in the distance. Where was the rest of our group? The lighter wavered in Lori's hand, casting weird shadows on the walls.

"Rowen?" she yelled. Her retreating footsteps clapped against the rock-hard floors. I turned just in time to see her enter the passage to the left where the stream flowed.

"Lori, wait up!" I called after her, echoes exaggerating my call, as if the walls were making fun of me. I sprinted after Lori as fast as the semidarkness allowed. I could hear some of the others dashing after me in the dark, intermixed with the sounds of water splashing and Tommy or Luke swearing. Together, we were creating a strange cacophony.

Somewhere ahead of us Lori screamed, the sound twisted, desperate. I still couldn't see her. When I caught up to her at last, I halted to a stop as I caught a glimpse of what lay ahead. My feet skidded against the ground and I came dangerously close to an open pit that yawned beneath me. Lori was crouching by the pit's edge, close to the drop. After I braved another step toward it, I could see that the bottom of the pit was covered with sharp objects, like spikes.

Rowen was down there, his body skewered on several spikes. Illuminated by some dull light streaming from above, Rowen's face stared back at us, eyes open but sightless. My own eyes were frozen and unable to blink; all I could see were the spikes coming out of his torso. The material of his T-shirt was turning dark red.

"No . . . ," I whispered.

The semidarkness wavered around me. How did Rowen end up in the pit? We were all together just moments ago—when did he wander off? This wasn't real. It couldn't be.

I was hit with the ghost of a pain in my own gut. Everything slowed down, the walls and the ground beneath my feet vibrating. I lost track of where I was, where my friends were. I was standing by the edge of the pit, but I was also *in* the pit. Everyone, Rowen included, was looking down at me from above. Their faces were twisted masks; and there were spikes coming out of Rowen's stomach and chest. I strained to snap out of it. There was a movement next to me, displacing the air. Stubbornly rejecting the new reality, I thought maybe it was Rowen. When I managed to tear my eyes away from my friend's unmoving body in the pit, I came face-to-face with Tommy. He was right next to me, close to the pit, and he was horrified. His hands were shaking.

To my other side, Lori started to wail. What came next was a mess. Chaos. At first, I couldn't move, petrified. I was losing time. I could've stayed down there for months or years. It didn't really matter to me. And then there were hands dragging me away.

As Tommy ushered me away from the pit, my eyes sought out Lori. She was fighting against Luke, who was, in turn, pulling her away. Before I gave in to Tommy and left the edge of the pit, I caught another glimpse of Rowen's body down below. I knew with absolute clarity that my mind would never be able to revisit this memory and not glitch out in shock. That lifeless mass of flesh on the bottom of the pit, that grotesque, bleeding rag doll, was once my friend. He was one of the good guys. Sometimes jaded, sometimes a jerk, but overall okay. And now, the Queen of Giants had claimed him as her sacrifice. *Better him than me*, a horrible part of me thought before it slithered back into the darkness from which it had briefly raised its scaly head.

THE POWER
OF DENIAL

I didn't know who broke into a run first, but one second I was immortalizing every detail of Rowen's body and the next we were all stampeding away from the pit and down, down, down the dark corridor. Aside from the pandemonium of our galloping feet, the only sound was Lori's nonstop sobbing.

My mind was fried, but I had to keep on moving. I knew that much. Stuck in fight-or-flight mode, my brain kept pumping fear into my veins, telling me that if I stopped, whatever had gotten Rowen would get me too. As I ran, I somehow broke away from Tommy and ended up way ahead of my friends. But I wasn't alone. There was someone else in the dark with me. I sensed an odd pattern of alien breathing, a sulfurous stench of burnt hair, a guttural laugh. I couldn't see her, but I knew that the blinding gaze of the Queen of Giants was on me once more. I also knew that all of this was her doing. She was controlling us, manipulating our every step, every thought.

I paused, and Minh bumped into me. I yelled into the darkness behind me, "We're up ahead! Slow down!" *Down . . . down . . . down . . .* Echoes repeated my words as the rumble of approaching feet lessened, came to a halt.

"Shush," Minh hissed at me.

I held my breath. My eyes picked out Minh in the dark. She was feeling around with her hands, looking for something.

She turned to face me. "We haven't been here! This is new!" She was pointing at the wall, indicating another one of those eerie drawings I could barely make out in the weak light. She was right though, this *was* new.

The image showed five pairs of hands surrounding that same white hexagonal object I'd seen before.

I ran a finger over the image, then had to swallow down a pang of guilt. As a child of two archaeologists, I knew it was poor practice to touch cave paintings. They were fragile, likely to get damaged by sweat and dirt. But I couldn't help myself. There was something immensely attractive about this particular drawing.

The cave's lighting intensified, or maybe it was just my eyes adapting to the dark, allowing me to see more detail to the drawing. Like how the white paint an unknown artist used to draw the hexagon had a greenish glean to it. It screamed organic matter. Algae maybe. Was it the same sludge I felt at the entrance to the temple? Some kind of primordial soup from which relentless life crawled out?

And then the painting also *spoke* to me, as if through some kind of osmosis. Its voice, as visceral as a tap on my shoulder, was saying, *Come to me . . . Alif . . .*

Luke, Tommy, and Lori caught up to us while I was drooling over the drawing. "Where should we go? Which way?" Luke cried so loud my eardrums reverberated.

I pulled my hand away from the wall, my trance broken. I said, "There was only one path leading in here. There's no way we could've taken a wrong turn, so let's just keep going?"

We proceeded with extreme care, stepping on the ground softly. The corridor curved, and instead of taking us back to the entrance, it led us to a new, low-ceilinged room. The temple was constantly changing, moving. An Ouroboros swallowing its own tail.

But I sensed we were safe now. This place had already claimed its sacrifice in Rowen. If it had wanted all of us dead, we *would* be dead by now. But I knew I shouldn't reveal my thoughts about this to anyone. Not even Tommy.

The sole source of illumination in this new room came from a column of light streaming down from a large crack over our heads. The light landed squarely on the center of a flat slab, waist-high. The way the light behaved around the slab seemed odd. Soon I knew why.

As we approached, I saw that the light was being reflected off the slab's surface. At first, I thought there was a mirror. As I closed in, I saw it was a hexagonal tablet, just like the one from the cave-wall drawings—only real, three-dimensional. The tablet's surface shone pale green, making me think of Tommy's eyes.

Lori reached out and, before anyone could stop her, touched the tablet. When her skin made contact, Lori yelped and jerked her hand back. Steam came off her fingers in wisps, and the stink of sizzling flesh tickled my nostrils and throat. Cradling her arm, Lori stepped back. When I looked at her in the semidarkness, her eyes were glazed over. I was expecting her to cry or whimper in complaint over her injury, but she was quiet.

"What do you think that is?" Luke's question was interrupted by a monstrous howl. Its sound multiplied, growing bigger with each echoed repetition. Noise of rushing feet against rock followed, something clicking violently through the cave. Taloned paws?

"We need to get out of here!" Tommy's quivering shout forced us out of our collective trance. I worried Lori was too out of it to be able to move, but she sprang back to life just like that—and she reached out for the tablet. Stunned, I watched as she picked up the tablet like it hadn't hurt her just seconds earlier, and then she was scrambling off in a loose-limbed run.

This time we managed to trace our steps back to the familiar large room. We didn't linger there, immediately tearing to the entrance corridor, which eventually led us outside. We didn't drop our crazed pace until after we were out of the caves. Somehow, it was already night outside.

I could barely see where my feet were landing. This was a recipe for a disastrous fall.

"Stop! Just stop!" I yelled. "No one's after us!" But only Tommy slowed down. I watched as the rest of my friends dashed away, merging into the dark mass of trees. I caught up with Tommy, and we continued side by side, lagging behind the main group. He appeared strong and unshakable to me, as tall and confident as always, but when our eyes met in the dark, his gaze was stripped of life, haunted.

As we returned to it, our familiar sleeping ground seemed malevolent now. The darkness would have been absolute if not for a handful of stars fighting for their right to shine beyond the heavy-hanging clouds. The space was crowded by the imposing palm trees, which seemed to have crept closer to our clearing while we were away. The spring's bubbling song was muted and distant. My breathing was erratic, and something was off about my perception of space and time. My movements, even my thoughts, felt delayed, like I had to work extra hard to make my body respond to my brain's commands.

I had matched my pace to Tommy's and stopped when he did. We remained standing, watching Minh and Luke crouching by the spring, about ten feet away from Lori. I could hear the nervous undertones of their conversation, if not their words. Lori, her back against a palm, was clutching the hexagonal tablet to her chest. She was smiling to herself, but just with her lips, while her eyes were staring at nothing.

When Lori spoke, her loud, clear voice was surreally casual. She could've been talking about a new top or a pair of shoes she'd just gotten in her favorite shop. She was giggling too. "And that's why she's got no friends. No one likes a gloomzilla." Lori was still staring straight ahead, clearly not addressing Minh or Luke. But it became obvious who Lori was speaking to when she said, "Now you're just being silly, Rowen."

My heart was slamming against my rib cage. Without putting much thought into it, I found Tommy's hand in the dark. He gave my fingers a light squeeze and didn't let go.

Together, we approached Minh and Luke by the water. It was as if Lori was repelling us all. Hesitantly, I let go of Tommy's hand and sat on the ground next to Minh. "Is she okay?"

Minh kept silent, frowning, and it was Luke who answered, "Of course she is not *okay*, Alif. She's in shock. Rowen is dead. Dead!"

Minh hushed Luke while I met his angry stare. The whites of his eyes were glowing, almost swallowing the blue of his irises. I chose my next words carefully.

"I know that. We're all in shock. Don't bite my head off."

"Oh, I'm sorry," he hissed. "I'm sorry if my unkind tone upset you."

Minh shushed him again and then said in an awkward semiwhisper, "Did any of you see Rowen wander off on his own?" She spared a look to where Lori was sitting and hugging the tablet, but Lori didn't show any interest in this conversation.

"No," I whispered back. Luke shook his head and Tommy just shrugged in the way of someone lost and no longer sure of anything. I explained, keeping my voice at half volume, "I heard the screams, so I followed the sound into the . . . pit room."

Luke pointed a finger at me. "If only we'd just stayed here and waited for rescue instead of going on your pointless quest to the caves, Rowen would be alive. It's all your fault! Your fucking fault!"

"Shut it, Luke," Tommy said. "Just shut up!"

The shouting attracted Lori's attention. She gave the four of us a long look. "What do you think?" she asked.

None of us responded. Finally, Luke stood up and crossed the distance between our group and Lori. He put a hand on her shoulder. "What do you mean, Lori?"

Lori stared at Luke's hand on her shoulder, then her gaze slid up to his face. "About what Rowen just said. That in the morning we should walk in the direction the cars came from. What do you all think about his plan?"

"*Rowen* told you that?" Minh asked from her spot by the spring. She was shrinking into herself, subconsciously moving as far away from Lori as she could.

Lori let out a frustrated exhale and started talking again, slower, as if explaining a complex math problem to a not particularly bright student. "Yes. *Rowen* just said that. You all must have heard him."

"Is Rowen here with us now?" Luke asked.

My *Shut up* glare in his direction was wasted, of course. He simply refused to acknowledge me.

Lori just shook her head as she slumped to the ground, eventually coming to rest on her side. She closed her eyes and stacked both hands underneath her head like a pillow, though not before tucking the tablet closer. I could swear the tablet, this *object*, whatever it was, glimmered. The four of us watched Lori until her chest was rising and falling in sleep. She looked so peaceful, she was practically glimmering herself.

We exchanged looks. No one was willing to speak first. Finally, Tommy was the one to break the spell. His eyes weren't focusing on anyone specifically, and his tone was matter-of-fact, mechanical.

"There was something wild in that cave. An animal. Perhaps Rowen encountered it, and when he ran, he fell."

There was no conviction to his tone, though his words made sense. I *had* heard some strange sounds too, suggesting an animal presence in the temple.

Uninterrupted, Tommy concluded, "We need to take turns keeping guard. How about I take the first shift and I wake up one of you to take over in a few hours?"

Minh nodded before quickly settling on the ground next to Lori. Luke shrugged, appearing disinterested, but he did spare a long look at the tablet Lori was clutching. Was there longing in his eyes—or was the tablet making him uneasy? I couldn't tell, but I thought I felt what Luke was feeling—a nervousness deep under my skin, squirming on the molecular level. There was no way I could fall asleep right now. So I stayed close to Tommy.

He looked at me, not unkindly. "You should try to get some sleep, Alif. It's been a very long day, and tomorrow will be an even longer one."

"I doubt I can sleep. How about I stay up and keep you company for a bit?"

He considered it before giving me a curt nod. Not like he had much of a choice. Together, we moved away from the sleeping ground and sat down facing the dense grove of trees separating us from the temple. Or was it a cave after all? I wasn't sure anymore. I leaned in to whisper into Tommy's ear, "Want to know what I'm thinking? All this is a mirage and we're slowly dying of exposure in the desert."

He stayed quiet for a long time before murmuring back, "Hey, if that's the case, at least we're not *aware* we're dying, right?"

"Maybe we're being punished for something we've done, only we don't know what it is exactly. Or this is a test or something. Or we're trapped in a Kafka novel . . ."

At that Tommy chortled. "I like the Kafka option. As long as we're not going to turn into bugs."

"Cockroaches," I corrected. "And I meant another Kafka novel. *The Process.*"

He said nothing to that. We watched the moon peek through the neon-gray clouds, only to disappear again, teasing us. I listened to Tommy's soft breathing. It kept me grounded. Tommy's breathing meant he was alive. My hearing him breathe meant *I* was alive too.

"We shouldn't have taken that tablet thing from the cave," he said.

"Why, do you think it's *cursed?*" I said in an eerie voice, trying for a comedic tone, which immediately seemed inappropriate.

In a voice more flat and tired than before, he asked, "Do you remember when we found Rowen with all that candy? He was mumbling something about it being his reward."

That wiped all future attempts at jokes from my system. I softly confirmed I remembered it.

"What do you think that meant?" Tommy asked, finding my eyes in the dark and not letting go until I felt naked and exposed.

"That he wasn't thinking rationally?" I said.

Tommy wasn't satisfied with my answer. He looked away, cutting off our connection.

To say what I said next felt like going up against a powerful current. "I've been having such strange dreams since we got trapped in here," I confessed, seeing again the giant woman seated on her giant throne, head hidden in the clouds. "Each time, it was as if someone—or some*thing*—was trying to communicate with me."

"And then you were shaking those poisonous yellow things into the stream?"

"I really thought I was dreaming . . . What do you think the tablet's got to do with all this?"

"It's obvious it had some importance to whoever lived here before this place became lost and abandoned. Someone planted fruit-bearing trees in here; someone did those drawings on the cave walls. The tablet has angles and a clear geometrical shape, which means . . ."

"Human design," I completed his sentence. He was right. And isn't that what occurred to me too—that the hexagon must've been man-made—back when we were in the temple? But there was something else . . . That *organic* feel to the tablet; its greenish undertone. Like maybe it was alive once. "Do you think it killed Rowen somehow?" I asked.

Tommy shrank away from me, his entire body tightening. "It was chaos in those caves," he said, his voice controlled. "Who knows what really happened. But the likeliest thing is that Rowen wandered off, then slipped and fell. It could've been any one of us. It could've been *you*, Alif."

The way he said it made my skin crawl.

After a moment he said, as if he were trying to convince himself, "I guess if there was anything really wrong with that thing—the tablet—it'd be obvious by now, right? I mean, Lori's been handling it for some time now and she is . . ."

"She's in total denial and hallucinating, that's what she is," I finished the sentence when he trailed off. "I want to have a better look at that thing tomorrow. That is, if we can wrestle it away from her. She seems pretty attached to it."

"Why wait?" Tommy stood up and beckoned me to follow him.

THE DREAM MAKER

We moved, quiet as thieves in the night, until we were hovering over Lori. She appeared younger in her sleep—innocent, carefree. As if she could sense our wicked intent, she murmured sleepily and covered the tablet with her right hand.

I crouched by Lori's side and reached for the tablet. Before my fingers brushed the tablet's surface, Tommy grabbed my wrist. We had to communicate with gestures and glances. Tommy signaled for me to wait and walked a small distance away to search for something in the grass. He returned carrying a flat rock, its shape roughly similar to the tablet. Tommy handed the rock over to me, and then, two fingers wrapped around Lori's slender wrist, he lifted her hand off the ground just enough to start tugging the tablet out. At the same time, I started to insert the flat rock underneath Lori's hand. The whole operation lasted less than a minute, but by the end of it I was sweating from the effort.

The deed done, we should have retreated, especially since Lori started to fret in her sleep, but Tommy lingered, so I stayed too. I tried to meet his eyes, but he was staring blankly at the tablet cradled in his hands. Not wanting to wake up Lori, I patted Tommy's shoulder. He was unresponsive.

"Tommy?" I leaned in and whispered into his ear.

He didn't flinch, didn't react in any way. It was the tablet, I realized. Its neon glimmer seemed brighter now, illuminating Tommy's skin. I reached out and, without thinking, snatched the tablet from him.

A wave of rocket-blast euphoria hit me so strongly, I ended up on my butt. The tablet was magnetic in my hands, my fingers glued to its surface, feeding on an electric discharge, not completely unpleasant. It was strong enough to reach deep under my skin.

My body became a shell, and I was trapped inside it. Yet my mind was flying free. I saw my father's face. Dad was smiling that crooked smile I used to see a lot when I was a kid. Mom was also there with us. Strong gusts of nautical wind were whipping her black hair around. The three of us, we were on a yacht. *I remember this trip!* I must've been about ten when we visited Rügen island, where Dad's grandparents were from. We toured the island, learning how people used to live their entire lives out there decades ago. The day we went sailing was particularly stunning, water so calm Dad took us around the bay and then out into the sea proper. Mom laughed a lot that day. This was two years before my parents separated, divorce soon to follow.

"Alif!"

A slight pressure against my right cheek. Was it that wind again?

"Shit . . ."

A stronger sensation—a touch?—on my face. Or more like a gentle slap. Dad's face started to melt away, merging with the blue horizon, out there where it met the sea.

"Alif, wake up!"

Mom's laughter dissipated into the wind that was now howling something scary. *Daddy, turn the boat back to shore*, I wanted to say, but my lips couldn't move. The sensation of flying and then falling overcame my body and I was whooshing through the air—in free fall. With visions of my parents cutting off abruptly, I was left reeling from the hurt of withdrawal. My skin was clammy, hot. I was lying on my back. Tommy's blurry face was over mine, and I stared at him, focusing on the movement of his lips until I regained my equilibrium. I sat up.

"What the hell happened?" I looked around. We were closer to the trees now and farther from the sleeping trio. I didn't remember walking here. Minh and Luke were quiet in their slumber, while Lori was fussing around, whimpering in her sleep.

"I'm not sure . . ." Tommy scratched the back of his head. "I must've blacked out for a second or two, and when I came to, you were on the ground, clutching the artifact like your life depended on it."

I was about to ask Tommy where the *artifact* was now, but then I saw it lying on the ground between us, shining its alien light. I said, "The last thing I remember is you staring at . . . this thing. You were totally out of it, so I grabbed it out of your hands and then, I think, it gave me a mini electroshock and I had a hallucination . . . or more like a vision."

"What did you see?"

"My parents. It was a memory actually, but one I thought was long forgotten." I wasn't sure I wanted to share the whole thing with him. Or with anyone. The vision I had of my family before its implosion was a personal, deeply intimate experience. I wanted to keep it to myself.

But Tommy was waiting for more of an explanation, and after another moment of hesitation, I added, "It was a memory of Mom and Dad, the way they were before they split up. Back when they were happy."

"I had a vision too," he said after a long pause. "Visions, multiple."

"Yeah? What did you see?"

"I'd rather not say . . . It's just that my things, what I

saw, weren't memories as much as . . . something I *want*. But I didn't know I wanted it until I had the vision, if that makes any sense. Sorry I'm being so vague. It's just so weird. All of it." He gave me a strange look that set my skin running with cold fire. "We've all done strange . . . things since we've been trapped here."

"That's okay. You don't have to tell me." But I really wanted to know why he was looking so uncomfortable. "Was it something embarrassing?"

"Alif . . . ," he spoke softly.

"Okay, I won't push . . . So should we try it again?" I indicated the tablet—or artifact, whatever it was—looking innocent now. "I mean, I think it's safe to say we've already established that this thing generates visions and that it's activated by touch. We both have now tested it once. We need to set up an experiment and try it out again. I'll go first?" My hands were starting to shake, eager to touch the tablet again.

"Alif, we don't know anything about this thing. It could be radioactive, for all we know. It could be making us sick, making us *do* things . . ."

I was beginning to feel the burn of impatience. I really *wanted* to hold the tablet again. My fingertips were practically twitching. "Come on, where's your spirit of scientific discovery?" Before Tommy could stop me, I reached out and picked up the tablet from the grass. This time I had a bit of a warning and held on to myself a little longer. As Tommy moved toward me, I waved him off, assuring him I was okay. He stayed tense, close to me, ready to slap my hands free of the tablet.

As a familiar daze pulled a curtain over my eyes, I was expecting to see another happy memory of my pre-divorce parents, but instead the tablet showed me something else. I didn't like this. Not one bit. It was a more recent memory, which was also my embarrassing little secret that no one knew about. This memory was one of rejection. It stung so much, I'd had to shove it to the very back of my mind and ignore it the best I could. I'd done a good job of it so far—until now.

Before high school ended, even before this trip to Dubai was in the works, I'd applied to a creative writing program at the University of Southern Melbourne. It was a bridging program, designed for students who showed talent but whose specific academic credentials weren't appropriate for mainstream admission. This was me. I loved to write, but all my high school electives were science- and history-focused. No one knew I'd applied for this program. No one even knew I was interested in creative writing. Everyone just assumed I wanted to study ancient history and become an archaeologist like my parents. Did *I* want that? I kept asking myself that question, and the truth was I didn't know. Not for sure. Maybe? I didn't have it all decided and lined up like Luke did, with his family's history of graduating from Dunstan

Law, or like Lori, who wanted to do a business degree at the "best Australian university" and then "see how that went."

When I got my rejection email from USM, I stared at my laptop screen in a stupor. This was just a bridging program, with no guarantee of admission. And I wasn't good enough even for that? How could this be happening to me? Was I irrational to expect to be accepted? Nothing made sense in that moment. A massive blow to my self-esteem, that email turned my world upside down. And I had to pretend like nothing was off with me for days and weeks afterward. I deleted the email and purged it from my "trash" folder. But I couldn't delete it from my mind. Now, this tablet, this *thing* glowing in my hands, was shoving that rejection back into my face. But then it was all changing. The letters in the email were rearranging. Instead of *unsuccessful on this occasion*, there was now *we are pleased to inform* . . . The memory stream cut off all of a sudden, and I was back in the oasis with Tommy.

Reeling from the experience, I saw the tablet once more lying on the ground. I knew it was irrational to project human emotions and feelings onto an inanimate object, but I couldn't help it. The tablet was mocking me. It could see through me. It fished my deepest regrets and wishes out of the depths of my mind and then used it all to torment me.

"What did you do?" I asked Tommy, my voice wavering.

My face was wet, and I looked up, wondering if it was raining. It wasn't.

"You started crying. Just silent tears. I don't know what the hell this thing was showing you, but I couldn't take it anymore." When I offered no response, he asked, "What was it showing you?"

"My parents, again," I lied.

It was Tommy's turn with the tablet now. I'd had enough of its twisted visions, I decided. Or at least that's what I told myself. Who was I kidding? My whole body was craving to touch the tablet again.

Tommy made a move for the tablet but then paused, fingers hovering over its surface but not touching it.

I said, "You don't have to do this, if you don't want to. Whatever this artifact is, it's playing with our emotions, bending our memories, maybe even our desires."

Tommy seemed miles away from me. "I do want to try it again. But if I do or say anything weird, can you please promise me you'll push it out of my hands? Just try not to touch it yourself. And I think, after this, it's better if we avoid direct contact with this thing."

"Sounds good."

First light broke and the sun began to ascend. Tommy picked up the artifact from the ground and, immediately, a euphoric expression spread over his face. I observed him, waiting for any sign of trouble, but then his eyes refocused and found mine. He was still holding the artifact, but at the same time he was also present here with me, not lost in some fantasy. It was eerie to see him like this, so I tried looking away but couldn't keep it up for long. I felt a pang in my chest, a whisper of a wildflower unfurling its petals. I wanted to kiss Tommy. *So bad*. My skin was practically electrified and singing.

I reached out for him and wove my hands around his neck, locking my fingers and bringing him close. He didn't resist. When his lips met mine, that flower in my chest exploded into thousands of pieces. Nothing imaginary about that kiss. It was immediately frantic, raw, as real as it gets. This was finally happening. I was doing it. Half dreaming, half waking, I opened my mouth a little wider and quivered when Tommy's tongue touched mine. Tommy shifted to embrace me, and, with a thump, the tablet fell out of his hands. The thrall I was under released me, and I broke away from Tommy.

We were still physically close, both breathing heavily. The tablet was lying flat on the ground between us. I released Tommy from my grip, and he let go of me too. We said nothing following the kiss, and as more time passed, nothing we could say seemed adequate anyway. So instead of talking, speculating, apologizing, or backpedaling, we gave in to our sudden fatigue and settled on the ground, curling up next to each other, forgetting all about keeping watch and being vigilant. We fell asleep holding on to each other.

I woke up to the sound of Lori screaming Rowen's name.

REALITY?
ANY TAKERS?

Suddenly, I was upright and stumbling, dashing toward Lori. She was sitting, messy legs splayed underneath her and pulling out her hair. One long torn lock was already hanging from her clenched fist.

Tommy was just ahead of me, but he slowed down and hovered over Lori, unsure what to do. It was Minh who acted—she appeared from the thick growth and rushed at Lori, half tackling, half hugging her. But Minh was lighter and weaker than Lori. Lori pushed her away and stood up.

With her hair sticking out and eyes red-rimmed, Lori was a twisted version of her usual well-put-together self. The oasis was driving us all to the brink of our personal collapse.

"Calm down, Lori . . ."

"Please stop it . . ."

"You had a nightmare . . ."

"You're awake now . . ."

We all talked at Lori at once, while, up on her wobbly legs and fidgeting like a panicked animal, she slowly backed away from Minh.

"Where is it?" Lori asked, eyes flitting between our faces.

She meant the tablet. I moved to the front of the group and took another step toward Lori. "It's on the ground over there. I think it was making you hallucinate, so we took it away."

She deflated and gave me a slow nod, actually meeting my eyes. I hoped this meant she was coming back to her senses. She unclenched the fist that was still holding a lock of her hair, letting it fall to the ground. Absently, she went on to pat the right side of her head. I watched her wince. The pain must've been kicking in right about now.

With our combined silence pressing on her like a heavy, dark cloud, Lori marched toward the spot I indicated. She steered clear of us, walking in a wide circle before dropping to her knees to pick up the tablet off the ground. As she pressed it tightly to her chest, Lori's mouth spread in a blissful half smile.

The rest of us, tied together by a common thread, started to approach Lori, encircling her slowly. She must've been in that in-between state, about to give in to the tablet's influence but still partly present in the now, because she looked up at us, sensing danger. Right then Lori was a trapped animal, and we were a pack of encroaching hyenas. But whatever half-hatched intervention we had in mind was interrupted by a distant roar.

Thunder? Wind?

Luke must've been thinking the same thing. His voice shook. "If another sandstorm is coming, we need to hide! Now!"

"It's not thunder," Tommy said.

We all became silent, listening and staring in the direction the sound was coming from—where the oasis ended and the sand began. Whatever it was, it was coming, and it was coming fast.

We stood in a semicircle around Lori, tense but reluctant to move. It was like we had more important things to do than run and greet the cars—I could swear they were the same ones we saw yesterday—speeding toward us. I'm sure all of us were expecting the first car to pass right through us.

But this time the cars didn't turn into ghosts. Their drivers hit the brakes just in time, the vehicles coming to a full stop amid rising clouds of dust. All doors on either side of each car opened, spilling out a bunch of people. Most of them were wearing the familiar khakis and white shirts from Dad's dig, but there was also a man and a woman dressed in blue scrubs, the latter also sporting a matching head scarf.

There was something staged about the cars' arrival, and I couldn't stop my uncontrollable grinning as I watched all these people running at us. I recognized Dad in the group, but I couldn't move, frozen in shock and disbelief.

The five of us stood still, staring at our rescuers. My eyes were misted with sweat or tears. I didn't know anymore what was real and what was a desert-generated dream.

Lori was first to react to our changing reality. Nervously eyeing the rescue team approach, she stuffed the tablet underneath her tank top and shorts. It bulged out, even when she covered it with her hands, hugging herself and bending over slightly, like she was about to hurl.

"Alif!"

Dad's shout carried in the desert air, reaching the very insides of my soul and teasing silent tears out of me. Dad was close now. There was some dirty piece of fabric in his hand that he was waving like a flag. The colors of that rag seemed familiar. Dad was smiling.

"We found the towel you kids left behind!"

We were packed into the cars. I ended up riding with Tommy and Lori while Luke and Minh were taken into another car. We were given a bottle of water each and instructed to drink it slowly. Dad, who was in my car in the front next to a driver I didn't recognize, kept turning to look at me. He was saying something, but I could hear only bits and pieces, my mind unable to put the whole picture together. One word stuck out from Dad's monologue: *Rowen*. A flicker of recognition raised its foul head in my mind. I strained to listen closely to Dad's stream of words, and it hit me he was repeating the question I'd been dreading: *Where is Rowen?*

I didn't answer. I couldn't. Instead, I hung my head low, resisting the urge to stuff it between my knees and sob. It was Lori who replied, her voice cool, composed. "Rowen didn't make it out of the camp with us. We got separated during the sandstorm, and the last time I remember seeing him was when something heavy landed on top of our tent. Rowen was running away from the tent, and we never saw him after that."

I looked at Lori sideways and caught Tommy staring at her too. I tried to catch her eyes to communicate my confusion without openly questioning her, but Lori's face betrayed no signs of her lie.

Then something else took my mind completely away from her and her alternative reality: In the car's rearview mirror there was no sign of our oasis. Only the desert, flat and endless, stretched behind. I gasped.

That got Lori's attention. She faced me, suddenly angry. She shook her head once and gave me a cold stare.

Don't, she was telling me.

I was thinking about the oasis as we drove to safety—how it sprang out of nowhere and how none of us were aware of any patches of life in the desert for miles and miles surrounding the camp. And how odd everything was about those fruit and berries and the temple . . . that horrible place with its drawings and the killing pit. Could any of that have been real? And if it wasn't real, then what happened to Rowen?

Exhaustion crept into my body. I struggled to keep my eyes open. I was drowsing when I heard Dad talking with someone on his satellite phone. His voice was soothing, affectionate. It was a tone of voice he used only with me and, long ago, with one other person: my mother. Like that distant memory of my parents being happy together that the tablet showed me, hearing Dad's voice now made me nearly delirious with contentment.

Before I gave in to a fretful sleep full of shadowy presences and illuminated by the fire of a hexagonal tablet falling from the sky, I overheard Dad say into the phone, "Yes, Dahlia, I agree. I think she needs us both. And I need you too."

My mind zeroed in on my mother's name, and I let my eyes close at last.

RECOVERY

We weren't going back to the excavation camp. Was there even still a camp after the storm raged all over it like a distraught monster, crushing electricity poles and throwing cars around like Ping-Pong balls? I dreaded to ask Dad about the fate of his grand dig project. He'd worked so hard to secure the funds, to liaise with partner universities and sponsors, and now it all could be ruined.

But I knew I had bigger problems. At some point, I'd have to talk to Dad—and probably the authorities—to answer questions about what had happened to us in the desert. Should I tell Dad about the oasis? But how would I even begin to explain its mysterious appearance and then its convenient disappearance?

I wanted to confer with my fellow survivors first. We needed to get our stories straight. I urged myself to calm down, to take deep breaths. There was no reason to be scared. We weren't on trial here. Or were we? We were just a bunch of exhausted, malnourished kids who'd gone through quite an ordeal and survived. Well most of us did. One of us was dead now.

His mother was going to demand answers.

My mind was completely shrouded in dark thoughts by the time we sped into the city. Dubai's glittering beauty of modernity was lost on me. I pressed my forehead against the cool window and watched the world outside blink by. I was looking for sure signs this was indeed *real*, not another mirage cooked up by the oasis and offered to us on an elaborate plate.

Our cars navigated Dubai's busy afternoon streets on the way to a hotel aptly named Jewel of the Sands. It sparkled in the afternoon sun. The five of us had to wait in the icy, air-conditioned lobby while Dad and Dr. Palombo secured rooms. Lori, Minh, and Luke were on the next couch over, while Tommy was splayed next to me but facing away, eyes closed. I was very still, eyes trained on the floor, watching the granules of sand falling from my clothes and settling into the lush carpet. The hotel cleaners would have a hell of a time vacuuming the lobby after us.

There was some commotion behind me where the hotel's main entrance was located, but I was too lethargic to turn around and check it out. Then a bright flash of light illuminated my face. There was an unfamiliar white woman in jeans-and-a-blazer business-casual attire, a serious-looking camera in her hands. The woman was being escorted off the premises while Dad was running toward me.

"Let's go!" he said.

I let him usher me away from the lobby and toward the escalators. Lori, Minh, and the rest were not far behind.

"Bloody vultures . . . ," Dad was muttering under his breath. I had no strength to care.

He explained that most of our luggage had been rescued from the dig camp and was soon to be delivered to the hotel. But all I could think about right now was a hot shower. The hottest I could tolerate. I would burn my oasis clothes. And then I would use up all the free body lotion in my room to soothe my sun-damaged skin. In that order. I knew I couldn't *actually* burn my clothes, but entertaining the possibility felt nice.

I was to share a suite with Minh, which made me selfishly grateful I didn't have to deal with Lori. I was operating on fumes by now, having to make an effort to focus whenever someone spoke to me. I nodded when I thought it was expected of me and smiled, hoping to reassure those around me that I was indeed okay.

Two paramedics who were part of our rescue effort had already done some basic checkups on us, and now they were doing rounds, attempting more thorough examinations, as much as their carry-on medical equipment allowed. I didn't know why we weren't being taken to a hospital, but I was glad of it.

It was at least a whole other hour before everyone cleared out of our suite, leaving me and Minh alone. Minh went to use the shower first, and after I had my turn, I emerged from the steam, cleansed but not renewed, to find Minh on the floor in front of a TV. It was set on some news channel, but the sound was turned off. Minh was completely engrossed by the screen. I got dressed and sat next to her on the carpet. Mindless, we stared at the flashing images together. The soundless lips of the telecaster were putting me into a daze.

When the news segment went to commercials, it was time for us to talk.

"On our ride here, Lori lied to my dad about what happened to Rowen," I explained. "She said the last time she saw Rowen was in the camp when the storm hit."

"That was a smart thing to do." Minh looked away from the TV screen and focused on her bruised knees sticking out from under her hotel bathrobe.

"Lori's clever. She's already cooking up her story in case they want to do mental-health assessments with us. I mean . . . we all hallucinated that whole oasis thing. Including what happened, or what we *think* happened, to Rowen. The sooner we admit it, the better."

Her bluntness had a shock-wave effect on me. My ears burned from all the blood rushing into my head. I struggled to control my quivering voice.

"You can't possibly mean that. We *know* what happened. We *know* what we saw. At least I know I do."

"But do you? Really?"

"It was all too real to be made up! The sensations, the smells, the hunger! And what, you're telling me we *all* had the same delusion? A delusion that maintained itself for the entire time we were stuck in the desert?"

"I'm sure it's not the first time it's happened. Mass hallucinations are more common than you think."

"Okay . . . But how do you explain our relatively good health? You heard it yourself from the paramedics— we're not nearly as dehydrated as we should be, considering the official story is that we've been rolling around in the sand, unconscious or whatever, for days!"

"Alif . . . the truth is that we don't really know what happened. We *can't* know that. We might've been unconscious, or seeing things that weren't there, but we could *also* have found some kind of water source and it sustained us long enough till the rescue came."

"I don't believe what I'm hearing. Okay, one last try . . . What about the *tablet?*"

At my mention of it, Minh edged a few inches away from me, a shiver shaking her body. Another news segment started on the TV, but Minh had lost interest. She was looking at me so intently now, it required an effort on my part not to look away. The truth was, everything about her—but especially her eyes, bloodshot and bleak—was starting to scare me.

Her dry lips squeezed out, "I'm not even sure *that* was real."

"It was real. It *is* real. I touched it and it screwed with my mind. There's something wrong with that thing . . . Lori's got it now, and she's so possessive of it . . ."

"Sure, but what if it's nothing but a piece of flat rock? We came across it in the desert, and it became a part of our group delusion. Our minds just imbued this rock with whatever power we think it has."

But she hadn't touched the tablet. She didn't know what it could do.

"Minh, I'm telling you, I touched that thing, and it showed me these . . . images. Like it was sorting through my head, searching for my deepest secrets and desires. It was scary . . . but also wonderful . . . And then Tommy held the tablet for a moment and *I* had this overwhelming *need* to kiss him. So I did. But when he let go of the tablet, the compulsion was over. But that sensation, that enchantment, it didn't just appear out of nowhere—I *wanted* to kiss Tommy before but was always too shy, too scared, or too proud to do it. All my inhibitions were lifted and it was just me, like pure subconscious-me took control."

"You kissed Tommy?"

I studied her. "I thought we were going to die anyway, so I had this nothing-to-lose attitude going."

"Whatever." Minh stood up and opened one of the closets. She untied her robe and dropped it to the floor. In her loose white singlet and boy shorts, Minh wasn't how I remembered her. She was always tall and slight but not skinny exactly. Now her ribs were protruding whenever she lifted her arms. Plus, her skin was painfully red all over. Seeing this physical evidence of our ordeal was heartbreaking. I looked away.

"Lori could see Rowen, alive again, when she held on to the tablet," I said, unwilling to let it go and also eager to distract myself from Minh's emaciated body. "She spoke to him."

"Lori wasn't exactly in control, was she?" Minh rummaged through the closet. "Plus she needs to have all the attention on her all the time."

I knew what she meant, but still, she seemed unnecessarily harsh. "Her boyfriend just died. Cut her some slack."

"Rowen wasn't her *boyfriend*," Minh said, suddenly annoyed. Or angry. I couldn't tell. "She just wanted someone to hook up with during this trip. He didn't mean anything to her. You know how she is."

This was getting personal. And uncomfortable. I never asked Minh about Rowen and what went down between them. But I also remembered Lori telling us back in the tent at the dig how she *really* liked Rowen. All of it felt unreal now, childish even, just like my own crush on Tommy, but now Rowen was dead and Minh was angry and Lori was unwell.

"Were you in love with Rowen?" I blurted out.

Minh's shoulders sagged, hands releasing her pile of clean clothes to the floor. "What does it matter now?"

"Of course it matters."

She sat down on the edge of her bed. "I thought I was. I loved him as a friend, and maybe that messed with my head. I imagined that perhaps I loved him in other ways too. I always found him good-looking and funny. I slept with him once, you know. Just once."

Stunned, I stared at her. Her words were simple, clear, and yet their meaning was unreal to me. How well did I really know these people I called my friends?

"You *what?*"

"I . . ." Minh's bravado was fading. I could tell she hadn't shared this with anyone. "I didn't love *that*. It was just . . . It felt wrong—with him. But I kind of mishandled it afterward. I just pushed him away because it felt easier that way at the time. I think he went straight for Lori as a way to validate himself or something. And now he's gone, and I miss our friendship so much. I don't care who he's with. I miss *him*."

She wasn't crying. Our time in the desert must've burned all tears out of us, leaving us with nothing.

"Minh, you still have me." I came to her and sat next to her on the bed. "You'll always have me. And it'll be okay, I promise . . . And we'll figure out what to do. And we'll figure out what's going on with the tablet." I was now mostly talking to myself.

At my mention of the tablet, Minh snapped out of it. "Okay," she said, returning to her usual self—or a version of it. "So we have a difference of opinion on this whole *tablet* matter. And this object, currently in Lori's possession, is your only proof that the oasis was real. That is, if the tablet really does what you say it can do."

Minh picked up her clothes from the floor and got dressed. A pair of denim shorts and a red short-sleeved blouse were hanging off her thin frame. But despite her diminished physique, Minh was brimming with renewed determination.

"Anyway, I agree that we gotta do something," she told me. "If that *thing* is from the oasis, then maybe it's somehow responsible for what happened to Rowen."

"And now you believe that the tablet has . . . powers?"

Minh shrugged. "I'm just entertaining hypotheticals."

"What do you want to do exactly?" I asked.

Minh's lips were tight, her damp hair long and ruffled. "I'm going to Lori's room, and I'm going to demand to see that tablet. I want to see it with my own eyes in the light of day, and I want to see it *now*."

"You and me both."

REALITY FISSURES

We left the room and headed for the elevators. What Minh had shared with me—about Rowen and herself—had brought us a little bit closer, I felt. In addition to my own grief, I was now also mourning Rowen with her, as a lost friend and perhaps something more for Minh that now was never meant to be.

The hotel's air-conditioner was set on freezing, and the fragrance of some bitter incense permeated the air. There were piles and piles of dried figs on silver plates positioned on chubby decorative stands along the corridor's walls. I grabbed a few figs and devoured them, without pausing to appreciate the taste. Nothing tasted right following our return from the desert. The shiny apples and gleaming strawberries the oasis gave us were more real than anything I'd eaten since arriving at the hotel. All food since was nourishing but kind of empty—just something my body needed in order to function. The taste of water from the stream was what *real* water tasted like. Nothing civilization offered could compare.

A muffled conversation wafted from Dad's room as we passed by. I wondered if he was talking to my mother on the phone again. It didn't even occur to me to call her. She was so far away, physically and emotionally. Thinking this, I was expecting a pang of guilt, something, *anything* at all, but I mostly felt nothing. For a moment though, I allowed myself to fantasize that my parents were getting back together and this wasn't just some temporary truce brought on by my near-death experience. Maybe I should get lost in the desert more often?

As we journeyed to Lori's room, I kept close to Minh, our shoulders almost brushing. She smelled of cherry blossoms. Her favorite perfume had spilled in her bag during the sandstorm, and everything Minh owned in Dubai was now infused with its heady springtime scent.

The echoing boom of an aggressive conversation greeted us as we approached Lori's and Luke's rooms. We paused—and then the sound of a bang followed by a whimper made me break into a run. We never should've allowed the tablet to stay with Lori—not after the way she'd been acting in the oasis.

The door to Lori's room was open. I exchanged a look with Minh as we advanced, our steps suddenly slow and cautious. Amid Lori's swearing, Luke's hoarse voice boomed, "Enough of this! It's draining your brains out!"

I froze in the doorframe, looking in. Disarray. Towels on the floor, a chair on its side. Lori, trapped in a far corner and crouching on the floor. No obvious signs of struggle on her. Her hair was styled into a chic wave and her face was made up to perfection, layers of makeup hiding the sun damage and patchiness of dehydration and exposure. Only her black mascara, already running down her cheeks, disturbed the perfect illusion.

Luke, on the other hand, didn't look great. Still wearing the clothes he'd been rescued in, his short hair dirty and matted against his scalp, he was standing over Lori. He was gesticulating as he spoke. A familiar object—the tablet, the *artifact*—was on the floor at Luke's feet. Lori reached for it, but Luke leaned over her and pushed her away.

I went in and tried to wedge myself between them. "Leave her alone!"

"I'm helping her!" Luke shouted right back. "Can't you see it's messing with her head?"

I was close enough now to see the deep frown lines around his mouth, his lips bitten badly and so dry, the skin was peeling off. Had I also aged so visibly over the course of only a few days? I was avoiding looking at myself in the mirror too closely, only catching stray glimpses here and there. Afraid of seeing myself truly. Afraid of how the oasis had changed me.

"What's going on in here?" Minh asked from the doorway. But we both knew exactly what was going on and what Luke was talking about. Minh was just stalling him, I realized, probably hoping he'd cool down enough to engage in a rational conversation instead of throwing chairs around and hounding Lori into a corner.

"That *thing*!" Luke pointed at the object on the floor, lying innocently at his feet. Luke's hand was shaking. "That alien . . . thing! Lori's been carrying it around with her this entire time, and it's messing with her. Didn't you hear her talking to Rowen, like he's right in front of her? Well she's been doing that again—here! I could hear her from next door!"

"Is that true?" I looked at Lori, not really wanting to hear her answer. "Do you really think you see Rowen? Do you talk to him?" *Does he talk back? What does he say to you? What promises does he whisper?*

"You don't get it." Lori's voice was calm now, free of tears and frustration. "None of you do. Rowen is the reason we're free. He was our sacrifice to get out of that demonic place. But I can bring him back!"

She launched herself out of her corner and made a grab for the tablet. In one seamless motion, she swept it off the floor and elbowed Luke's knees. Caught off guard, Luke crumpled down. I spread my arms wide in an attempt to latch onto Lori and take her down, all the while wondering if Minh was still blocking the only way out of the room. We had to stop Lori from hurting herself. At least that's what my rational mind was telling me. What was lurking deeper inside just wanted the tablet.

Locked in a fight-or-flight mode, I went for it, my fingers brushing the fabric of Lori's top but not taking hold. She evaded me with almost supernatural ease, jumping over the overturned chair like a pursued gazelle before ramming into Minh and throwing her out of the room and into the corridor. With a muffled *oomph*, Minh landed on her butt. *Ouch.* With Luke still down and rubbing at his knees while Minh was also scrambling to get up, I, by virtue of being the last woman standing, took off after Lori.

By the time I exited the room, Lori had already reached the end of the corridor. I was expecting her to call the elevator, but she swerved left, going for the fire stairs instead. I slid into the stairwell after her. "Lori, wait!" I could see her below, hair flying in a blond halo as she raced down the steps. Carrying the tablet was slowing her down—and I could only imagine what it was showing her.

I was gaining on her when she attempted to open the door to the second floor of the hotel, but it was locked against reentry. Lori roared, scratching and banging at the door with her free arm, the tablet pressed against her chest.

"Enough!" I cornered her. Where the hell were Minh and Luke?

Lori faced me, her back to the door. Her pale blue eyes, circled in black mascara smudges, were glowing silver in the fluorescent light. "Stay out of it, Alif!"

"Lori, I don't want you to hurt yourself! This . . . this thing is doing something to you. To all of us. You haven't been yourself since you started carrying it around!"

"You just want the tablet for yourself, just like the rest of them. I know what you're all planning! I heard Luke talking to Minh. I even saw how Tommy eyes the tablet when he thinks I'm not looking. You *all* want it! It promised something to each and all of us, but there's only one tablet and six of us!"

"You mean five, Lori. There are *five* of us left, not six."

She didn't contradict me, but I could tell she really didn't care what I had to say. Still, I had to try reasoning with her. "Lori, you're confused by what happened to us . . . by what happened to Rowen. He died in the oasis. It's horrible, but it's what really happened."

She appeared briefly disoriented, bright eyes clouding with a dreamy haze, her whole body growing slack.

I used the distraction to come closer. "How about we just drop this and go back to your room?"

"I can't."

"Why not?"

"Luke wants the tablet. He'll end up taking it from me one way or another. He wants it for himself. But his dreams are so mundane. Mine are more important. Why can't you see that?"

"Lori, you're not making any sense."

"Oh, stop it, Alif!" She snapped out of her confusion. "Haven't you figured it out yet?"

In her fidgeting hands, the tablet's surface was never still, catching the artificial light and reflecting it at peculiar angles. The faintly greenish gleam of it brought memories of my own interactions with the tablet. Seeing my parents laughing, dancing . . . Me getting a letter of acceptance rather than rejection . . . Kissing Tommy and being kissed back . . . What else was there that I didn't retain—other wishes and promises of fulfillment? With aching clarity, I recalled how gentle Dad had sounded when he was talking to Mom on the phone earlier. Could the tablet really do that? Bring my parents back together? Could it give me other things I wanted? But what *did* I want? Maybe the tablet knew my deepest desires better than I did. The prospect of that chilled me.

Like Minh said, there was only one way to know. I had to get the tablet away from Lori. Out of the five of us, she seemed the least stable. A decision was made in my head, and without another thought, I went for the tablet. A dim kind of light started to seep from its surface—the tablet was anticipating my approach. It was egging me on. It liked being fought over.

I saw Lori's eyes widening, pupils shrinking in size, making it look like she had no pupils at all, just whiteness where her eyes should've been.

She shifted sideways, my hands meeting hers over the tablet and slipping and tugging and not letting go. Growing colder and colder to the touch, the tablet was now full-on glowing with greenish light—and too slippery to hold on to. Lori grunted in frustration when the tablet slipped out of our hands.

It met the cement floor, breaking in two.

We stood frozen still, staring down in shock and disbelief. There the tablet lay, broken into two uneven pieces.

One piece was bigger, and that's the one Lori went for the moment she snapped out of our mutual shock. She knelt and swiped the larger piece off the floor. Moving on autopilot, I picked up the other one before she could grab it too, just in time for Minh and Luke to find us crouching on the stairs as they descended from above. I expected the tablet to hit me with visions the moment my skin made contact, but there was only a faint buzz—and even that fizzled out after a few moments. My piece of the tablet was no longer glowing. It was just a rock, rough to the touch now that it had a jagged edge.

"What the hell?" Luke demanded, looking between us, venom in his eyes.

I showed my piece of the tablet to Luke, but not too closely. I was starting to share Lori's suspicion that Luke was after the tablet.

"It fell," I said.

Luke stared at the fragment in my hands, and then his gaze slid up to my eyes. "What does this mean? For us?"

The plaintive look on his face confused me—did he mean "us" as in he and I, or "us" as in our group of survivors?

I said, "I'm not sure yet. But we're taking these pieces to Melbourne with us. We'll figure out what to do then."

"And you two have self-nominated to be the guardians of the broken tablet?" he asked, while Minh stood silent by his side.

"You got a better idea?" Lori scoffed, her eyes back to normal.

"We all have to guard it together," Minh said sternly. "We can take turns. Lori and Alif can take the first few days, so they're responsible for smuggling the pieces to Melbourne. You all agree?" Out of our group, she appeared the most coolheaded. I wondered if that was because she really didn't believe in the tablet's powers.

Or was she just pretending not to? I met her eyes, wishing I could see inside her head and read her thoughts, but she remained closed off.

Slowly, I nodded, and so did Lori, but judging from her expression, she had zero intention of giving up her piece of the tablet to anyone. And I knew exactly how she felt. My own piece was slowly returning to life, pulsing in my hands to a rhythm only I could perceive. It was setting roots into my flesh and blood, growing on me and on my will while bending mine to its liking.

THE *REAL* TALE OF
THE DESERT MAN

The rest of my night settled into a flutter of mundane activity amid the promise of some supernatural doom. I hid my piece of the tablet in my messenger bag, which was going to be my carry-on on the flight to Melbourne the next morning. I decided to carry the bag everywhere with me, keeping it by my side while feeling more and more suspicious of every look thrown my way.

My mother managed to get ahold of me, the room's phone ring making me flinch. She was about to board her flight to Australia, and, after expressing her relief about me being alive and all, we talked about things of little to no importance, things that had nothing to do with my ordeal. Either she could sniff out my unspoken reluctance to rehash my desert nightmare over the phone or she was just out of sync with reality, but the most consequential question she asked was whether I was using sunblock.

I was standing while we spoke, swaying on my feet. Or maybe it just felt like I was swaying. Or maybe the room was. My blinks were long, as my eyes needed extra soothing. Regaining my view of the room after one of those long blinks, everything wavered, and there was mist drifting over the furniture, clinging to the walls. It was a nice-looking mist, I thought.

In this mist, autumnal yellow particles sparkled. I looked closer. They weren't particles at all but semi-translucent golden dewdrop berries. I touched one and it disappeared into my finger as if by osmosis.

Mechanically, I answered Mom's next question, my eyes no longer wanting to blink. My retinas were reflecting the yellow glow that was suspended in the air. I wondered if Minh and Lori could see it too. They were in the bedroom part of the suite. I couldn't hear them at all. When I finally forced a blink, the apparition of the mist and the berries dispersed. I immediately longed for it to return.

With Mom's boarding delayed, our conversation was starting to go in circles. Hoping to hasten things toward a conclusion, I asked Mom bluntly if she and Dad were getting back together. There was a sudden silence and then an audible click, as if the line went dead. But then

Mom was back on and delivering some vague but at the same time enthusiastic response that I interpreted as "maybe." I was so ready for Mom's dismissal of the possibility that I took too long to process her response. My extended pause spilled out over the distance and Mom abruptly rushed to finish the call.

I asked myself if I was happy now that I knew there was indeed a strong chance my parents were getting back together. But all I felt in the moment was emptiness. Just *nothing*. Was it because, after wanting this to happen for so long, now when I finally was about to get it, I was left underwhelmed?

Soon after I spoke with Mom, I could hear Minh on the phone—with her father by the sound of it. Everyone's families were waiting for them at home. Only Rowen's mom wasn't going to see her son ever again. Rowen's body was likely never to be recovered, left to decompose in that pit, in the cavernous temple hidden in the oasis—which perhaps no longer existed.

Later, Dad ordered room service for dinner, and everyone—including Dr. Palombo and Rufus—piled up in our suite. Being in a fairly small space with so many people at once felt claustrophobic. I kept wanting to retreat somewhere, but there was nowhere to go and my absence would be noticed.

Dad kept glancing my way, concern paling his sunburned features. Whenever he looked at me, I'd force myself to eat something, to take another bite. In the happy house of my childhood, having an appetite was considered a sign of good health. Eating heartily and together meant the family was functioning well. After my parents' divorce, when Mom moved out, my meals with Dad became affairs of utility, no longer joyful feasts. Now, in this hotel room in Dubai, I was stuffing what looked like delicious food into my mouth and feeling no satisfaction. When he wasn't staring daggers at me, Luke was fiddling with something on his plate. Lori was focused on cutting up her chicken into a dozen little pieces. Minh wasn't eating at all, wasn't even attempting to pretend to.

"Let's go get some fresh air." Tommy had snuck up on me, my hand halfway to my mouth.

"It's probably hot outside," I told him, though I wanted to go. I wanted to get away from here, from Dad's concerned looks and Luke's prolonged stares. Earlier, Lori told us she didn't want to be by herself, especially since her room was next to Luke's. We decided she'd stay with Minh and me. It meant I had to give up my bed and move to the couch, but I didn't care—as long as I didn't have to sleep on the ground again.

"I'm sure it's not that hot," Tommy said, voice lowered. Conversations in the room weren't exactly flowing, so it was easy to hear what he was saying all the same. "Come on?"

I stood up, my movement immediately drawing Dad's eyes, then Luke's, and, as a chain reaction, everyone else's.

"Just going for a walk," I said, rushing after Tommy before anyone could stall me—or try to tag along. My tablet piece's presence in my bag was heavy and heady. It was calling for me to touch it.

Tommy and I didn't talk till we reached the hotel's elaborate open-air terrace, home to al fresco dining and relaxing by the swimming pool. As the hour was late, the area was deserted. Only a few lights were left on over-night. Though there was still lingering heat in the air, there was a cool breeze flowing in. Somewhere in the distance, I imagined, the sands rippled, forming waves. There were no trees out here on the terrace, just fancy potted plants lining the perimeter, but in my ears was the unmistakable rustling of palm fronds in the wind.

I headed for the pool and sat in one of the sun loungers facing the water. Tommy took one next to me and pulled out his phone. That reminded me that my phone was still missing in action somewhere, but I couldn't tell if I needed or wanted it. There was a cer-tain kind of freedom that came with not having that constantly pinging extension of my online life on me at all times.

"I wanted to show you something," Tommy said, scrolling through something on his phone's screen.

I stared at him while he frowned in concentration. Did I really kiss him when I thought we were both dying in the desert? Or was that a dream? Ever since we'd returned from the oasis, he was behaving . . . differently with me. Our status quo was definitely gone—he was now more to me than my father's assistant whom I was crushing on, and I was . . . What *was* I to him? I drifted off, looking away.

"Alif?"

I sat up straighter and faced Tommy. In the eerie light, his eyes were so green, the color didn't look real. *So beautiful*, I thought. Or did I just say it out loud? I might've, because Tommy's face rippled in response, the sides of his mouth bending a little, suppressing a smile or a groan.

"There's something I want you to see," he insisted.

When I accepted Tommy's phone, it was open to a browser display of search results. A few of the links were darker in color, indicating items that had been read. The search terms were *Noam+Delamer+Dubai*. I met Tommy's eyes over the screen.

"Read the ones I've selected first," he urged me.

The most recent internet search results dated back a few days ago, to reports of when Noam Delamer, dehydrated and close to death, staggered into my father's dig camp. In the news, there was talk about massive book and movie offers, both centering on Noam's story of surviving in the desert alone for *years*—hailed as the ultimate survival story on steroids, *Robinson Crusoe*, *Castaway*, and *Alive* all rolled into one. All of that, including the snippets of his interviews and even a few photos of his face—always hidden behind large sunglasses—made clear Noam was an enterprising man who gave away little for free. He was keeping the circumstances of his miraculous survival close to his heart, saving it for the big payout. Or perhaps his evasiveness during interviews suggested he had something to hide— like the truth about the fate of his fellow victim of the desert, Alain Pinon.

Under Tommy's watchful gaze, I looked through the rest of the news stories, going further back in time, until I came across an old syndicated feature informing the world of the tragic disappearance of *two* men who were visiting Dubai for a conference. This was the only mention of Alain Pinon that I could find. With Noam getting so much attention, it was odd that so little was being said about Alain. It's like the world just forgot about him. Was Alain like Rowen, left in the desert by the survivors and eventually edited from collective memory? I refreshed the news feed and was about to share my thoughts with Tommy, but then I glimpsed a very recent piece by a local newspaper that had *Dubai Five* in its title. The first photo that accompanied the piece was of a young woman slumped in a chair in a familiar hotel lobby. Her face was frozen in a stupor, eyes staring into space.

I did a double take. The woman was me. I looked older in this picture. Sadder. I felt sorry for myself in this photo.

I clicked on the link. The piece itself was short. Six Australians stranded on the sands, five of them rescued—the lucky ones. One suspected fatality, the body yet to be recovered. And photos of all six of us, plucked randomly from the web, including a younger version of Tommy with a beautiful brown-skinned woman in her fifties, an elegant scarf wrapped around her head. Both of them were grinning, but there was sadness clouding this photo. How little I knew of Tommy, of his life outside of my dad's orbit.

"Some fuel for your next blog post?" I asked, giving the phone back to Tommy and pointing out the Dubai Five article. He scoffed at the news piece and put the phone away. There were no more distractions between us. Just the two of us sitting out here alone, by the pool, its surface dead, unmoving.

"Yeah, I think I'm done with blogging for now," Tommy said. "I never mentioned it to anyone, but that post I wrote about Tell Abrar . . . I had weird dreams about the site, from the moment I first knew Dr. Scholl was going to lead an excavation there. I . . ."

"What kind of dreams?" I asked carefully.

"It was more of a feeling than some specific dream, really," he started, uncertain. "It was like I was approaching this glow in the desert, at night, and the closer to it I got, everything in my life became more . . . perfect. Just the way it was always supposed to be. Celeste was alive and healthy, and . . ."

He stopped, and I wondered who Celeste was. The grinning woman I just saw in the photo with Tommy? I wanted to ask him but didn't want to pry. He seemed to be carrying so much weight on his shoulders. I used to feel jealous about his relationship with my father, but I was being petty. If my dad was the presence in Tommy's life that was going to make things a little bit better for him, how could I stand in the way of that?

We both stayed silent as a full minute ticked away.

Tommy spooked me when he started talking again. "But then the dream changed. It became . . . like, perfection's only possible at a cost, if I'm making sense. Like, for example, if you want eternal happiness, you gotta do something ugly first. Like murder."

Where did that come from? I stared at Tommy in the nocturnal glow and barely recognized him. His face was sharper now, more angular, his bronzed skin paler, green eyes appearing darker in the night. I pressed my bag with the tablet closer to my side. "Murder?"

He didn't look at me. His silence was haunted. Despite my better judgment, I left my sun lounger to sit next to Tommy. I was close enough to feel his body heat. He flinched at our sudden proximity, but then his body immediately went slack, relaxing. He turned to face me, his expression returning to its normal, kinder features.

I said, "Tommy, we're all different after the oasis. Minh doesn't even think the oasis was real. Lori and Luke are obsessed with the tablet. And I . . ." I stopped myself from confessing my own obsession. Tommy didn't even know the tablet got broken. Could he feel the presence of one of its pieces in my bag?

He shrugged. "I don't blame Minh, to be honest. If it's healthier for her to imagine that none of it was real, then it's okay. I know what *really* happened. I was there. But I've been feeling odd ever since we came back. Like I lost a part of me, or like someone I cared about dearly has died. And this is different from watching Rowen . . . seeing him dead. It was awful what happened to him, but I barely knew him. The only way to explain it is . . . I went through five foster families when I was a kid, but the only time I actually felt like I belonged was with family number four. I was close to my foster mom, Celeste, but she got sick and I had to be moved into a different home. When Celeste passed away and I heard the news, I got this pain in my chest, and it wouldn't go away for months. Like I was completely scooped out, turned inside out, a piece of me erased. It still comes back sometimes, that pain. Like a bone that healed after being broken, but it still hurts when it rains. Or like the phantom pain of an amputated limb; I've read about that."

I reached out and touched him on the shoulder, to reassure him. But my hand lingered. "We all saw Rowen dead, and now we have to deal with it. We just cope in different ways. And then there's PTSD or survivor's guilt or whatever. Isn't it natural for us to feel that? We're all going to need professional help when we get home. And the things we did in the oasis . . . That wasn't really us. Those were *versions* of us who were placed in unbeliev-able circumstances and forced to react to unprecedented events."

He considered it, my hand still on his shoulder. Who was I, trying to rationalize what happened when I myself needed help understanding it? But perhaps it worked for Tommy, because his features smoothed out.

"Are you saying that kiss wasn't really *us?*" he asked, an eyebrow subtly quirking up. Tommy was watching me intently, like he could see through me. But maybe he didn't see me at all—just a version of me he wanted to see. All the same, I melted under his scrutiny. The tablet piece in my bag pinged. And then I was kissing Tommy, our hands tangling, hearts beating in erratic unison.

Like a long blink, there was a moment of absolute nothingness between our lips not touching and then our lips touching, two states of being that were bridged by a breathless second. Tommy was embracing me, hands sliding over my back. He was a good kisser, excellent even, and I was eager to melt into the sensation of his mouth moving against mine.

When we let go of each other, he was looking at me the way I'd seen people look at their objects of desire in movies. In the moonlight under the starry sky over Dubai, this was the most real moment I'd experienced ever since escaping the oasis. I patted my bag, and the tablet within it, when Tommy wasn't paying attention. If all of this was really the tablet's doing, did I really care?

GHOSTS AND SMUGGLERS

All was quiet and gloomy in the shared suite upon my return. The room service feast was long over, leftovers piled upon the delivery cart and exiled outside. Lori and Minh must've already been in bed, but I found Dad waiting for me in front of a silent TV. There was a movie on. An old one, from the look of it. A scraggly white man, desperate-eyed and worse for wear, was sitting in a shallow puddle in what looked like a room filled with sand. There were well-defined dunes inside that room, and it was dark but the sand was glowing—or maybe it was just the glare from the TV screen. The man was looking across this long, wide industrial room filled with sand dunes at two other people at a distance. They were staring back at him. The subtitles on the screen revealed the man's words, something about immortality and god. I couldn't place the movie, but the sand dunes felt real to me, prophetic even. I looked away in alarm, searching for any of that mist I thought I'd seen earlier, but the room was normal.

The couch was made up with fresh bedsheets, a lacy pillow waiting for me. Upon seeing me, Dad stood up awkwardly. He turned off the TV, cutting short the miserable man's perilous travel across the room of sand. I was never going to learn whether he made it safely to the other side.

"I got your phone, Alif," Dad said in a low voice. I accepted it, the plastic of it cold, unpleasant to the touch. "Try to get some sleep," Dad added. "I've arranged for a wake-up call for all of us at eight and in-room breakfast for eight thirty. You and the girls need to be ready to check out by nine thirty."

I nodded, searching for anything to say to him. This was my dad, someone I adored. But I felt empty, my insides scooped out.

"It's going to be okay," I said, more to myself than to Dad. He reached for a hug. Our contact was brief but very real. *Too* real. I was relieved when he let go of me, irrationally concerned he was going to tease my secrets out of me via touch. I knew my thoughts weren't logical, that Dad had no reason to suspect anything bad of me.

But I was also acutely aware of the tablet in my bag and how it was meant to be mine and mine alone.

After Dad left, I got ready for sleep and stretched out on the couch, the bag containing the tablet squished under my pillow. I played with my phone a little, though its bright light was hurting my eyes. There were dozens of missed calls and hundreds of social media notifications across my accounts, but I just couldn't bring myself to care. But I did check my email. There was *a lot* in there. From Mom and Dad, from strangers requesting interviews, and from random school acquaintances I had barely spoken to in months—or ever.

And then there was an email from the University of Southern Melbourne. Its date stamp was fairly recent. But with timelines all muddled in my head, it took me a long moment to place the email's delivery to the day of the desert sandstorm. I then just stared at the subject line: "Notification of your application's outcome." But they'd already notified me. They'd already rejected me. I'd deleted that email permanently. Was this some sick joke? Or an administrative oversight?

Despite my better judgment, I clicked on the email, preparing myself to feel the sting of rejection once more. But something was different now, this particular moment in time laying over my memory of the very same moment months ago. This email started off with "Due to an administrative error . . ." and then instead of "unsuccessful on this occasion" as a similar message had informed me in the past, this one said "we are pleased to inform."

I got in! I got in! I got in! I wanted to get off the couch, to scream and shout and dance. To shake Minh and Lori awake! To celebrate! And I wanted to come clean to Dad—I didn't want to follow in his footsteps; I wanted to pave my own path. It was all very new and scary, but that's what I *wanted* for myself. I had a luxury of choice, after all, and it felt nice to be in the position to choose.

But my body was heavy, and growing heavier with each breath my shuddering lungs took. I didn't jump up, didn't scream, didn't do any of the things I wanted to do, but instead I read and reread the email, each time checking that it was still there. And it was.

I must've fallen asleep with my phone in my hand. I woke to the glow from the TV. That weird movie was on again, still silent and subtitled. The man was once more sitting in his miserable puddle, and the sand dunes were very still around him. The man was saying strange things about god and immortality like it was all totally normal, like that's what you did in a room full of sand.

Someone was sitting on the far side of the couch, where my feet were. I didn't feel any weight on my legs. This was a dream, I realized. My hands were frantically searching for the tablet, relaxing only when they scraped

231

against its shape under the pillow. Even in my sleep, the tablet was drawing me in.

The longer I stared in the direction of the weightless phantom, the more its features came together.

It was Rowen. The second I made that realization, he faced me. He could see me. He was trying to tell me something. No, not tell—*yell*—he was screaming at the top of his lungs! He was angry, veins and muscles bulging on his neck and face. But no sound was reaching me as I watched in terror. Glued to the couch, I couldn't move. Rowen was wearing the same clothes as the last time I saw him, his shirt torn and stained with blood. There were gaps in his stomach and chest where the spikes had pierced through him. Invisible flies were buzzing. I focused on Rowen's mouth. Could I read lips? *Murderer*, Rowen was screaming over and over. *Murderermurderermurderer.*

Rowen was gone, but so was the hotel room. Over my head was the sky full of stars. Hanging low, oppressive. Against my back was the harsh ground, and in the wavering night air, I could distinguish the outlines of Minh, Luke, Lori, and Tommy. They were sleeping not far from me.

No, no, no, no, no! Please don't send me back there, I begged and cajoled, offering the Queen of Giants everyone and everything in exchange for my freedom.

In response, the indifferent stars brightened, heralding the inevitable approach of morning. But the glow wasn't coming from above. Rather it was coming from the TV, its screen glimmering in the room's darkness. Creeping shadows danced on the walls. My blanket was on the floor. Shivering, I leaned down to pick it up and saw a few of those unmistakable white-and-gold Al Nassma candy wrappers, scattered on the floor close to where Rowen's ghost had been sitting.

I slid off the couch and came to crouch on the floor. I picked up one of the wrappers, but it melted away. My fingers were left curling over thin air.

I whimpered, a soundless cry that stirred me awake—for real this time. My heart was beating and my clothes and blankets were soaked with sweat. I was lying faceup on the couch, staring at the white, featureless ceiling.

The days of Western archaeologists and explorers taking their finds out of the countries where they were excavated were long gone now. And the international pressure for the return of ancient treasures to their countries of origin was mounting—a movement that might leave most European and North American museums half empty. Both my father and mother were paragons of ethics when it came to working with ancient sites and negotiating fair agreements with local governments and communities. So where did all of this place me, the archaeologists' daughter who was about to smuggle a mysterious tablet from Dubai to Australia?

I compartmentalized it all and tried to keep my

face calm and not at all suspicious as I walked into the international-departures zone in Dubai's airport. Still shaken up by my dream from the night before, I tried not to make eye contact with anyone while keeping one hand casually inside my carry-on bag, my skin tingling against the tablet's jagged side. Mere physical contact used to trap me in visions, making my head spin, but now the effect had ebbed, reduced to a faint buzz. Did it mean the tablet's power was weakening now that it was broken? Or was I just desensitized to its influence from prolonged exposure? Regardless, I was now asking the tablet for a safe passage, not in specific words but in fears and desires—the language I knew it understood and spoke well. Somehow I knew this was also something Lori was doing with her own piece of the tablet. The rest of our group were flanking us two, but casually so.

Sweat coated the insides of my palms when I got my first glimpse of the security checkpoint, swarmed by uniformed officers. They were going to scan my carry-on, and they were going to see the tablet. They'd take it away. Of course they would. These days, Dubai's airport workers were trained to be extra vigilant, what with the increasing cases of trafficking of cuneiform tablets and the like looted from Iraq and other countries in the region. Smugglers were profiting off wars and human misery, selling precious artifacts to greedy private collectors. I despised them all for it, and yet I was about to break the law myself. Regardless of the circumstances and my reasons for smuggling the tablet, I felt guilty and probably looked it.

Pulsing, the tablet grew cold against my fingers, so cold I had to let go of it, afraid it would freeze my sensitive fingertips. Having my hand semihidden in my bag would be suspicious at this point, anyway. Carefully, I placed my carry-on bag on the conveyer belt and watched it disappear into the mouth of the scanner. I stiffly walked through the metal detector and waited for the bag to reappear on the other side. I picked an angle from which I could watch the stern officer assigned to the task of inspecting whatever passed through the machine. I watched her frown deepen and then . . . relax, disappearing completely.

I was getting away with it. The tablet did as it pleased, and for now it was pleased to remain in my keep.

I picked up my bag, muttered my thanks to no one specifically and proceeded to my gate, not daring to stick around to see if Lori was going to replicate my success.

TO MANY STRANGE RETURNS

Our flight to Melbourne was fully booked, and because Dad and Dr. Palombo had secured our tickets at the last minute, none of us got to sit together. I was in an aisle seat in the middle of the plane, next to a stranger. My bag rested on my knees until a smiling hostess asked me politely but decisively to put it underneath the seat in front of me or in the overhead compartment. Hesitantly, I put it down in front, but I kept the bag's strap wrapped around my ankle, a half-assed antitheft measure in case I drifted off.

Tommy sat in the row in front of me, and my dad was behind me. The rest of our group was spread out across the front section of the plane. I liked it this way—this accidental isolation. I didn't feel like talking to anyone, and I bet they all felt the same way anyway. Everyone seemed exhausted and uncomfortable in their own skin.

That morning I had eaten my breakfast with Lori and Minh in mournful silence, both of them red-eyed and hollow-cheeked, though Minh more so. I didn't have to ask—I knew their sleep wasn't a pleasant affair, same as mine. Minh had barely touched her breakfast, her already fragile frame appearing even thinner now.

Though not looking as brittle as Minh, Luke and Tommy hadn't fared much better. Haunted didn't begin to describe their eyes. At least Luke had taken a shower and changed his clothes. He was also back to his passive-aggressive staring mode, but it was more scattered now, as if not focused on anyone specific. He was one man versus the world, and the world was winning.

Tommy was quiet all the way to the airport, but I kept finding him close to me, in the car on the drive over, and later as we walked toward the departure gate. I wanted to reach out and touch him, to make sure he was real. I wondered though if Tommy, apparition or not, was more interested in the contents of my carry-on bag than in me, the girl who carried it.

On board, I mindlessly scanned through the entertainment options on my screen. I half expected to find the film Dad was watching yesterday. I didn't know its name or anything about it, but that silent moment of a bedraggled man trapped in a strange sand room had burned itself into my mind. In my head, it was Rowen who was trapped in that dark room. It was Rowen who stared wistfully into the abyss that yawned at him from across the sands. And in that abyss there were us five— Lori, Minh, Luke, Tommy, and myself—and we were staring back.

I found my favorite London Grammar album among the entertainment choices on the flight and put my headphones on. I waited for the music to carry me away, but my anxieties were stronger. The lyrics of one of my favorite songs didn't sit well with me anymore. "I'm gonna show you where it's dumped" made me think of Rowen and his body deteriorating in the pit.

I couldn't stop thinking about what was going to happen upon our return to Melbourne—coming to terms with Rowen's death (gone too soon, so young, so full of promise), explaining it somehow to his grieving mother (how could *any* death really be "explained"?), helping organize some kind of memorial service. *It. Sucked.* All of it.

But what sucked more was that I felt like a garbage human for even being bothered by these things. *Excuse me, Alif, did my untimely death inconvenience you? One thousand apologies!* And then, of course, I felt like an even bigger garbage human for feeling grateful that I wasn't the one who'd ended up in that pit of spikes.

Being brought up by two atheists meant I was grounded in *this* life. At least, I tried to be. So, naturally, I was suspicious about the idea of any sort of afterlife. But . . . all of this, the tablet, my hallucinatory reality shifts post-oasis, and my friends' physical deterioration, made me wonder what was out there and whether it was just waiting for an opportunity to get us. In the end though, I just wanted to close my eyes and listen to the music.

I drifted in and out after picking through the food on my tray. I mourned the loss of my appetite, but what could I do—keep forcing myself to eat? Every bite was bland and hurt my throat on the way in. I wondered if Minh was eating. She'd been so shaky on her legs that morning, her eyes hidden behind sunglasses that didn't come off until the moment of boarding.

I drowsed and didn't dream, or if I did, I had no memory of it. I woke up to someone shaking my seat, the plastic of it creaking in protest. The shaking grew more intense. The cabin was dark when I opened my eyes, the FASTEN YOUR SEAT BELT sign on and glowing.

"We're just passing through some turbulence, folks," the captain's soothing voice called from the speakers. "For your own safety, please remain in your seats."

Automatically, I checked my seat belt and tightened it. I tried to relax. I had no fear of flying. Flying was safe. Turbulence was normal.

A particularly violent tremor made me dig my fingers into the armrests. A baby started wailing somewhere at the front of the plane, another nearby joining in to form a duet. I suddenly yearned to be close to someone I knew. Dad or Tommy or any of my friends—yes, even Lori or Luke, even though both of them had changed into near-strangers to me in the past twenty-four hours.

But then everything became dead quiet, so quiet I wondered if I'd imagined all the ferocious shaking. Scattered murmuring went through the cabin, passengers releasing their breath, laughing off their fears.

I started to drift off again. But before I could fall back into half sleep, two flight attendants rushed along the length of the aisle, headed for someone seated a few rows ahead of me. Minh and Luke were somewhere in that section.

I unbuckled my seat belt and stood up, trying to see what was going on.

"Is there a doctor on the flight?" one of the attendants asked the passengers, while another rushed away, disappearing into the next section of the plane, presumably to search for a doctor there. I looked behind me and met Dad's concerned eyes. Technically he was *a* doctor, just not the life-saving kind.

"Minh, ohmygod, Minh!" The hysterical note in Lori's voice carried all the way to where I was standing. My heart fell deep and deeper and kept on falling.

I left my seat and proceeded down the aisle. "Please return to you seat!" the flight attendant closest to me barked. I obeyed but not before catching a disturbing glimpse of my friend splayed on the floor in the aisle. Minh was having some kind of seizure. Her eyes were rolled back, and her lips were white-blue. I stared at her in confusion, my presence irrelevant, helpless. My eyes were glued to Minh's face. I couldn't look away.

Lost to the throes of her convulsions, Minh was coughing up sand. *No.* It was blood.

In the flickering light of the airplane cabin, everything shimmered in the wrong kind of way.

Not thinking, moving on instinct, I returned to my row, fell into my seat, and grabbed my bag off the floor. The passenger next to me, a middle-aged woman in a comfy tunic dress and a pink head scarf, appeared sound asleep, so there were no questions, no inquiring looks thrown my way.

I reached inside the bag and found the tablet piece, its cold surface pumping calm into my veins. Fingers tingling, lungs filled with apprehension, I placed both hands flat on the tablet, sandwiching it between my palms. I hoped, prayed—*Oh, hear my atheist prayer of despair!*—that Lori was doing the same, that she was asking her fragment of the tablet for Minh's recovery, begging that whatever was happening could be fixed, prevented, reversed.

Minh didn't believe in the tablet's power, and I didn't blame her. I couldn't even describe what this power was or how it worked, but I did know that my parents were talking again and I was now miraculously accepted into a writing program despite my earlier rejection. Did the tablet work miracles? Grant wishes? If yes, then I wished for Minh's health, for her life. I couldn't imagine losing another one of my friends.

A query swirled in my mind. *But is it your deepest wish?* Was the tablet questioning my desperate request to save Minh?

Yes, yes, please save my friend! I was thinking irrationally, a storm of emotions rather than concrete thoughts.

But what if your friend doesn't want to be saved?

I rejected that—*Nonsense!*

What if saving her will have terrible consequences for all of you?

I didn't care!

The plane started to shake again, turbulence kicking back in. The seat belt sign switched on again. When was this hellish flight going to end? A particularly bad shake caused the oxygen masks to fall from above. Someone screamed, and then passengers clambered all around me, reaching for the masks. The air in the cabin acquired a metallic taste of fear, and I could hear prayers in different languages, directed at different gods, but all begging for the same thing, unified by the act of staring death in the face.

I reached for the mask dangling in front of me, the skin of my hand rippling in my vision. With a delayed reaction, I realized I was light-headed—there was not enough oxygen. The flight was losing pressure.

I must've blacked out, and when I came to, everything was calm again. There were no oxygen masks flying around, no signs of panic among the passengers. The calm atmosphere was . . . too calm. With a start I realized I was seated in a window seat, with Lori to my left. When did I manage to change seats? I rubbed at my eyes. Through the window glass I could see a sky so clear and bright it hurt my retinas. Puffs of pearlesque clouds dotted the view. Sunshine everywhere. I closed the window's shutter with unnecessary force.

Lori was asleep, her body leaning into her neighbor on the left. I blinked the rest of my sleep out of my eyes and took a closer look. Lori's head rested on Rowen's shoulder.

Rowen himself was awake and, as if feeling the heaviness of my gaze on him, he raised his eyes from the entertainment screen and returned my look. Was I asleep? Still in Dubai, lying flat on the couch and seeing things that weren't there?

Without taking off his headphones, Rowen leaned forward to rummage through the pocket of the seat in front of him. His hand returned with a fistful of Al Nassma candies, which he offered to me. Automatically, I accepted. His hand was ice-cold to the touch, like the tablet when it was busy at work.

Days and nights that I had lost to the desert flashed through my mind. There was that moment I'd first laid eyes on the oasis, its massive outline claiming the horizon. There was the harshness of sleeping on the ground, and there was my unfortunate sleepwalking incident that led to my poisoning our only water source. None of that made sense, but all of it had *happened*. And also . . . the sinister temple cut deep into the rock. The tablet. Rowen's body at the bottom of a pit, bloodied spikes coming out of his stomach and chest.

I knew what was real (all of the above) and what wasn't (my dreams about the Queen of Giants). And yet . . . here was Rowen, cramped in the seat next to Lori. He looked exhausted and banged-up but very much alive.

I looked away from him and focused on the candies in my hand. I waited for them to melt away into the air, leaving only the ghost of a sensation on my skin. Yet they remained. Real. Mocking me.

Rowen was leaning forward once more, this time to readjust Lori's bag, seated between her feet. I watched him pat the bag carefully, as if checking it was still there, verifying its existence—or rather the existence of its contents.

My body became slack, heavy and weightless at once. The plane was preparing to land. Was Minh okay? Or at least no longer suffering? A voice inside me said, *Just give in. Stop fighting it. Take what the oasis gives you and make the best of it.*

After landing in Melbourne, we were told to stay in our seats, even after we'd docked at the gate. When a group of medics entered the cabin, carrying a stretcher, my heart started to hammer in my chest. Lori was awake now but barely paying me any attention, all her energy aimed at Rowen.

The rest of the world drained to near black and white as I watched the medics carry Minh away. Dr. Palombo, his eyes wrinkle-rimmed, followed the solemn procession off the plane. I didn't let my gaze leave the stretcher until it was carefully maneuvered outside. Minh was motionless on there the entire time, but her chest was moving. She was alive, but the tablet didn't make her better. Instead, it brought Rowen back.

Lori picked up her bag off the floor and placed the bag's strap across her chest, ready to disembark. When our eyes met, she looked away guiltily. Or maybe it was just my imagination.

"All right," my dad said when the FASTEN YOUR SEAT

BELT sign switched off. "Let's all keep together. Don't talk to anyone. And don't let anyone slow you down. The sooner we get out of here, the sooner we can find out what happened to Minh and which hospital they've taken her to."

In silent determination, our diminished group gathered in the arrivals area. "Did you actually see what happened to Minh?" I asked Tommy, but he just shook his head. "Something went down on that plane," I continued. "I mean, aside from Minh's . . . seizures. In all the chaos, I could swear I changed seats somehow, but I don't remember doing that. And also, you know . . ." I didn't want to say it, as if articulating our new reality was going to solidify it.

Tommy studied me, his gaze assessing me. "That turbulence was the worst I've ever experienced," he finally said. "When the masks fell down, I was kind of saying goodbye to it all in my head."

I reached out and squeezed his shoulder to reassure him, though he wasn't getting what I really meant. Leaning into Tommy's personal space, I murmured into his ear, "Rowen is here." I carefully shifted my view to Rowen himself. He was in line to use one of the self-service immigration kiosks. Lori lingered nearby. I watched her reach out and hug him from behind, saying something into his ear. She wasn't laughing exactly, but she exuded joy and playfulness. Was I the only one who saw Minh carried away on a stretcher? The only one who found Rowen's presence among us impossible? The only thing that was keeping me together right now was the very real possibility that I was seeing things. Could it be me who was carried away from the plane on a stretcher?

"Why wouldn't he be?" Tommy asked.

His response made it obvious I was on my own here. Still, I wanted to press him, to push him to recall our experiences in the temple, but we were now being ushered past the self-service kiosks and my questioning had to wait.

As we were about to exit the Tullamarine airport, I noticed movement in the crowd gathered to greet the arrivals. People I didn't know were running toward us, cameras at the ready, flashes blinding me from afar.

"Quick, don't slow down," Dad said. "Let's go."

In a flurry, we exited the airport, though not before I caught calls of "Dubai Six" and "desert survivors" coming from the mob of reporters. *Dubai Six*. Six of us. Rowen was back, and the rest of the world seemed to have no memory he'd ever been gone.

THE RIFT

A rift formed in our group the moment we woke up in the desert after the storm. Whatever glue that held us together started to melt away, evaporating under the blinding sun. It made sense: We were still *ourselves* but also new versions of ourselves in crisis. We were relearning the basics about who we were—near-perfect strangers drawn together by terrible circumstances.

Now, we were in the airport's multilevel parking garage, where cars filled with anxious parents were waiting to take us all home. Dad told me my mother's flight was landing in a few hours, and she was going to make her own way to our apartment. It was getting late, and I struggled to stay upright and functioning.

The moment Rowen disappeared into his mom's car, I felt like some dark weight was lifted off my back. With him out of the picture, even temporarily, I could pretend like he didn't just come back from the dead. As if my brain just glitched and made it all up.

Lori didn't seem to share in my relief. Edgy, her hands were constantly moving, constantly digging in her bag. It was taking a lot of my diminished focus not to do the same. The tablet's presence was tugging at the strings of my very being. It was in constant turmoil, pulsing, chilling my side through the material of my bag.

Lori turned to me to say goodbye, but when she started to approach for a parting hug, she halted, bounced on her heels a little, and pulled back. Responding to her closeness, my tablet piece pulsed violently, making my skin crawl. Lori's eyes widened with understanding. Did the pieces want to be reunited?

I stepped away from Lori and gave her a nod from a safe distance. She mimicked me, and then her parents were ushering her away from our thinning group. With her gone, I felt an ache, a kind of emptiness in my chest cavity. Like hunger, only not for food, not for human contact.

"Bye, I guess?" Luke's words jolted me out of my stupor. His dad was waiting for him in a car.

"Bye. Drive safely," I replied, my tongue struggling to move in my parched mouth. This thirst came and went, leaving me constantly seeking out fluids but never feeling completely satisfied.

As Luke lingered, I caught an impatient look from Tommy. He was waiting for me by my father's car. Dad was already inside, hands on the wheel. I wondered where Tommy lived and why nobody was here to pick him up. Perhaps my dad indeed was the closest thing Tommy had to a family. Did Tommy want from the tablet the return of his foster mom Celeste? If so, it didn't work. Perhaps the tablet's power had limits.

Or maybe it granted only specific wishes, driven by an agenda we could only guess at and probably never get right. *The lonely spark*. A meteor that wasn't a meteor. *What are you?* I asked in my head, not really expecting a response.

I'm your deepest wish, the answer came.

But I couldn't tell whether it was my own mind giving the response or something external. *Was the oasis real?* I asked, deciding there was nothing to lose.

The oasis is me.

And that was that.

In the car with Dad and Tommy, radio tuned to some news station, I drifted off in the back seat. I woke up to Tommy saying my name. He was about to get off in what looked like Hawthorn, though it was hard to say; a lot of older parts of Melbourne sported the same kinds of terraced buildings and old pubs.

Tommy passed me a piece of paper as he got out of

the car. "Here's my number." I watched him run up the stairs of an old apartment building.

I switched seats, taking the one next to Dad as we continued home. More or less awake now, I listened to the newscaster droning on. . . . *Dubai Six . . . Originally vanished from an active excavation site in Tell Abrar four days ago. Six Australians have now been recovered, alive and well. The search effort was accomplished in collaboration . . .*

At this reaffirmation of my new reality, all the mismatched moments in my head were compressed into a multidimensional one: the visual of Rowen's body at the bottom of the pit merging with a more recent one—of Rowen smiling my way, Lori's head on his shoulder. Rowen dead. Rowen alive. At once. Maybe it was like Schrödinger's cat, its state of being subject to it being observed. But why was I the observer? And were Rowen's two states one and the same, interchangeable? What did it mean for my own status as a survivor?

"Your mother would've eaten me alive if something bad happened to you," Dad was saying. *He's been trying to have a conversation with me*, I realized with some delay, but all I could manage was a smile and a nod.

By the time we made it home, night was crawling in. After the divorce, my parents sold our family home and Dad downsized into a smaller but comfier apartment, not quite in the suburbs but in that liminal space between the city and its outer edges. We still enjoyed the relative quiet and all the trees and saw an occasional possum at night, its eyes burning white from a tree branch or an open dumpster. I loved living here, even though it was time for me to start looking for a place of my own soon, moving in with friends perhaps. I had been talking with Minh and Lori about getting a rental together, but all of that seemed far away now.

Since we had only canned food in the house and were in desperate need of a grocery run, Dad ordered delivery for dinner. But even with a mushroom risotto and a Greek salad, my favorite food combination in the whole world, it was hard to muster an appetite. Still, I stubbornly ate it, washing it down with water, as Minh's emaciated body and bluish lips flashed through my mind. What was happening to her? I had to see her, tomorrow if they'd let me.

Dad was going to stay up to wait for Mom's arrival. I was anxious about seeing her but not exactly excited. Having Mom here meant my time and energy had to be redirected at her—she was going to expect it. But the mere thought of it made me tired. I told Dad I was too exhausted to wait up for her and headed for bed, trying not to cower under the weight of his concerned gaze.

I threw my bag, the tablet piece still in it, under my bed and took off my travel clothes. After changing into my pj's and brushing my teeth, I braved a long look in the bathroom mirror.

A stranger glared back. Some reversed Wonderland version of me, older, eyes like a ghost's. But I was alive. The image in the mirror wavered, like I was staring into water. The rustling of the palms filled my head with longing.

When I lay down to sleep, nothing felt right. My bed was too soft, too comfy. Even after my last night in a Dubai hotel, my back still wasn't used to the many comforts I used to take for granted. Maybe I was even nostalgic about the feel of bumpy ground against my back. My mind kept wandering off, listening for the sounds of Mom's imminent arrival and then sliding to the tablet's presence under my bed. I didn't know if it was the best idea to keep the tablet so close, but putting it farther away felt more wrong. As if in response to my thoughts, a subtle buzzing came from underneath the bed, my back tingling in tune with it.

I sat up. I wanted to grab the tablet but feared it'd overpower me and flood my head with its invasive visions. But I needed it, I realized. In hopes of distracting myself, I grabbed my phone and entered Tommy's number.

I realized none of my friends had called or messaged me, but I guess I hadn't contacted anyone either.

Tommy picked up on the first ring. "How are you holding up?" I asked.

"Don't think I can sleep tonight," came the response,

some kind of white noise enveloping his words. "Not after the nightmares I've been having."

I stiffened. "What kind of nightmares?" I lay down on the bed and waited for the room to start dancing in my vision, for the golden-specked mist to drift in. None of it came. Maybe the tablet, broken in two and torn out of its lair in the desert, was losing its power after all, its grip on me loosening.

"It's about those caves. Mostly," Tommy said. I waited for more, while that background white noise grew stronger, then subsided, then returned once more, flicking in and out of my range of hearing. The tablet under my bed was pulsing again. Or perhaps it never stopped doing that. Its heartbeat. Only I could hear it.

Tommy went on. "In my dreams, I keep running through those caves. I'm being chased, but I'm also pursuing someone. A predator and prey at once. It always ends the same way, the dream. I halt, freezing right on the edge of that pit. I stare down at the spikes, balancing on my heels. I'm about to fall in. I can see the bones down there, on the bottom. And then it hits me—*I've done that*. I've killed someone. I'm a murderer."

Tommy's words caused sweat to coat my hands, my back, my forehead. I was parched again too, but I didn't want to leave my room to get water. I could tell my mother was here, in the house; whispers suggested a conversation going on outside my room. I wasn't ready

254

to face her, to deal with the shock in her eyes at seeing the new me, ravaged by the desert.

"I have strange dreams too," I said to Tommy. I didn't call those dreams "nightmares," because they weren't exactly that—more like distorted reality. "Not about the pit though. But, Tommy . . . those weren't *bones* in that pit," I said, immediately wondering if I was making a mistake. My memories of seeing Rowen at the bottom of the pit were become fuzzier and fuzzier. Still, before I completely forgot, I had to find out what Tommy remembered.

"If they weren't bones," Tommy said, confused, "then what were they?"

I lowered my voice, afraid my parents would overhear me. "I might be remembering it wrong, but I could swear it was Rowen in there. Killed by that pit." I stopped. I should've had this conversation with Tommy in person so I could see his face, his reactions. But it was too late now.

"Rowen?" Tommy repeated the name of my friend like it was a word from a foreign language. "No, no . . . That makes no sense . . . But . . ."

The rest of Tommy's words were swallowed up by that white noise I kept hearing. It spiked in intensity, giving off a pulse that was hurtful to my ears, even to my eyes. The phone in my hand started vibrating. I let it go, pushing it away from me. I had to touch the tablet now. It'd make everything better. It'd make things right.

I slipped off the bed, to the floor. Holding my breath, I reached for my bag. Hands shaking, I almost tore my bag to pieces. When my fingers touched the tablet's surface, I felt a sense of overwhelming relief. Of rightness. But it didn't last.

The tablet in my hands showed me images, memories of the oasis and the temple—memories I hadn't seen before. They weren't *my* memories.

There was Noam Delamer, his skin sunburned, eyes red with despair. And there was Alain Pinon, the other victim of the desert, the one who didn't make it out. Noam and Alain were trapped inside the temple, frantically searching for a way out. They were rushing down the twisting corridor, perhaps chasing someone—or some*thing*—and also being chased.

Alain came to a halt at the edge of the killing pit, balancing on the balls of his feet. Relief washed over his face—this was a close call! But something rammed into his back, and then Alain was losing his balance and falling over and into the pit. His death was instantaneous. I felt it, the suddenness. Burning agony in my chest and then nothing.

I was now inhabiting Noam. He was standing on the edge of the pit, looking down at the impaled body within. Noam's right hand was shaking.

"Why are you showing me this?" I whimpered.

I tried dropping the tablet, but it seemed glued to

my hands. It made me live through the same sequence of events over and over, like it was playing charades and couldn't come up with an alternative way of explaining things when its audience drew a blank.

Instead of resisting the flow of memories, I tried focusing on the images flashing before my eyes, hoping that if I decrypted the tablet's message, it'd release me. But my time to come up with an answer was running out. A cold sensation was spreading from my fingers upward, numbing my hands, slowing down my heart rate.

I zeroed in on Alain's face, frozen at the exact moment the man knew he was going to die. What did I see? Surprise, confusion.

I dug deep into Noam's perception of events. I sensed some remorse from him, but mostly relief that he wasn't the one to die. Though what ran in the background of this unfolding drama was the overall feeling of dissatisfaction. The Queen of Giants, the lonely spark, wasn't quite sated after she had pushed Noam to sacrifice Alain. This murder was too cold, too clean-cut. The two men didn't really know each other before the oasis, so whatever relationship they'd developed while stranded in the desert together wasn't enough nourishment for the hungry little spark.

The spark wanted more. Much more. Its pulsing desire overwhelmed me, its want becoming my want. But there was also something else, something more immediate. My tablet piece wanted its other half. It wanted to be whole again. Or as whole as its state of existence allowed. The realization was a monstrous shiver shaking my whole body. Once the tablet was sure I got its message, it released me.

WHERE IS THE INTERVENTION BANNER?

I was groggy despite what I thought was a full night's sleep. The morning was almost obnoxious in its brightness. Not a cloud in the sky. I stretched my limbs. No dreams last night, at least nothing I remembered upon waking.

Out of my window, I could see a trio of banksia trees slowly moving in the wind. There was the loud, cheerful chirrup of birds too, and the distant moan of traffic in the distance. The distinctive laugh of a kookaburra, an uncommon but not unheard bird within the city limits, reminded me: I was home. But . . . my memories were a mess, a tangled ball of yarn. I may have returned home, but my home was not the same as before, and I was also different.

Uncertain what the day would bring, I quickly

showered and put on some makeup, concealing my sunburned spots. Having access to my closet, with its abundant selection of clothes, presented too many choices, and it took me longer than average to dress myself. I finally settled on some light blue jeans and a pale lilac button-down shirt. I'd always loved the way its color contrasted with my skin. But now, with my sunburns still healing, nothing could fully hide the consequences of my desert wanderings. I wore my hair down; it had lost its shine and thickness since the oasis and looked messy and felt frail to the touch.

Delaying going outside of my bedroom, I repacked my bag, taking out some unnecessary items. The tablet was in there, hidden in the zippered pocket. I avoided touching it, but the skin on my fingers was practically singing in anticipation of contact.

My phone was missing. Last time I used it was when I spoke with Tommy before bed. Something about dreams and nightmares and the pit filled with bones.

I *needed* my phone. On cue, it pinged from under the bed covers. As the phone's screen came alive in my hand, notifications flooded it. It was a group text from Lori that immediately hijacked my attention.

Tablet emergency. Something's wrong. Meeting in Silver Crescent to discuss this afternoon.

I frowned. What was Lori's experience like last night? Was her family reunion bustling and satisfying? Or did things get weird quickly, sending Lori into some foggy maze of tablet-induced nightmares?

I reread Lori's short message again. Silver Crescent meant her parents' summer house. She probably wanted to meet there because being away from adult supervision meant we wouldn't have to pretend everything was all right. But this little trip to the coast was going to be difficult to explain to my parents, especially with my mother here and wanting to see me. I could hear her laughing in the living room. Plus the place was starting to smell of pancakes and coffee. The scent combination that used to soothe me years ago now was sending me into a near panic attack. Maybe my parents' reunion wasn't what I *really* wanted.

I texted back to the group:

I'll see if I can get away. But what about Minh?

While I waited for anyone to respond, I scrolled through my social media and even googled Minh to see if there were any updates about her health. There was nothing. Like *at all*. Even all those Dubai Six news pieces were old now. I guess we were being forgotten already. Or maybe the tablet didn't want any extended attention on us. On *it*. Growing impatient, I stared at the screen of my phone and compulsively hit refresh on the group chat. I was beginning to expect some reality shift to occur, for someone to ask "Minh who?" And maybe it was a valid question. After all, everything in my head was covered in thick smoke.

Relief came from Tommy, who texted me privately, offering me a ride first to the hospital to see Minh, then to Silver Crescent for our secret tablet meeting. Though I had a bad feeling about the latter, Lori was right—we did need to meet and discuss what the hell to do next. Did we just go on like nothing had happened? Did we try to study the tablet, research its true origin? Did we tell our parents? The last two possibilities made me deeply uncomfortable, my stomach actually roiling.

Okay, no external people then. The tablet was *ours*, and regardless of how we felt about it, the six of us were now connected. The tablet was our seventh. And it was a part of each and every one of us.

But first I needed to leave my room and face my parents. I braced for it and opened the door.

I walked into the living room and straight into a trap. Mom and Dad were perched side by side on the couch. From the faux-causal expressions playing on their faces, I knew they'd been waiting for me to come out of my room. Three mismatched ceramic mugs and a family-size glass coffeepot (almost empty) were the only items on the table. The TV was off. Just like old times, and I mean *old*. But what really stood out to me was that Mom and Dad were holding hands. I don't think my parents had been in the same room since I started high school. The sight of it should have been happy and fulfilling, but instead it scraped me the wrong way. A migraine started at the front of my head, making me cringe in pain as it spread.

"Where is the intervention banner?" I asked this strange couple on the couch. A fake smile was on my face, while I was mentally hurrying Tommy to get here, ring the doorbell, and rescue me from whatever this was.

"Come. Take a seat, Alif." Mom patted the love seat to her right. The simple gesture made me break into an uncomfortable sweat. I hadn't had a single meaningful conversation with either of my parents since before Dubai, and besides, the psychological distance between me and my mother was too long to bridge in one leap. But right now in this moment, it was that she was obviously brimming with uncontainable joy that weirded me out the most.

I stayed up on my feet. "I can't stay long. Tommy's picking me up . . . to go see Minh."

"Oh." Mom's face fell at the mention of my friend. "I heard she had some kind of incident on the flight over. You and your friends have been through such horror. But Archer is in contact with her parents, and he updated us this morning. Minh's stable and conscious. I can give you a ride to the hospital today, if you want."

"Tommy's taking me," I reiterated. The possibility of spending quality time alone with my mom in the tight space of a car came with a fresh dose of dread.

"Tommy, huh? You two seem cozy together lately,"

Dad said, his expression turning quizzical. "And I thought you weren't Tommy's biggest fan."

"I guess being lost together in the desert has changed my perspective," I replied.

"Who's Tommy?" Mom asked, looking mischievous.

"He's a good kid. My research assistant—who Alif apparently fancies."

"I don't . . ." I started to deny it but then thought, *Whatever*. It wasn't a lie—I did fancy Tommy, even though Dad's word choice to describe it made me want to giggle and roll my eyes simultaneously. "Never mind. It's not like I'm going out with him or anything." I was about to say "We're just friends" when my eyes landed on my parents' hands again, their fingers intertwining. Time for a topic change. "And what exactly is going on with you two?"

They exchanged looks. Or more like, The Look.

Mom smiled and said, "You're like a skittish deer! Come. Sit. Please?"

"This will only take a minute." Dad's enthusiasm echoed hers. He winked at me, his face glowing with contentment.

I surrendered, doing as I was told, lowering myself onto the love seat and facing my parents. My bag was wedged between my side and the armrest, the close presence of the tablet anchoring me in this slice of reality. Further delaying the inevitable, I reached out for what was left of the coffee and poured it into the only clean mug, dregs and all.

After I took a big gulp and set down the mug, Mom grabbed ahold of my hand and said, "Your father and I, we've been doing *a lot* of talking ever since you went missing and especially after your father brought you back to safety . . ." She let go of my hand, but only to weave her fingers back with Dad's.

And apparently it was Dad's turn to speak. "And we decided that . . ." He looked at my mother.

She finished it off. "We're getting back together."

I stayed motionless and looked on with what I hoped seemed to be happiness in my eyes, while all I felt was emptiness. This idyllic picture before me was . . . too much. Too soon. Too perfect.

But isn't this what I wanted?

"I hope we didn't ambush you with this," Mom said in a cautious voice. "How do you feel? I know this is sudden, but it also feels right to us. I've already quit my job in Birmingham."

"You *what?*" I nearly choked on my second large sip of coffee. Mom just gave up her long-coveted tenure and was—what?—moving back to Melbourne, where academic jobs in her field and at her level were close to zero? Next was she going to say she'd be opening a coffeehouse or becoming a long-distance marathon runner?

"Oh, don't look so terrified, Alif." Mom laughed.

There was a stench of something burning, and a deafening white noise in my ears, not quite painful but uncomfortable. The room swam, the air moving in rough waves.

The doorbell was ringing. It took me a moment to register that.

I stood up too soon, wavering on my feet. Thankfully neither of my parents noticed—Mom had left her seat to open the door, and Dad was staring at her, his eyes not quite glazed over but . . . hypnotized into adoration? I was stuck trying to digest how I really felt about them back together. I never really knew the main reason they split up. There were many little reasons that accumulated into a relationship-killing avalanche, but I always suspected it was their off-the-charts competitiveness that drove them apart. They were both brilliant people working in the same field. Maybe it was all great at first, but eventually one of them must've gotten more of *something* and the other felt left out, and then it snowballed from there. And now Mom was quitting her job because of what—love? *Right.* Still, I tried to muster some glee at this new reality in which my parents were back together and failed. I just couldn't swallow it, this sickeningly sweet pill.

But I had to keep it together. Tommy was now in the room. I'd missed the part when Mom invited him to have breakfast and he accepted. Fast-forward to the most awkward gathering at our kitchen table yet, where Tommy was treated like he was my long-term boyfriend. I studied his reactions, trying to catch him in any moments of WTF confusion—at seeing these doppelgängers of my parents or at being treated like the son they'd never had—but he seemed to be adjusting pretty well. A faint, distant memory unfurled in my head. Back in the oasis, when Tommy and I had been experimenting with the tablet and I kissed him, I just assumed that being with me was his "wish," something that the tablet granted, but what if his deepest wish was something else. A family? Belonging?

Amid our pancake- and coffee-devouring frenzy, Tommy found my eyes and shrugged, as if he were trying to tell me, *Well, what can you do, huh?* But I couldn't ignore that my stomach was in knots and my hands were cold and tingling.

WE ARE ALL DYING

"What's so interesting in there?" Tommy asked when we were in his car and I, not ready to talk, was trying to look busy on my phone. I was rereading my acceptance into the USM writing program. Eventually I was going to have to mention it to my parents and my friends, but for now . . . I was half expecting the email to vanish. But it was still here, and now I was skimming through my writing sample that I'd sent along with my application. It had been a long time since I'd read that piece, and I remembered how it felt like it was something that ought to set the world on fire. Rereading it now just felt awkward. The piece was overwritten, dramatic, a story full of "gasps" and "gazes" and "releasing breaths I didn't know

I was holding." I must've been delusional thinking this was good enough for USM.

"Alif? How about some music?" Tommy's cheerful tone was gone. Now he just sounded concerned—his apparent default state when he was with me.

I fiddled with the radio, but nothing appealed to me. I gave up and went for Tommy's digital player, wedged in the cupholder next to his phone. Tommy wasn't that much older than me, but, aside from the compass watch or whatever the device on his wrist was, he must've possessed some kind of special immunity to the ever-present appeal of high-tech gadgets. His phone, now that I was taking a closer look, was an old model. Not a flip phone or anything, but still pretty outdated and banged-up. Plus Tommy was using a separate device to store his music. It was sweet. *He* was sweet.

"Knock yourself out," he encouraged me.

I flicked through Tommy's music collection, my jaw dropping at his highly organized folders. He had about fifteen of them, grouped by time period and then genre. My eyes landed on the very last folder, called "Alif."

My breath hitched, and I gave Tommy a sneaky side glance. He remained oblivious. I plugged in the device, opened the Alif folder, and hit play.

When the first notes of London Grammar's "Hey Now" started, Tommy swore under his breath and reached for the player but stopped midway, bringing his hand back to the wheel. He stared straight ahead, a red blush spreading from his ear down to his neck. "I forgot that was there," he said.

"Should I even ask you about your secret flaming love for me?" I deadpanned amid the flutterings of my heart. Too impatient all of a sudden or maybe just latching onto any excuse not to discuss our real problems, I pressed on. "Or is it just a coincidence that you have a mix with my name on it hidden away on here?"

"You know," he said, still not looking at me, "I'm waiting for a giant eagle to sweep down from the sky and carry me away."

"It *is* pretty embarrassing indeed."

He pretended not to hear me.

I gathered up my courage. "You know, after our kiss in the desert, I kind of suspected my giant crush on you was reciprocated. And, you know, it's okay to admit things like that once in awhile; you don't need to be all stoic all the time. I mean, it couldn't just be me wishing on the tablet that made you kiss me, right?"

I was joking. Kind of. But Tommy's blush trickled away, replaced by a sickening paleness that drained his skin of color.

In fact, Tommy didn't just look sick, he looked . . . dead. Like Rowen's apparition looked when it showed itself to me in the hotel in Dubai, invisible flies buzzing in my ears. Alarmed, I looked away, but my gaze landed on my hands and gave me something else to worry about. What I could see of myself didn't look that great either. My skin was so pallid, it appeared paper-thin, with bluish veins showing through. I blinked it all away, the illusion fading, but slowly.

"Alif . . . ," Tommy was saying. "The tablet. Do you have it? Or it's with Lori?" A quiver in his voice made me grip my bag with the tablet tighter. Briefly, his eyes traced my movement, and I wanted to stop the car, jump out of it, and run. But I knew Tommy, I reminded myself.

At least I thought I did. But did I? Did I really?

Tommy continued, "I'm only asking because maybe . . . it can help Minh get better."

"Maybe," I said. "I mean, it's worth trying, but . . ." I recalled Minh's aggressive stance on the tablet, her skepticism about what it could do. "But we still don't really know anything about the tablet and how it works." I was going to tell him about the tablet's current broken state but held back, worried how he'd react.

"We'll figure it out. I'm certain of it," Tommy assured me, but I wasn't buying his sudden optimism. I couldn't be the only one weirded out by this mysterious chunk of flat rock that vibrated with power and whispered promises into our ears. I couldn't be the only one to hear said promises.

"Yeah, I guess," I said, moving to the first thing that came to my mind that didn't threaten to circle the conversation back to the tablet. "So . . . my parents must be high on their own renewed romance, because they seem really excited about the possibility of us . . . dating, you know."

"Wow. You've totally changed the topic," Tommy noted. "But it's okay, because we're here."

Tommy found a parking spot across the road from the hospital and, my heart sinking deep with dread, we proceeded to the reception desk.

Minh didn't look good. If I saw only vague signs of our ordeal here and there on my own body—the burns, the veins showing through my damaged skin—there was nothing vague about Minh's sorry state. Her eyes were the scariest part of her, dark and bottomless against her pallor. What happened to her? She'd been barely eating ever since we returned from the desert, but she still seemed mostly okay up until I saw her convulsing on the plane.

We'd gotten to Minh when she was alone in her hospital room, but the signs of her mom being nearby were there—in the half-read book left on the floor and a blazer stretched over the back of a chair by the bed. I was grateful for our good timing. I didn't think I could look into Mrs. Quoc's eyes and pretend like I didn't see Minh's deterioration.

"You look terrified, Alif," Minh said, the croak of her voice making me flinch. "It's okay, I'm not dead, so no need to mourn me just yet."

Minh was hooked to an IV filled with some transparent liquid. A monitor nearby was measuring her heartbeat. *Beep. Beep. Beep.* Slow and steady. *Alive.* I approached her bed and leaned in for a hug, gently, so as not to break her. She gripped me, arms thin and pale. Her hot breath scalded my cold skin. By the time she let go, I was shivering. I felt this way around the elderly. I was ashamed to admit it, but it was what it was. Something about shriveled skin and wispy hair made my insides curl. The physical effect of seeing Minh right now was the same.

I took one of the chairs next to Minh's bed, with Tommy occupying another. My bag and the tablet were at my feet, but even its proximity wasn't enough to assuage my twitchiness. It didn't help that Minh had a full-body shudder when her eyes sought out my bag and lingered on it.

"The rest of the gang is on their way," I said, "and then we'll be heading off to Silver Crescent for a reunion of sorts. Maybe we can have you on video-chat there or something . . . You look good, by the way." I gave her a fake smile.

"Liar," she scoffed.

I could barely contain my tears. Guilt. It was guilt. Perhaps of all of us, Minh was getting the worst end of the deal. Whatever the deal was, it had landed her in the hospital. Maybe it was because she was resisting the tablet, denying its influence, or maybe all of this was random—just me trying to rationalize events that could never be comprehended.

Without a warning, the hospital room rippled, all sound disappearing, then rushing back in, its quality improved, magnified. *Beepbeepbeep*. Minh's heart monitor was going faster. Did she feel the brain-liquefying shift that had just occurred? The morning pancakes and coffee didn't sit right in my stomach.

When Minh spoke again, the words came to her slowly, like every sound she was making cost her too much energy. "And how are you two feeling? Any strange dreams? Garbled memories?" She reached out for me, and her skin was so cold.

The hold of Minh's hand on mine strengthened, her fingers digging in, nails drawing blood. "You died in that cave, Alif," she said. "Lori pushed you in—it was either you or Rowen!"

It was Minh's voice and also not Minh's voice. It was in my head and also everywhere. The tablet was the one speaking. I was frozen, and I was melting, disappearing, starting with my feet, then my legs, and then moving up, up, up. A sand castle dried out by the sun, I was falling apart. Particles that made me into what I was were starting to forget their reasons for holding together. Minh was right: I wasn't meant to be here; my existence was an affront to the fabric of reality.

All the fuzziness in my head solidified into stone-cold focus, and I saw it with clarity then, the image the tablet had since all but erased from my mind—Rowen's body on the bottom of the pit. Only now it wasn't Rowen's body. It was mine.

"That's bullshit!" Tommy launched out of his seat and grabbed Minh's hand, pulling her fingers off my aching flesh. "Rowen was the one who died! Because I got to him first! To save Alif!"

Tommy's outburst made me flinch. He'd totally snapped; this was something I'd expect of Luke, not mild-mannered Tommy. But then the meaning of Tommy's words reached me. Tommy *killed* Rowen? No, no, no! That made no sense. That wasn't how I remembered it. Rowen was on the flight home with us, and I recalled seeing him even before that, in the suite I shared with Minh and Lori in Dubai.

"But Rowen is alive!" I was shaking my head. My chest hurt. The tablet piece in my bag was pinging and I rested my hand over it, seeking reassurance. It was all Minh's fault. She was clouding my mind with her twisted perception of things. I needed to get away from her, from this room. I picked up my bag, but a bout of dizziness swept through me, making me reach out for the edge of Minh's hospital bed. Disoriented, once again I saw networks of dark blue veins circling my wrists and spreading in all directions.

"You're dying," Minh said after studying my wrists.

"We're all dying," I protested. "Eventually?"

"That's true." Minh nodded, and then, her reflexes

lightning fast, she slid out of bed and rushed toward me, going as far as her IV tubing allowed. She grabbed on to my bag. Caught off guard, I relinquished my hold on the bag. In moments, Minh was holding the tablet fragment in her hands, her eyes open, unblinking, while her skin regained its glow and blush.

The hell? Minh, the nonbeliever in the tablet's powers, had caved in?

Moving fast, Tommy reached out for the tablet. Our eyes met over Minh, and I nodded at him. He took a long breath and grabbed on to the tablet.

Minh started to scream. Full-on, deafening, horror-movie screaming that was surely going to bring nurses in here. "You have to destroy it!" Minh was crying as Tommy tore the tablet from her shaking hands. "Before it destroys all of us. It feeds on us, can't you see? Our angst and torment as we're dying are its food source!"

"Alif, we've got to go," Tommy was saying to me as he stuffed the tablet piece back into my bag.

"We never really left the oasis, did we?" Minh was becoming calm and pensive again. She returned to the bed and pulled the covers around her tall, skinny frame, all the way to her neck despite the warm sunlight streaming through the room's open windows.

"What do you mean?" I asked, words coming out hoarse from my bone-dry throat while Tommy urged me out of the room.

My question was swallowed by the roar of distant thunder. The room darkened ominously. Minh closed her eyes and didn't respond. A nurse stuck his head in, eyeing Minh and then zeroing in on me and Tommy with suspicion. "Did I hear screaming in here?" he asked. Tommy shrugged away the nurse's concern, and the two of us quickly left Minh's room.

After giving Tommy an abridged version of the events surrounding the tablet's being split in half, I sent a group message to Lori and the others warning them of Minh's scary new disposition. It turned out that Lori and Rowen were on their way in to see her but had now changed their minds, driving to Silver Crescent directly instead. We could only hope Luke was going to do the same.

Despite what had happened with Minh, Lori's mention of Rowen in her text didn't have the same effect on me that it had in the past. The discombobulation I'd experienced ever since Rowen's return was turning into a distant dream now. Perhaps the tablet was immunizing me to the reality rifts it was causing. Or perhaps this was just my new state of being. If Minh was to be believed, Rowen and I weren't so different after all—both back from the dead, both alive against all odds.

IT ENDS.
OR IT BEGINS.

The rain was sudden and violent, spectacular in its fury. Unexpected weather shifts were common in Melbourne, but this? This was something *different*.

We were completely soaked by the time we made it to the spot where Tommy parked near the hospital. It could've been a cute romantic moment, which, in any other circumstance, might've led to a kiss, but I was too consumed by what had happened with Minh, while Tommy . . . Well, whatever Tommy was thinking probably wasn't helping either.

"So Minh says we should destroy the tablet," I said as we got in the car. "But the tablet's been broken into pieces and yet it still works . . ." As if hearing my words, the tablet fragment in my bag vibrated with what I interpreted as anxiety. My fingers twitched, wanting to touch it—to reassure it of its safety in my keep. If Minh was right and the tablet was indeed somehow using us to ensure its own existence, what did that mean for us? An uncomfortable memory resurfaced—of Noam Delamer wandering into my father's dig camp, skin burned into a red pulp, hair bleached white. But as the tablet's former victim, Noam wasn't faring too badly now, was he? But then again, there was also Alain . . .

"What do *you* think we should do?" Tommy asked, pulling me out of my thoughts as we began to drive.

And just like that, it all snapped into place. I had clarity. It was simple, really. What I wanted was for things to go back to normal, for my friends to be okay, and for us all to stick together. But could we have our pre-oasis lives back now that the tablet was among us, pulling and tugging at our heartstrings, messing with our heads—and possibly devouring us in the process?

"We need to find out what the tablet really is and what it wants with us," I said, although the possibility of finally learning the truth filled me with uncertainty and, frankly, dread. The tablet was something out of this world; I was sure of it in the same kind of instinctual way I was also certain that the tablet was communicating with me. "Maybe it can be manipulated. Or reasoned with."

"So your plan is to try and negotiate with a chunk of rock," Tommy concluded.

"It's not just a chunk of rock, and you know it." I spared a look at my bag, half expecting it to move, but it remained still. Nonetheless, the tablet's subtle vibrations washed over me in gentle waves. "I don't think Minh's theory is totally off—in fact, I'm sure the tablet has latched onto us and now depends on us for its survival. But it also saved us."

"For all we know, it orchestrated that sandstorm in the first place," Tommy said, frowning. The mood in the car was darkening with each passing second.

"I guess there's no way of knowing for sure. What we do know is that the tablet is giving us what we've been wanting for a long time. I think it brought my parents back together."

The moment I said that, I thought of all the other times I suspected the tablet showed its power by bending the reality around us. It seemed to work as some kind of magnet, pulling our unarticulated, deepest wants and desires out of us and, in the process, shaving away at our very beings until our cores were exposed. But was any of it truly *real*—these wishes the tablet granted? I thought I had wanted my parents' reunion and my acceptance into USM, but now with both those things coming true, my new and improved reality felt shallow, undeserved. And by extension, I also felt shallow and undeserved, less than a whole person.

"I've been thinking a lot about that, actually," Tommy said as we left the city limits and merged on to a coastal highway. The view's beauty was lost to a wall of rain. My clothes and hair and shoes were damp, but I could barely feel it.

Tommy continued, "Perhaps the tablet knows what's on our minds better than we ever will. Maybe it burns through our obvious wishes and desires first, like fixing your broken family and . . . making me feel like I at last belong, and then it gets to your deepest core, and that's when it becomes really interesting."

"And it devours us in the process," I said darkly, unable to dismiss Minh's concern.

"But are we really sure of that? Maybe we're just adjusting to having all our dreams come true."

I didn't say anything to that. It was a lot to take in. And the only thing that could give us answers was currently broken into two pieces. At least the piece in the bag at my feet was no longer transmitting anxiety. The tablet's presence had taken a different form though, and it was intensifying, making the air inside the car heady. I wondered if Tommy could hear the tablet's steady heartbeat. *Beep. Beep. Beep.*

Through the window I could barely see the ocean, but what I could see was disturbed, waves high and frenetic. Even with the car's windows rolled up and the rain drumming up against the roof and sides, I imagined I could hear the ocean complaining. My own insides were in turmoil too, and it was growing.

"This is a bad idea." I edged to the end of my seat.

The closer we got to Silver Crescent, the stronger the tablet's waves became and the more my concern grew.

"What is?" Tommy asked.

A wave of irrational fear, the strongest I'd ever felt, surged through me, filling me with suspicion and dread. Lori was my friend, and though we needed to stick together right now more than ever, I didn't think her judgment could be trusted where the tablet was concerned.

"Alif?" Tommy's voice was clouded with worry. "Are you feeling okay? You're turning pale. Do you want me to stop the car?"

"I'm okay," I said, though I didn't feel okay. "I know we need to meet with Lori and everyone, but maybe it's a bad idea to bring my tablet's piece there."

"It'll be all right," he said.

"You can't know that."

Tommy just shrugged in response, but I could tell he was as tense as I was.

"As a kid I used to play on these cliffs with some of my foster siblings. We didn't have a lot of adult supervision," Tommy said. We'd parked not far from Lori's summer place in Silver Crescent.

I'd never been here, never even been invited for a visit, though I'd heard a lot about the house from Lori. The rain had turned into a drizzle, making the landscape—the ocean beach, dark waves encroaching on the shore, rocky sand dunes towering over it all—moody and foreboding. The house was seated on an elevation, not far from the cliffs, where the dunes plunged into the water, rocks sticking out at random from the ocean froth.

We walked toward the house, while Tommy kept on reminiscing. "My very first host family used to own a house out here. More of a shack, really. But they had a boat, this ancient paddleboat that my foster dad improved by attaching a motor to it. I wonder if it's still in its boathouse down there . . . There are caves out there too, you know." He was looking in the direction of the cliffs almost wistfully. But it was the tablet piece in my bag, awake and demanding, that dominated my attention.

"I've had enough of caves to last me for the rest of my life," I said. I'd used *caves* automatically, though it still pained me to think of the temple as a mere cave. "However long that is," I added as I took Tommy's hand and led him toward the house. One car was already parked there—Rowen's. Or Rowen's mom's, rather. I wondered what lies he and Lori and Luke fed to their families about coming out here. I was hoping my own parents weren't going to the hospital to check on Minh, only to find out my visit didn't last as long as they'd thought it would.

I rang the old-fashioned brass doorbell. There were muffled voices coming from inside the house, which we took as an invitation to come in; the door wasn't locked.

Lori and Rowen looked like a prim and proper couple, waiting on their poorly behaved children and ready to discipline them. They were seated at the far end of a long table in the dining room. The half of the tablet in Lori's possession was placed on the table before her, while her right hand and Rowen's left were intertwined and resting on it. The pupils of their eyes were large, making me think of addicts or adrenaline junkies. Acknowledging its other half, the tablet piece in my bag pinged in excitement, or anticipation. I could swear Lori's piece pinged in response.

"Your text from the hospital sounded like Minh was on the attack," Lori said, not quite sounding like herself. As usual, her makeup was well done and her hair flawless, but something about her posture or maybe the angle of her mouth brought the sense of possession to my mind. Like she was being inhabited by some force that was still learning how to properly move her body and manipulate her vocal cords, still working out the kinks. Was this the tablet's influence? Did I look and behave this way too, without realizing it?

"She's doing worse than I thought," I replied, struggling not to come off as alarmed. "I feel terrible for leaving her, but I don't think my presence was helping her heal."

"We've got bigger problems than Minh. Way bigger." Lori fidgeted in her chair.

"Take a seat." Rowen nodded at the chairs by the table. His even tone was a counterweight to Lori's anxious one.

Tommy took a seat on Rowen's right side, and I perched on the edge of the chair next to Tommy. My tablet piece was now full-on crying, moaning, just like the powerful wind outside. The tablet wanted to be whole again.

"Should we wait for Luke?" Tommy asked. I doubted he cared that much about including Luke in whatever this gathering was; maybe he was just stalling for time.

"Luke's not here. I haven't heard from him," Lori said angrily. "Maybe he's dead in a ditch somewhere. He's not the one with a fragment, so I can't see how he matters to us if he doesn't seem to matter to her."

Up until that last word, Lori was starting to sound like her normal self again—impatient, a little obnoxious, ready to pounce. But the way she ended with *her* was a wake-up call. It couldn't be coincidental that both Lori and I had gendered the tablet as female. If I thought of the entity that toyed with me on the sands as the Queen of Giants, how did the lonely spark appear to Lori? And what about the rest of our group? It was time we found out. We needed to put an end to this. The uncertainty was crushing, suffocating.

"Fine," I said, connecting with the tablet fragment in my bag, running my fingers against its jagged line as if to pacify its incessant pinging and pulsing. Could Tommy feel it too? As if reading my mind, Tommy brought his chair a little closer to me.

"You must have something to say, so let's hear it," Tommy addressed Lori.

It was Rowen who answered, slurring words a little, like he was powering through a sudden drug haze. "Noam Delamer, or whoever that man really was, has died. He had a seizure and collapsed in his apartment." Rowen was stating the facts, no emotions involved. "Or maybe he was dead all along and that was some kind of illusion of a man walking around, running on fumes. But the thing is, he could've lived on and had a great life, with everything he's ever wanted, if only he listened to her. If only he took her heart out of the desert, if only he cherished her and her gifts."

If I didn't know better, didn't know exactly what Rowen meant, he'd sound like he was saying nonsense. But I knew. So Noam Delamer was no more. The man who walked into my father's dig camp what felt like years ago didn't get to enjoy his good fortune after all. This is what happened to those who rejected the gifts of the oasis.

"This is what's going to happen to Minh too. She had seizures on the plane, and she seems to be getting worse," I said out loud.

286

"Yes, and it's going to happen to all of us if we don't do something." Rowen exchanged looks with Lori. "We're all connected. We're all her children now, in a way, because she created us—and we her. But she *needs* to be made whole again."

His words were turning my blood cold. And now the tablet piece in my bag and the one on the table were vibrating, filling the air with mechanical buzzing. I looked at Tommy, seeking reassurance or advice or anything, but he was nodding, as if whatever Rowen was saying didn't weird him out at all.

I studied my friends' faces, our group fractured, incomplete. But we were all looking for answers. Only the tablet could tell us what was really going on, what was happening to us. There was only one way to resolve this. We had to finally meet our maker, the Queen of Giants herself, head-on.

I pulled my tablet piece from the bag and gingerly placed it on the table in front of me. It was strange to remember how not that long ago touching the tablet knocked me into visions. Now that the tablet had already stripped away those exterior layers of my being, it was attempting to connect with the very core of me. It promised to be a mirror to my soul, an answer to the question—what was my deepest wish? But before I could see the answer in its heady emanations, my tablet fragment vibrated and lifted off the table. Lori's fragment mirrored mine, levitating, vibrating, buzzing.

Then, as if magnetized, the two pieces rushed toward each other. They collided in the middle of the table with a bang that deafened and blinded me. Everything was fiery white, the color of cosmic matter crashing and burning, sending its pain out as far as it could reach.

COMMUNION BY
THE CLIFFS

The four of us, acting as one, stood up, hands reaching for the tablet that was now whole again. There was nothing, not even a faint seam, to indicate that it was ever broken.

When my fingers reached its surface, an electrical discharge went through me. Instead of pulling away, I held on. We were all holding on. If my friends' dazed faces were any indication, they were as out of it as I was. The house, its walls, its windows, all of it was the same and not the same. It had transformed into a better version of itself—*too* real, colors saturated, sounds enhanced. Everything, from a lonely fly buzzing in the corner to the roaring of the distant waves on the beach, was magnified to the max and then some. *What are you really?* My mind formed the question, my intent spreading to the rest of our group, as we were all connected.

Suddenly, while I was still present here, in the company of Tommy, Lori, and Rowen, I was also up *there*, in the vacuum of space. I was the lonely spark as well as something else. Something bigger, infinitely more complex. And I was moving. Fast. Through space. But then I was dragged off course by the gravity of a strange world, which I knew could mean death, but also the opposite of death. I couldn't die. There was no death. *I* was death. There was nothing *but* death, and in this dying, there was life. As I approached this alien world, it welcomed and rejected me at once. It hurt so much, the pain of entering this unfamiliar atmosphere eating me up whole. Though infinitely diminished, I was still alive, my entire essence now packed into this one little piece. And I fell and I fellandIfellandIfell. The only thing I knew for sure was that I still existed. Reduced to a little fragment of the former whole, one out of thousands of plates covering my outer body, each hexagonal form green with life and breathing and thinking. I was now my own prison. But I learned to exist—by shaping this foreign world to my specifications. I found a way to sustain myself.

The longer the moment lasted, the more I let go, allowing the tablet's essence to merge with my bloodstream, my cells, the very core of my being. Now that we knew the tablet's past, our hive mind was complexifying, growing layers upon layers upon layers. I could recognize individual thought patterns in the way different ideas formed in my head. There was Lori, her brain waves punctuated by impatience, by her urgent need to have things go her way—and also by her fear of loneliness. There was Rowen, self-satisfied but also, surprisingly, hiding some feelings of inadequacy behind his easygoing facade. And there was Tommy, his brightest light being his hunger to belong, to be needed, to be a part of something bigger. Torn between these three, I tried to focus on my own consciousness, to know myself. And what I saw there, deep inside of me, was that I strived to make my own meaning, to create, to breathe life into things, be it a friendship between people who were seemingly too different to be friends or a blank page begging for words. I thrived on that, but it could also be my undoing, broken relationships leaving me alienated from the people who cared about me, and from myself.

It dawned on me then that the tablet, this alien mind that thrived on human interactions, did so because it couldn't create anything new. Rather, it made things clearer for its host while it fed on the host's thoughts and feelings.

And so in our moment of communion, we knew everything about ourselves and about one another. We knew every possibility. Every deep secret. This everything included the lonely spark and her secrets. But as its dark doings were revealed to us all in one infinite instant, we felt no anger. She was our tablet, our oasis, but *also* the Queen of Giants to me, a monstrous shadow to Lori, a dark pair of angelic wings moving in the wind to Tommy, and a sentient tree to Rowen. She appeared to us all, filtered through our perception, our experiences. As she took many shapes, she kept whispering into the ears of those willing to listen. She made me poison our only water source in the oasis because she wanted us to fight over it and for me to torment myself with shame. She showered Rowen with food because she wanted him to feel guilt—and for us to judge him. And she tormented Tommy with an impossible choice—to sacrifice Rowen or to watch Lori do it to me instead. Perhaps, in an alternate reality, Lori succeeded in saving Rowen from the pit. But it didn't matter now. We felt no vengefulness toward our queen. She was our lonely spark, just trying to survive. Weren't we all?

Lost to our shared trance, time became twisted and turned inside out. We floated together, and in this moment everything was right in our closed-circuit world. But then . . . something else pushed in, forcing itself into the mix of our combined thoughts. A burning desire to be important, to matter, to lead, and to be respected. A desire so strong, it was violent in its velocity. And then there was another *something*—a yearning to make a difference, to do the right thing, even if the thing in question was going to break you. Neither of these felt like evil aspirations, but nonetheless the tablet didn't react well to these new additions to our hive mind. My fingers were burning against the cold as my stomach coiled. The tablet was resisting—buzzing in protest and lifting off the table again.

No, not lifting—being taken away!

The tablet's abrupt absence was like a vicious attack on my body. My skin, joints and muscles, rib cage wrestled wide open, exposing my heart to the world. I heard the others crying out and realized I was whimpering in pain and loss as well. I could no longer hear and see everything at once. I was deprived. Empty. Inadequate.

"It's Minh and Luke! They took the tablet!" Lori croaked amid violent coughs.

She didn't have to say what the four of us already knew from the brief moment Luke and Minh joined our hive mind while scrambling to tear the tablet out of our combined grip: their plan to destroy it. Or at least, that's what Minh planned to do. Luke? I wasn't so sure . . .

I was still reeling from the shock of separation when there came the unmistakable bang of the front door swinging shut. Everything wavered around me. The living room had floor-to-ceiling windows and, like in a fever dream, through the glass I followed the movement of

Luke's athletic shape as it rushed by outside. The tablet was in his hands. Minh was lagging behind him. She was wearing the same clothes she'd worn on the plane when she collapsed, her hair was a mess, and her legs were thin and wobbly. And yet she was strong enough—or determined enough—to conspire with Luke, to come here and take our lonely spark.

Moving as one organism, the four of us left the table and ran after the thieves. As our weirdly coordinated group exited the house, Lori yelled after Luke and Minh, "You're going to kill us all!" followed by a string of profanities.

I found myself at the forefront of our pursuit, my legs hurrying over the grass in long strides, practically flying, like in a dream. The wind was helping me one moment, pushing me back the next. When I saw Luke reach his car—parked a block away from the house—I knew I wasn't going to get to him in time to free the tablet. But unexpected help came from Minh, who was near Luke. She surprised him with a kick in the knee and latched onto the tablet, grabbing it for herself. Luke's cry of pain was swallowed by the wind. I guessed Minh's unlikely partnership with Luke was over now.

I switched the trajectory of my pursuit as Minh raced away from Luke and toward the cliffs, her intent painfully clear: She was going to destroy the tablet. Whatever empty fumes her frail body was running on would expire soon. She was weak when I last saw her. It was a miracle she was even moving.

Trapped in Minh's hands, the tablet was emitting a high buzzing that hurt me from afar—sending my ears pulsing, my eyes tearing up. Through our connection, the tablet was screaming in my head, its cry intensifying as Minh approached the cliffs. I could already see it—the shadows of my own demise in the foamy dark waves raging below the drop. They say your life flashes before your eyes when you're near death, but that wasn't exactly the case with me. What I was thinking in that moment was that I should've been nicer to my mother, more forgiving maybe. I didn't know where the thought came from, but the regret was crushing.

But if I got the tablet back from Minh, I could make it all right again. I could fix everything—I could beg the Queen of Giants for another chance. For me. For all of us. "Minh, wait!" I yelled, losing my breath in my mad dash. Others were right behind me, but it was up to me to stop Minh now.

Minh paused on the cliff's edge, dangerously close to the drop. The winds were battering her from all sides, her hair wild and her body about to fly away. I was less than ten feet from her when Minh turned to face me. A mask of pain and struggle made her face unrecognizable. Who was this girl?

"Don't come any nearer!" Minh warned, and I halted,

Tommy almost bumping into me. The others must've been behind us—I could sense their combined tension with every bit of my skin.

"Minh, listen to me," I said, struggling to speak against the wind whistling in my ears. "If you destroy it . . ."

"This thing is evil," Minh cried out. She angled her body so she could hold the tablet in one hand, over the edge of the cliff.

"It might be the only thing that's keeping us alive right now!" I begged her with my eyes to listen to me, to reconsider. "Noam Delamer is dead, and we all might be next!"

"This isn't life," Minh said, no longer yelling. I could hear her all the same, as if she'd said the words directly into my ear. Awkwardly, she shifted her weight again, bringing herself even closer to the drop. The dark desperation in her eyes was what moved me. Without giving it a second thought, I tackled her. I knew full well we could both end up falling, but I also knew I wasn't about to let someone else decide my fate for me.

The world around me darkened. I grabbed on to Minh with everything I had, my hands going around her waist. There was a sudden pain in my stomach, the kind that I somehow knew came with stabbing—the piercing of flesh, with the blade burning its way in, disrespectful of internal organs, of bones. In our struggle, I looked down and saw a gaping hole in my stomach, blood gushing out. I couldn't even scream. This was an illusion. It had to be. The tablet was misfiring, terrified. But I was weakening quickly. My feet were slipping on the wet grass. The yawning drop below me beckoned.

"Let go, Alif . . . ," Minh hissed as I kept reaching for the tablet, my fingers sliding against it.

Another chance . . . I begged the Queen of Giants. *For me and my friends.*

My thoughts were all tangled, a messy ball of yarn, all emotion, no logic.

And what are you willing to do to get what you want? came the answer, calm and quiet but also deafening. For a moment, I was back in the white-walled throne room without a ceiling, where a throne made of human bones and possessions towered over me. The Queen of Giants was there, seated on her throne, her head lost to the clouds. I could see myself through her eyes. She was always watching.

My response came easily, like the last piece of the puzzle falling into place; there was only one spot where it could fit. *I'll do whatever's necessary.*

Then came a sizzling noise, followed by a whooshing sound. The sensation of my ears popping. I was still holding on to Minh when the tablet slid out of our combined grip and fell into the watery abyss below.

WHISPERS, PROMISES

Lori cried out behind me, and then there was no sound but the howling wind. I looked down. The tablet's descent was excruciatingly long, and every cell of me, every atom that made up my body, was feeling the terror the lonely spark felt as she fell to her death. This was so mundane. Our spark had survived the vacuum of space and her perilous journey to Earth—how could her ultimate ending ever be adequate? But all the same, her pain was my pain, her fear my fear. I hated her and, in a way, I loved her. In her own twisted way, perhaps she loved me back.

And then she finally met the rocks below. My heart constricted, and slowly I collapsed to my knees. I searched the swirling water below, but there was nothing down there but jagged rocks and dark waves frantically attacking everything in sight, vicious and hungry, a pack of rabid beasts fighting over prey.

I strained to listen, to feel for the tablet, and for a moment I thought there was a signal, like a faint echo of something. But it was gone before I could zero in on it. The tablet must've shattered into pieces, and I couldn't even cry—that's how stunned I was, how emptied out by grief. My friends were equally silent as they surrounded Minh and me in a loose semicircle. It must've been Tommy's hand resting on my shoulder. It provided little in the way of reassurance.

The wind was unforgiving, and yet all I could feel was the clammy heat, the kind that makes clothes stick to skin. My face was tight and burning now, and my throat was parched—the kind of thirst I learned in the desert.

"Alif . . ." Minh's voice was weak. I turned to her just as she lowered herself down next to me, then came to lie on her side, facing the point where, up ahead, dark water met dark sky.

"I'm here. We're all here," I said. "Together."

Minh's body jerked as she coughed up sand. Tearing against the wind, I blinked my eyes to clear this vision, but it stayed the same. I closed my eyes again, keeping them shut longer this time, and something must've changed. The wind had stopped, and I could feel bright light all around me. It was bothering my vision even through my eyelids. There was a part of me that knew what was happening. It knew this entire time but didn't want to admit it. A self-preservation mechanism. A human way to cope in the face of a decisively alien threat.

Everything that happened to us was a test, I thought, and by the looks of it we'd failed. Maybe this was our second chance? A rerun of the game so that we could do better? One thing was certain in my mind: We had to stay together if we were to sustain her, in order for her to sustain us. We were linked now, forever.

A familiar voice reverberated inside my head. *Open your eyes.* I did as asked.

I was lying on my back, facing up to the blinding, cloudless sky. Up above, the heads of wild palms swayed in the wind, their shapes black against white.

I was back. We all were. Perhaps we'd never left.

I could hear the others as they came to their senses.

Nothing was real. Everything was real. Never. Forever. Words and concepts didn't matter here. The oasis enveloped us like a mother cradles a baby close to her chest, heartbeats synchronizing. The tablet was nowhere in sight. Perhaps it never left the temple. Perhaps it never even existed outside of our hive mind. But I knew the lonely spark was watching. It was always watching. It chose us, and it wasn't done with us. Not yet. Did it really hear me when I asked for a second chance? What else did I promise it in my burst of desperation?

I sat up and looked around me. The achingly familiar palm trees towered over me, their heads swaying gently in the wind, fronds rustling. As my eyes adjusted to the light, I noticed flowers and multicolored fruit everywhere, shiny and perfect, glistening in the breezy heat. There was the unmistakable noise of a burbling spring. And then also those darker, shadowed gaps between the trees, from which something invisible was staring back at me.

My friends were close by, wild-eyed and dazed but also alive. Slowly, I met Minh's eyes, healthy color having returned to her cheeks, and she looked away, clearly disappointed with me but also resolved. Tommy came close and sat down on the grass next to me, wrapping an arm around my shoulders. I looked up and found him smiling. He leaned in and placed a sweet little kiss on my nose, then on my cheeks, and finally on my lips.

Not far from us, Lori and Rowen were locked in a hug, while Luke just stared on, focusing on nothing in particular, his expression unreadable.

A sound of distant thunder brought us all to our feet. The sky above was clear, so the noise must've been coming from the desert. If any of us felt fear, none of us showed it.

"Our rescue is here," Tommy said, focusing on the space beyond the trees, where our oasis merged with the desert. As if his words had the power to reshape reality, the thunder transformed into the roar of engines. With a pang in my chest, I thought of my dad. Of Mom. Of my life back in Melbourne. All of it was far away now. Still part of me, but also belonging to some other Alif—my doppelgänger in a parallel universe.

We all exchanged looks. Our bodies were still tense as our minds adjusted to our new reality. But one thing was certain—we weren't running toward our rescue. It wasn't our time to leave. Not yet.

The darkness that lurked in the depths of the oasis beckoned us. I took Tommy's hand and gently pulled as I started moving away from the noise of the cars and toward our salvation, down where the heart of the oasis was beating slowly but surely. My friends followed close behind. The tree branches and thorny shrubbery moved out of our way. The deeper in we progressed, the more I could hear it—in my chest, in my heart—the lonely spark whispering the promise of eternal life and unmeasurable treasures and everything that I could wish for and more, now and forever.

AUTHOR'S NOTE

This book is a work of fiction, and while it is set in real places—the United Arab Emirates and my hometown of Melbourne, Australia—places and institutions described in this book are fictionalized. Tell Abrar, where the archaeological excavation at the heart of this book takes place, and Silver Crescent, where the book's latter parts unfold, are imaginary places partially inspired by real locations. As an author I have to alter reality a bit to put it in harmony with the events of this book. For similar reasons, I have created two Melbourne-based universities—Dunston and the University of Southern Melbourne.

ACKNOWLEDGMENTS

How can this be? Five years ago, as I was fighting my way out of query trenches, I started drafting a new NaNoWriMo project driven by my love of archaeology and Andrei Tarkovsky's movies. That project eventually became *Oasis*. Here I am now, writing acknowledgments for this book that I'm immensely proud of. Mind blown.

So many amazing and talented people have worked tirelessly to make this book the best it can be, and it's one of my biggest publishing-related anxieties to forget someone vital in my thankful gushing. But I shall try nonetheless.

John Morgan, my editor extraordinaire. I swear, sometimes you know exactly where I'm going way before I know that myself. Or is it *all* the time?

Erin Stein, my stellar publisher. Thank you for making my publishing dreams come true—again!

Amy Tipton, who was instrumental in guiding this book in its metamorphosis from an unpolished manuscript to a good-enough-to-show-to-editors almost-book.

Jeff Miller at Faceout Studio for creating yet another mind-blowing cover.

Rena Rossner, my agent (and a talented writer herself), whose multifaceted work never ceases to inspire me.

Everyone at Imprint and Macmillan Kids, but especially Hayley Jozwiak, Erica Ferguson, Dawn Ryan, Kristin Dulaney, Nicole Otto, Brittany Pearlman, and Kelsey Marrujo; Natalie C. Sousa and Elynn Cohen for the stunning book design. I'm lucky and happy and privileged to be working with you all.

Ellen Peppus at Signature Literary. Erin Cashman, Rachel Caine, and everyone at 1st5Pages workshop—I learn from you and with you every day. All my friends at Electric Eighteens and Renegades (or are we Rena-Gates?); Melanie and Sarah at Unplugged Book Box.

My author friends, in no particular order. Thank you for being infallibly excellent and always there when I need you: Astrid Scholte, S. Gonzales, Ella Dyson, Rachael Craw, Sarah Epstein, Sara Faring, Lucia DiStefano, Candace Robinson, Jess Flint, Shivaun Plozza, Lee Kofman, Kayla Ancrum, Adalyn Grace, Kristina Perez, Alison Evans, Lyndall Clipstone, Dana L. Davis, and Wendy J. Dunn.

Sarah Robinson-Hatch as well as the YA Room's Shaun and Bianca deserve a special mention for all the tireless and enthusiastic work being done for Melbourne's thriving and ever-expanding YA community.

To all the readers, booksellers, librarians, reviewers, bloggers, and various other kinds of book people (book people are the best people!) who picked up my debut and loved it and spread the word and then got excited about *Oasis* way before it was anywhere ready. In no particular order: Mike, Vicky, Katherine x2, Cherry, Kate, Kait, Meg, Leah, Tracy, Tasha, and Jayse (and everyone over at the Nerd Daily and GeekCon), Annie (and everyone at Read3er'z Re-Vu), Austine, Joel, and Ian (and everyone at Speculate), Angela (and Readings as well as Readings Teen Advisory Group), Emma (and all of Dymocks), as well as wonderful booksellers at Galaxy, Kinokuniya, Harry Hartog, Paperchain (hi, Claire!), and so many others for welcoming me and offering support and being awesome.

My "day job" book-loving friends who are pretty much the reason I don't spend my days at work sobbing in despair: Antoinette, Ay Sian, Barbara, Carol, Gertie, Min-Hui, Kerina, and Effie. Also Liz, who has now left for better (academic) pastures but who's been the best and most supportive boss ever.

And, of course, Jorge—thank you for making sure not all of my weekends are spent hunched over a laptop and that I get to experience the world outside and feel the sunshine on my skin, even if I have to be tricked into leaving the house for that to happen.

Last but not least, I thank my parents, who brought me up to love books and crave knowledge; and my extended family spread across two continents and three countries: Lydia, Angela, Paola, Jaxson, Roberto, Simi, Miguel, Jason, and Clery.

And Augusto—we miss you terribly.